THOU SHALT NOT

MURDER

THOU SHALT NOT
MURDER

A NOVEL

CRAIG S. MORGAN

Silver Creek Farm LLC

Thou Shalt Not Murder
Copyright © 2023 by Craig S. Morgan. Second Edition. All rights reserved.

No part of this publication may be reproduced, stored in a retrieval system or transmitted in any way by any means, electronic, mechanical, photocopy, recording, or otherwise without the prior permission of the author except as provided by USA copyright law.

Scripture taken from the Holy Bible, New International Version®. NIV®. Copyright© 1973,1978, 1984, 2011 by Biblica, Inc.™ Used by permission of Zondervan. All rights reserved worldwide. www.zondervan.com The "NIV" and "New International Version" are trademarks registered in the United States Patent and Trademark Office by Biblica, Inc.™

This novel is a work of fiction. Names, descriptions, entities, and incidents included in the story are products of the authors imagination or are used fictitiously. Any resemblance to actual persons, events, and entities is entirely coincidental.

The opinions expressed by the author are not necessarily those of Silver Creek Farm LLC.

Published by Silver Creek Farm LLC
PO Box 754
Magnolia, MS 39652
www.CraigSMorgan.com
Book design copyright © 2023 by Silver Creek Farm LLC. All rights reserved.
Cover design by Colleen Sheehan
Interior design by Grace Morgan

Published in the United States of America

ISBN: 979-8-9891295-0-8
1. Fiction / Suspense

For Kathryn

CHAPTER 1

Jerry Hargood pulled an afghan up to his neck when the air conditioner kicked on; his little toe was numb. The den, illuminated only by a television true-crime documentary, flashed with the degrees of light depicted in the changing scenes.

"But this night," the narrator said, "Serena would come home to find her mother beaten, lying in a pool of blood, gasping for life…"

Hargood's pulse rose; his ears burned as tiny moans and creaks surfaced from his brand-new beachfront home. A 911 call replayed for the viewing audience.

"It's my mother…someone has…something has…happened…"

The light in his den flashed red and blue as the scene changed to file footage of police surrounding the horror inflicted on a small home somewhere in the northeast.

"And when we return…"

Hargood took this opportunity to channel surf. When the program returned from commercial break, he cranked up the volume to cover the disturbing pops coming from the foyer.

He jumped when the doorbell rang.

Rolling out of his lounge chair, he glanced at the clock and moved quickly toward the front door. Into the hallway and along the stairwell, he tiptoed on bare feet that were swollen from sitting for so long. With the back of his hand, he slid the curtain away from the window beside the door.

The man was clean shaven, and his eyes had dark circles under them. His hair was greasy and combed out of his face with his hand. He looked familiar; Hargood knew everyone in Pascagoula.

"Are you broke down?" Hargood yelled, as he began to unlock the door.

Hargood turned the knob, opened the door to the full length of the chain, and stuck his face in the crack.

"Are you broke…"

A spray blasted him.

Stumbling backward into the foyer, Hargood grabbed his eyes. He screamed. Chemicals filled his mouth, blistering his tongue and lips. The substance clung to his palms.

With a deafening crash, the chain ripped from the casing, throwing splinters throughout the foyer. The door slammed against a table, throwing a glass tray onto the tiled floor. Hargood cried out; an intruder entered his house.

Fumes stung his throat as he drew in a deep breath. He screamed once again, but for only a split second; his throat tightened around the vapors. He swung his arm out violently to catch his balance. Striking a mirror in the hall, shards of glass crashed to the floor.

"Careful now." The voice was cold.

Spinning to face his assailant, Hargood fell backwards into the mirror.

The door slammed shut.

Hargood's legs weakened. As he slid down the wall, glass carved his bare back in streaks.

The intruder engaged the lock and dropped a backpack at Hargood's feet.

Hargood covered his face with his hands. The intense burning in his sinuses and eyes overpowered the pain in his back. As he began to lose consciousness, he gasped for air.

"Now Brother Jerry, don't die on me yet."

The high pitch of duct tape tearing from a roll echoed through the hall. Hargood's arms weakened; he dropped his hands to the floor. He struggled for one good breath.

Through blurred vision, Hargood saw the outline of his assailant move toward him. Kicking violently, he inched his way down the hall, keeping his back pushed into the wall.

The duct tape moved closer to his face.

Hargood's right hand found a large piece of glass.

"Just settle down. I need to make this quick."

The mirrored glass sliced into Hargood's palm, as he squeezed it tight.

"I need that heart of yours to keep pumping. Boy, that stuff really burns."

Duct tape was pressed to Hargood's temple.

"I'm just going to cover your eyes so you won't…"

Taking one last deep breath and lunging forward, Hargood lashed out with the glass toward the tape and collapsed along the baseboard.

"What the…?" the intruder screamed. "Oh God! No! Hargood!"

With the exertion, Hargood was suddenly paralyzed. Darkness engulfed him, as his head was jerked back by his hair and duct tape was wrapped around his eyes and mouth.

"Now look! We're getting blood everywhere." The intruder's voice raised in pitch. "Hargood, if you've messed this up, I'll…"

A tourniquet was wrapped around Hargood's left bicep.

"Okay, calm now. Calm. I've only practiced on a pot roast, so be patient. No. Let's try again. Ah, there we go. Okay, good, now she's got a flow…"

Hargood sensed pressure in his chest, as the tourniquet was removed.

"Shouldn't be too long now. Dammit, Hargood! You got my knee good. I don't suppose you have any gauze?"

Through the pounding in his ears, Hargood heard the intruder walk toward the kitchen. The volume of the television in the living room weakened with each heartbeat.

Within minutes, Jerry Hargood was dead.

CHAPTER 2

Pastor Cooper Dupree stepped off the elevator into the world of hospice care—quiet, cold, with a hint of ammonia cleaner wafting through the air. Mrs. Brewer was in Room 3003. Dupree looked at his watch. Twelve hours of ministering to criminals, on a stiflingly hot Friday, had him operating on fumes.

One of Dupree's duties, as the pastor of Christ Church, was to serve twice a month as a chaplain to those doing hard time at the Greene County Maximum Security Prison. Earlier that day, during his visit, Dupree almost made a real, spiritual connection with Clive Brewer.

"Will you let Jesus into your heart?" Dupree had asked, separated from Clive by a plexiglass barrier.

"Will you visit my mother at Singing River Hospital?"

"Uh…yes, I'll try."

"You promise?"

"Yeah sure," Dupree said. "Clive, if you confess your sins, God who is faithful and just, will forgive you all your sins and forgive any unrighteousness."

"I ain't confessing to nothing. I didn't kill none of them people. I'm innocent."

"Do you have other sins to confess?" Dupree prodded. "Certainly there are things you feel sorry for doing."

"I'm sorry I can't see my momma and that they got me holed-up in here."

"We'll work on it," Dupree said, placing his little Bible in his pocket. "Can I pray with you?"

"Will you visit my mama?"

"Yes, for Christs' sake. Let's just pray. My next appointment is in a couple minutes."

The endless hall on the third floor in Singing River Hospital was vacant, silent, daunting. Dupree took one step forward, looked at his watch once again, then turned back toward the elevator and punched the call button.

You've still got to deal with Mrs. Frisk.

His appointment with an elderly ballroom dancer was at nine o'clock.

Breaking his "promise" to Clive Brewer would allow him time to swing by his house before his lesson.

"Can I help you?" a female voice came from behind Dupree. When he turned to address her, he was stunned, speechless. Planted in a field of the dead and dying was a beautiful flower.

"Uh…yes," he said, as he took a few steps toward the nurse's station. The elevator dinged behind him. He ignored it. "I'm here to see Mrs. Brewer."

Dupree ran his finger inside his clergy collar to release a little heat. Drenched with sweat for the third time that day, he desperately needed a shower.

"Mrs. Brewer?" she asked, walking past Dupree. Taking a seat at a computer terminal, she began typing frantically.

"I think she's in 3003," Dupree said, shifting his stance at the counter to get a view of the badge hanging around her neck.

"Yep," she said, looking up at Dupree with a beautiful smile. A few years younger than Dupree, mid-twenties perhaps, her green eyes sparkled against the backdrop of her freckled nose and auburn hair.

"I'm Cooper," Dupree said, extending his hand across the counter. "And you must be…Kelly."

"That's right, Kelly Mitchell," she said, taking his hand giving it a firm shake. "Thank goodness for badges."

Dupree returned a smile. His day-old whiskers bunched on his lip.

"I took mine off earlier," he said, shaking her hand gently. Dropping his head toward his other hand, he brushed a clump of dark hair out of his eyes. He kept his elbow as low as possible to keep from exposing his underarm.

With dark, penetrating eyes and a hard jaw bone, Dupree was almost as pretty as nurse Kelly, except his nose had been broken a couple of times. This cut through the pretty and gave him a rugged, handsome, intimidating look. He towered over most at six-feet two. He was, however, able to appear open and humble. The clergy collar helped this perception.

"I didn't know Fathers wore badges," Kelly said, standing. Keeping a hand on the counter, she circled around the work station toward Dupree.

"Oh sure, I wear one all the time," Dupree said, reaching into his pocket for his nametag. "I must have left it in the car." He smiled and brushed his hair back with both hands. Getting a whiff of his shirt, he dropped his arms quickly. "Uh…so how's Mrs. Brewer doing?"

"Mrs. Brewer is comfortable. She's not in any pain," Kelly said, walking past Dupree. "Are you here for 'last rites'?"

"Oh no, I'm not Roman Catholic. I…uh…I'm here as a favor. I told her son I would check on her."

"You know she's dying," she said, as she continued down the hall.

"Yes, I'm just going to sit with her for a minute," Dupree said, a little louder.

"Let me check on her first." Kelly disappeared around the corner.

Dupree shook his head. His heart was racing; his fingers tingled. *You're dehydrated.*

He checked his breath by breathing into his cupped hand. *You're just exhausted.*

Kelly Mitchell had Dupree's mind scrambled. Buried in a prison, with the worst criminal offenders, for most of the day, Dupree was now conversing with a J-Crew model in scrubs. Six inches shorter than Dupree, her waist was at the perfect height for his arm to wrap around in a well-choreographed dance. She was absolutely the prettiest woman he had seen…since…

Sarah.

Dupree smiled at the thought of his wife.

Thank you Lord for the reminder!

Dupree was thumbing through a small pocket Bible, when Kelly rounded the corner.

"She's okay," Kelly said, walking up beside Dupree. "So…Cooper… I was wondering…if you're not Catholic, why are you wearing a collar?"

"Oh, a lot of churches have pastors that wear collars," Dupree said, giving a half smile. He ran his index finger around the inside of the collar. It was strangling him. "But I'm not…I mean, we're not Fathers. We don't take vows of…well, you know." He began to blush.

"Like poverty?" Kelly said, smiling.

"Yes, exactly," Dupree said, nodding. "I haven't taken a vow of poverty." He smiled and held out his hand. "Just check out this watch."

"It's a Timex," Kelly said, taking his hand and giving it a light squeeze.

"I spared no expense." Dupree gave her plenty of time to read the watch.

"It's time for my rounds," Kelly said, releasing Dupree's hand and flashing a smile. "3003 is just around the corner on the right."

• • •

The door to Room 3003 slammed shut like a coffin lid, rattling the walls. Dupree tried to cover his ears; Mrs. Brewer didn't budge.

Unlike a normal coffin, the walls were not padded and covered in satin. They were painted a deathlike grey, that absorbed every uplifting band of light. A fine, bleak film of doom covered the entire contents of the room, including Mrs. Brewer.

Dupree placed his hand on the door handle. Mrs. Brewer's chest rose and fell to the rhythm of the giant machine that beeped beside her. Using his free hand, he grabbed the Bible from his pocket. Turning to Psalm 40, he read a few lines before moving to Mrs. Brewer's bedside and taking a seat on a little stool.

As a shadow moved underneath the door, Dupree sat up straight. Nurse Kelly was going to burst in and pull him back to the land of the living.

"I waited patiently for the Lord…" he said. Mrs. Brewer's chest expanded and contracted. Her ears were deaf to his words. Her eyes were blind to his presence. She belonged in a real casket.

Dupree fought to continue the grueling task of finishing the reading. He watched the shadow move in the corridor.

When the door handle appeared to jiggle, Dupree leapt up and ran to the door. He flung open the door. The hallway was empty. Returning to his stool, he placed his little Bible back into his pocket. The shadow had disappeared.

For the first time since Sarah's disappearance, Dupree thought about spending time with another woman.

It's too soon.

Dupree sat forward with his forearms on his thighs. He studied the cords running beneath Mrs. Brewer's machinery. Mrs. Brewer was comatose; she had been brain dead for a month. He touched one of the cords with the tip of his right shoe. If he "accidentally' kicked the plug, Nurse Kelly would be forced to rush to the rescue.

His rescue.

Instead, he pulled back his foot and took the Bible out of his pocket.

"You placed my feet upon a rock…" he said, as he pushed the pages of the Bible flat with his thumbs.

We could just go out for a coffee.

In the awful-smelling room that contained no flowers, he sat back in his chair and stared at the ceiling. His eyes were heavy. Outside the door to Room 3003, a beautiful auburn-haired nurse brought ice chips to a patient, or placed a blood pressure cuff on an arm. As Dupree contemplated ways to ask Nurse Kelly to share her break with him in the cafeteria, he dozed off to the rhythmic hum of Mrs. Brewer's ventilator.

· · ·

Pastor Dupree ran from the hospital refreshed, but troubled, by his little nap. Late for his standing Friday date with Mrs. Frisk, he worked his way through the parking lot. As his lean hips dodged side-view mirrors, he slowed to a jog. His hands pushed off the hood of cars to maintain balance and propel him quickly through the turns. As he gained speed in a parking lot aisle, running against a traffic, arrow his "prison" shoes slapped the pavement in rhythm with his breath.

Kelly was not at the nurses' station when he sprinted to the stairwell next to the elevators. His prayer for a cordial exit had been answered. It would have been impossible to tell her that he really didn't have time for her tonight.

Dupree jumped into his six-year-old Toyota Camry and cranked the engine. Breathing heavily, he grabbed a water bottle from the floorboard, while pushing his face into the air conditioner vent. The day had been stifling hot. Now, soaked with sweat for the fourth time, he ripped off his collar and threw it in the backseat.

Mrs. Frisk's studio was located on Chicot Street about a mile from the beach. Dupree's standing lesson was at nine o'clock. Pulling out of the hospital parking lot, he checked his watch and cringed. It was ten minutes to nine. Mrs. Frisk demanded promptness.

"Dancing is timing," she would say. "Why must you be late?"

In the six months he had been working with the new instructor, his flexibility had improved dramatically.

When he entered Mrs. Frisk's studio for the first time, she had mistaken him for a parent.

"Why do you want to take ballet?" Mrs. Frisk had asked in a heavy East German accent. "You are quite old to start dancing."

"I've been dancing for almost two years." Dupree said, taking a seat on a chair that was too small for his frame.

"Uh-huh"

"My first class was ballroom dancing at the YMCA," Dupree said.

"Why ballroom dancing?"

"I promised my wife that we would go dancing on our third wedding anniversary."

"How did it go?" Mrs. Frisk asked.

"She didn't make it," Dupree said.

"I've heard," Mrs. Frisk said, as she stacked matts in the corner of the dance studio. "I'm sorry for your loss."

Dupree never got the chance to keep his promise. Sarah's time was cut short; her body never found. Evidence pointed to her not surviving the attack—the amount of blood in the utility room of their apartment was excessive. Dupree and the Mobile, Alabama, police exhausted every effort to find her. However, when his third anniversary arrived, Dupree was alone.

"So again, I ask. Why ballet?" Mrs. Frisk asked, from across the studio.

"Well, I've perfected tap, jazz, and hip-hop," Dupree said, smiling.

Mrs. Frisk let out a little laugh. "Yes, I'm sure you have." She walked across the studio. "Stand up." She studied Dupree. "You have the build for a fine dancer. But not a ballet dancer."

"I'll work very hard."

"You'll have to. You will first learn to crawl, then walk, and then maybe…run."

"So, you'll teach me?" Dupree asked. "I do insist on private lessons. I don't want to draw attention."

Mrs. Frisk laughed. "For sure, you would draw attention. You're three-feet taller than the others in your class."

Six months had passed since their first meeting. Dupree had taken twenty-four lessons.

He was late for half of them.

"Dancing is timing," Dupree said, as he pressed down on the accelerator. "Why must you be late?"

Pulling into the lot at the studio, he parked quickly and grabbed his dance bag from the passenger seat.

Opening the ashtray, he removed his wedding ring and slipped it onto his finger—finally keeping a promise.

CHAPTER 3

"**J**esus, Janna," she said to her reflection. Her effort to fight back tears had made her eyes red and swollen. She ran cold water over her fingertips and gently daubed her eyes, trying to cool them off.

"Of course, she leaves a lucrative veterinary practice to follow him…"

An older lady entered the restroom and gave Janna an empathetic look before entering a stall.

A rom-com, really?

Mocking the conversation she and Lawrence had when studying the movie offerings, Janna pushed her chin toward the mirror and bobbled her head, as she exaggerated the words "…let's see something light and fun."

Entering an empty stall, she unrolled three feet of industrial-grade bathroom tissue and blew her nose. Dropping it in the commode, she pulled off another wad.

It's over. You know it. Do him a favor!

Moments earlier, as Janna felt Lawrence put his arm around her shoulder, she realized that she would never leave her job to follow Lawrence.

And my job isn't even that great.

Expecting the night to end early, she pulled the phone from her purse and dialed her mom.

"Hey Janna," her mom said, picking up after the first ring.

"Hey Mom," she said. Her voice was weak.

"What's wrong, sweetie? Are you okay?"

"Yes." A long pause followed. "Mom, I've decided to break up with Lawrence…"

"Oh my God, what did he…"

"No. Mom. It's not like that. It's just not working," Janna said. Moving from the stall, she brushed her hair back with her free hand. Putting the phone on speaker, she placed it on the bathroom counter. "Can I spend the night with you guys?"

"Sure."

Janna washed her hands.

"Dad will have to take us home tomorrow morning, and I'm on call, so there's a chance that I will need to get my truck tonight."

"Whatever you need sweetheart. I'm sorry it's not working out."

Janna smiled at her reflection in the bathroom mirror.

"It's fine. So, is Katie asleep yet? Can I talk to her?"

"Yes, she's been sleeping for a half hour."

"Then never mind," she said, with a new confidence. She dried her hands and picked up the phone. "I'll call if I need you. Okay?"

"Be safe."

"Will do," Janna said, cradling the phone in her shoulder. She started searching her purse for make-up. "I'll call if plans change. Love you, Mom."

• • •

Janna and Lawrence exited the movie theater into the parking lot, avoiding the crowd of teenagers loitering at the marquis. Janna folded her arms in front of her as she stepped outside. Lawrence offered his hand to her by swinging it up a little higher than his normal stride. Janna gave a weak smile and avoided contacting the tuft of reddish-blonde hair on the back of his fingers. He placed his arm around her waist as they moved toward the car.

The smell of asphalt replaced the musty odor of curtains and padded chairs. The air was heavy, saturated; it blanketed the cars with an eerie haze illuminated by bluish halogen lamps. Lawrence's glasses fogged up as soon as they stepped outside.

"I couldn't help notice that the movie got to you," he said, removing a handkerchief from his back pocket.

The movie was condescending and stupid. Its plot? Boy meets girl, boy loses girl, boy gets girl in the end. Lawrence and Janna would play two of the three acts.

"Lawrence, we need to talk," she said, without looking up.

Lawrence opened her door; Janna settled into the seat and dropped her hands into her lap.

She stared toward the parking lot as Lawrence got in and buckled his seatbelt.

"Lawrence," she said, turning to look into his dimly lit eyes. His nose began to twitch. "I think I would like this to be our last date." She held the glance for just a moment then turned her head toward the passenger side window.

Lawrence sighed.

"Janna…I…you're serious."

"I'm sorry."

Lawrence said nothing.

Janna grabbed her cellphone—the call would be a short one.

She reached for the door handle.

"No, Janna, I'll take you home," Lawrence said, as he placed the car in reverse. "Buckle up."

"You don't need to drive me all the way back to Pascagoula," Janna said. "My parents live just a few miles from here."

"Don't you need your truck? You said you were on call."

"I am, but…"

"I'll take you home. It's no big deal."

Janna pulled a tissue from her purse. She touched the corner of her eyes and blew her nose as indiscreetly as possible.

The date was over. Janna and Lawrence's three-week "relationship" had officially ended.

She had met Lawrence when he came over from Ocean Springs to help distribute meals-on-wheels after the storm. Janna's church, being north of the railroad tracks, had survived the storm surge and became a central distribution center for providing food to the community.

Lawrence's enthusiasm, his genuine love for helping people, and his work ethic were admirable. He had a great sense of humor and laughed, often excessively, at Janna's witty observations. When he asked her out for a date a month ago, she had no reason to say no. Lawrence was a perfect gentleman.

However, Lawrence was plain. Tall and awkward, he walked with a stiff lower back, which proved handy in stacking several Styrofoam lunch containers along his exceedingly long arms. His eyes opened a little too wide, giving him the appearance of an insect.

But Janna overlooked the straight back, the insect eyes, the hairy fingers. She admired his character, and they could have built a long, happy relationship on that alone. But, Lawrence had waited until last night to call her for the date, and this first character flaw was the chink in Lawrence's armor.

Taking a quick glimpse over at Lawrence, she returned her stare outside.

On just their third date, the relationship had grown as stale as the rolls they stuffed into the care packages. Janna didn't even bother to wash her hair after work.

For an actual date, she would clip her blonde mop up on her head, allowing the natural curl to give the impression of controlled chaos. Her blue eyes, accentuated with a hint of light make-up, would be framed nicely with a high-collared blouse with blue undertones and a set of super-dangly earrings. For this date with Lawrence, however, she was tempted to wear her work uniform in a blatant display that she didn't have time for a social life.

"Jeez, Janna, we could've taken a little time to allow you to change," he would have said.

"Lawrence, you can't imagine what it's like. I don't see why anyone would want to get involved with me. I'm always on call."

Lawrence pulled out onto Highway 90.

Janna glanced over to see his expression. It was blank.

This was only the second time she had ever broken up with someone, not including her divorce. She combated the low tug of pain in her chest with the anticipation of being free from Lawrence in about twenty minutes.

• • •

The storm changed everything in Pascagoula. Nature, the great equalizer, leveled the playing field. Rich bankers waited in the same FEMA lines for a formaldehyde-laden trailer as the shipyard workers. For the first time since World War II, when Pascagoula was placed on the map, the residents looked outside of themselves for strength. They were reduced to rubble.

Janna's profession opened new doors in this time of trial. She seized the opportunity and accepted a calling to invite people to attend her church.

"Thank you so much," nearly every customer said, when she mentioned that she was helping her church distribute meals.

"You're welcome," Janna responded. "I can bring a few more on Saturday or, if you like, you can pick up some at the church on Sunday—after the service. Church is at 11:00."

However, now, after the recovery, it was business as usual, and no one wanted a free meal or an invitation. No one wanted to relive the humiliation that destruction brings. There was no good in returning life back to its basics.

• • •

With clear eyes, Janna studied the Pascagoula River Bridge. The red warning lights flashed; the guard arms dropped in front of the car in front of her. The drawbridge rose slowly before her.

"Great," Lawrence said. "Prolong the agony."

"I'm sorry Lawrence."

He didn't respond.

The grating elevated, pivoting on invisible hinges that ran beneath the road. The little man in the gatehouse, whose entire career involved watching the traffic on the river and pushing the "up and down" buttons, appeared to be sleeping. Outside the passenger-side window, the river was dark. The lights on the banks widened as the river flowed south. Once at the gulf, the lights disappeared.

A pogy boat moved beneath the bridge. Lights from the crow's nest blinked as it moved past the grating. Janna sighed. Why couldn't she have been born far away from the Mississippi Gulf Coast, far away from the river, and the drawbridge, and the movie theater, and the storms and the…

"What the hell is he doing?" Lawrence shouted, snapping Janna out of her daydream. He hit the power locks on the doors.

Janna jumped as a figure flashed by the window. Someone was running for the rail.

"Oh, my God!"

"He's going to jump! I think he's…"

Suddenly a stockier man grabbed the first man as if he were going to tackle him on the bridge. He secured him to the rail; they were shouting at one another. Janna wanted to roll down the window.

A flash of light from the high beams of the car behind them allowed Janna to recognize the would-be jumper.

"I know him. That's…" Janna said, squinting to make sure she was correct.

"Who?"

"Franky."

"Which one? The first guy or the other one?"

"The first guy. Him, right there. That's Franky Stevens; we went to high school together."

Franky was being led back to the car. His legs wobbled under him. His eyes were slits.

"Jeez, I wonder what he's on?" Lawrence asked. "He looks wasted."

"I don't know."

Janna watched the side-view mirror, as the spans of the bridge descended in front of her. It had been ten years since she had seen Franky.

"What's he doing home?" Janna asked, letting her thoughts slip into spoken words.

"He's your age?" Lawrence asked, placing the car in gear. "He looks older. Who's the other guy?"

Janna's mind flashed with vivid images of Franky.

"I don't know. No, we're the same age. It's just that…well I haven't seen him since high school. I didn't realize…" Janna's voice trailed off.

High school was easy for Franky. With his infectious laugh, cute friends, and an abundance of confidence, he strolled the halls like he owned them. Passing him, Janna would smile. Franky rarely noticed; his cackling entourage demanded his complete attention.

Oh, God. Wilson's party. Janna's mind flashed to the only time they rode together.

Lawrence pulled into Janna's driveway; she wanted to say something sweet. Lawrence was a fine man, but she was not attracted to fine men. She wanted to say something like, "Lawrence, I'll never forget you. You're terrific, and I wish you all the best."

The fact was that she would forget him, and the elegant dismissal came out sounding more like, "Well, I'll see you around. Let's stay in touch."

"Okay, Janna, goodnight."

She climbed out of the car and walked in the side door.

"No," she said aloud, stepping into the living room.

"Lawrence, I might forget you."

Grabbing her senior annual from a bookshelf, Janna thumbed to the graduates' pictures.

"But Franky Stevens is a different matter."

CHAPTER 4

Dale and Franky flew head first off the decks of the gambling barge in what spectators called a post "Impressions" spectacle. Although the impersonator show at the Isle of Capri Casino included Madonna, Roy Orbison, and Elvis, Dale and Franky were real. They screamed, they fought, they cursed, they spit.

The "Impressions" show was little compensation for depleting an entire social security check in a single slot machine. However, the little old ladies watching the fight, between a couple of drunks and security, felt like VIPs. Having racked up tons of players-club points, they now treated themselves to another free show.

Dale landed on the concrete, bounced on his hip, and rolled several times, before jumping to his feet. Brushing himself off, he limped up to Franky.

Franky didn't bounce or roll. He just hit the ground like a bag of wet rags.

"I got him," Dale said to the bouncer, who was pushing Franky toward the curb with this foot. "I got him."

"Keep him out of there."

"Yeah, yeah."

Dale grabbed Franky around the waist and pulled him to his feet. Another night ended badly.

Dale should have expected it from the moment they stepped into Tres Rancheros earlier that evening.

• • •

"Yeah, one more, gracias," Franky said, to the waiter who was bowing politely.

Franky raised his fork and carefully placed a mouthful of enchilada in his mouth.

"Ugh, this is authentic Mexican food?" Franky asked, his words muffled by the chunks of tortillas and sauce filling his mouth. "It's authentic Mexican crap."

"Whatever, man," Dale said, shoveling in another forkful. "Keep mouthing off and they'll kick us both out."

"You think I care?" Franky said, looking around.

Franky had ordered the Baja—a meal made up of a taco, enchilada, and tamale with rice and beans. He picked at the tamale and dropped his fork onto his plate with disgust. Puddles of grease rose to the top, separating the main entrees into tiny masses of unidentifiable food stock.

The waiter returned with the beer and handed it to Franky. He pulled the lime wedge from the top and lifted a mock toast, chugging half of the beer in his first swig.

"The only thing authentic in this joint is the cerveza," he said. The third one went down as fast as the first.

Franky tossed the lime into his plate; it didn't add enough taste to compensate for the time wasted squeezing it into the bottle. He rarely ate. Food hurt his stomach, and he suffered the first symptoms of liver disease—his yellowish complexion was more noticeable with the lack of sun exposure. In the spring and early summer, his tendency to look jaundiced was cured with a healthy tan. However, in southern Mississippi in August, like winter in Duluth, no one went outside.

"We could've eaten somewhere else."

"No, I like this place. It's okay," Franky said, watching Dale take another bite. He threw his napkin onto the plate. Immediately, the yellowish-red grease wicked to the top.

"Hey, I'd have eaten that," Dale said, looking up.

"It's still good."

Franky removed the napkin, handling it like toxic waste.

"You know man, we really don't need to go to the casinos." Dale began working the paper wrapping off a tamale.

"What do you mean?"

"I'm just saying…we don't have to go. My old lady's already…"

"Your old lady? Tell me you did not just say 'your old lady,'" Franky said, sitting forward. He polished off his beer with another long drink. "It's been forever. Listen, man, I've been sitting in my office all day thinking about this. I left early just so I could get ready."

"You're still wearing your work clothes," Dale said, looking up and smiling. For Franky, getting ready meant spending the last two hours of the workday in Castaways Bar.

"Whatever man, all I'm saying is that Fineburg came in and started busting my chops about something, and I had to cut out. That guy's going to kill me one day."

"He's going to fire you one day," Dale said, shoveling the remaining mixture of Franky's refried beans and rice into his mouth.

"Hey Poncho! Yeah, come here. One more cerveza, por favor. Just one more."

"If we're going to go, we need to go," Dale said. "We'll take the check."

The waiter nodded and placed the bill on the table.

"Never mind then," Franky said, pulling out his wallet. "Let me get this."

• • •

Drunk beyond the point of pleasure, Franky fell to the pavement at the trunk of his car. Flaccid, unconscious, he drooled from the corner of his mouth. The little puddle shined blue and yellow with the glow of neon from the front of the casino.

"Jeez Franky, what have you done now?"

Dale searched Franky's pants for the valet ticket. He consoled his inebriated friend, who communicated nonsensically in grunts and snorts. Dale gently placed his free hand between Franky's head and the pavement, as he handed the ticket to the valet.

"You got to help me, buddy."

"Five, really, five?" Franky mumbled.

When Franky's car pulled up, Dale dragged Franky to the passenger side door, loaded him into the car, and buckled his seat belt. After tipping the valet, Dale drove east on Highway 90 toward Pascagoula.

"Hey man, I mean are you sure, $500?" Franky asked. He slurred another sentence, inaudibly. With his eyes shut, his head bobbed with the movement of the car.

"What are you saying?"

"Five hundred dollars is that…I mean…come on, man, I don't… whatever, if you say so, man." He collapsed deeper into the seat. His head struck the passenger door window.

They drove through Gautier without incident. When they stopped at the drawbridge marking the city limits of Pascagoula, the road rose in front of Dale.

In the dark with the lights tracking along its rails, the span of the bridge became a newly constructed skyscraper. Ships sailed in from a late evening pogy run, weighted down, smelling of fish. Below, the water flowed invisibly, its edges illuminated by the lights of barges parked on the banks. The slow-moving river fell silent against the hum of the engines of waiting cars and the whir of the cables of the lowering section of bridge. Car exhaust lingered forever in the heavy, humid air.

"What the…Franky!" Dale shouted.

Without warning, Franky grabbed the door handle, shouted something, and fell out of the car.

Jumping up, he staggered from the idling car, toward the top of the bridge.

"Franky!" Dale shouted. "Franky!" Dale followed quickly behind, waving at the others in their cars to show that he had everything under control.

"Check that out man!" Franky shouted, as he moved toward the side of the bridge. "That's a long ways…"

"Franky, hold on! Just settle down!" Dale pinned him against the rail and jammed his leg between his friend's legs. Dale spoke with a shortness of breath. "We're going back to the car. Okay? Calm down, okay? C'mon, let's go!"

"Dale, check out the river. Man, that's a long way down."

"Come on, come here," Dale said, moving him away from the rail. He talked in a calmer voice. "Let's go home. Let's get back to the house, all right?" He patted his back and hugged him tightly. He talked directly into his ear.

"Yeah man, whatever," Franky said, nearly collapsing. "Whatever."

CHAPTER 5

Kenneth Schultz crossed Beach Boulevard and leapt into the chest-deep water on the other side of the seawall. Keeping one hand on the concrete and one hand on the straps to his backpack, he pushed eastward toward the pier.

He groaned under his breath. The wound across his left knee, sliced open and bleeding profusely, refused to coagulate. The gauze, that had been wrapped round and round so tightly, was soggy. The duct tape, used to secure it, stretched into a silver ring that slid down his calf.

Initially, Schultz planned to casually stroll along the seawall and dive into the water if he saw a police officer. But, nothing went right. Hargood slashed his knee; blood spewed everywhere when the tube popped out of the milk jug; dragging the body to the stairs nearly broke Schultz's back. He cut his losses and ditched the idea of a casual, early morning stroll home.

Schultz bit his bottom lip; he tasted blood. Pain surged through his knee and shot up the back of his leg into his spine.

His moans and heavy breaths bounced off the water. Submerged in darkness, the concrete wall to his left guided his path. A distant light illuminated the entrance to the recently destroyed Pascagoula public pier.

With each odd-numbered step, the wound in Schultz's knee tore open. It closed every time his left foot sank into the muck—the straightened leg allowed the skin on both sides of the wound to come in contact. But as soon as the foot found solid ground, in mud six inches deep, it was time to tear the flesh apart.

Schultz fought the wound.

"Stop! Rest! Let me coagulate," the knee screamed.

"No! I can't stop," Schultz yelled, moving with more determined steps. His voice hugged the rippling surface. His mouth was full of salt water; he spit toward the south.

"If I've figured the distance correctly, and if I was correct on the number of steps it took to get to his front door, then you'll have to open and close another three hundred and twenty times. But there now, it's one less and still one less; three hundred will soon be two and then one—and soon the pier. I see it!"

The pier designated completion.

"It is finished!" Schultz said, exhausted. "So to speak."

Once Schultz touched the pier, he would be free. Free to live a life of pain and happiness, suffering and praise; free to exercise his awakened conscience. Years had separated events that warranted repentance. At the pier, this would all change—a fully mature psychopath would once again feel the sting of remorse.

Schultz pushed onward, occasionally hiking up the backpack. A putrid smell made his eyes water.

A tear ran down the side of his face and mixed with the drops of sea water sprinkled on his cheek. Schultz rubbed his eyes with the back of his hand. He blinked wildly to grab any speck of light.

"A psychopath? Not hardly, not me, not anymore, not at the pier..."

He took in a deep breath. A splash of water hit the side of his head; he remained low. He fought back a gag reflex.

Schultz spoke, gasping for air, struggling with each step. "My senses are already returning! My nose, my sinuses, aaghh! They burn. Just like old Hargood's, hee hee."

Headlights appeared on Beach Boulevard. Schultz sunk low into the water; the backpack was getting wet. He straightened his left leg, as he waited for the car to pass.

As the car approached, he took a deep breath and went under water.

One one thousand, two one thousand.

Slowly, raising his head out of the water, he began his trek again, counting down each step.

"Just a few more! Ah, there it is. Yes."

Schultz reached out toward the pier and lost his footing. "Ouch, son-of-a…!" His arm scraped along a piling as he fell forward into the water. Submerged oyster shells sliced his hand. Coming out of the water, he gasped for air. The straps of his backpack wrapped around his throat.

Climbing over the seawall, he crawled beneath the pier. A squad car with its lights flashing raced down Beach Boulevard. Schultz crawled on one knee, hidden by the pier above. Rolling over, he sat with his legs straight out. His sinuses filled with the putrid odor of decaying fish, chemical foam, and diesel fuel. The scene of his crime was a quarter mile away.

"Only one car?" Schultz held his knee tight with both hands. "Ah…bye, bye, officer." The police cruiser raced past the Hargood house. "You should come back tomorrow. You might get a little shock. Doesn't it look a bit like Golgotha?"

The next 100 yards were critical for escape. With one witness or another patrol car, Schultz would spend the rest of his life on death row.

"One minute. One minute is all I need."

With a shot of adrenaline, Schultz took off from below the pier. Running down the middle of Beach Boulevard, with his left leg perfectly straight, his elbows keeping the backpack centered, he was totally vulnerable, totally alive. He started to laugh.

The one hundred yards passed in seconds, and Schultz leapt into the canal that ran behind his house.

Breathing heavily, he took an inventory of his surroundings. The dim lights from the surrounding houses worked their way through thick brush and reflected off a trickle of water at his feet. Weeds and garbage surrounded him.

"The leg is getting infected," he said, as he stood and began moving north along the canal. "It's wonderfully infected!"

He crossed the canal to a clearing. Pushing weeds aside with the back of his hand, he kept his left leg perfectly stiff.

Up the canal, along the dry banks, Schultz hiked. He wanted to skip, but the wounded knee rejected the notion. Choking weeds made it difficult to take one clean step.

If it were light, he would fear snakes.

Fighting brush and crunching down razor grass, he stepped across the dry bed. He slid into a clearing and then crisscrossed to the other side. Another five hundred paces to his back porch, another five hundred paces to…

"No, oh God no!"

Schultz's left foot sunk into a mud hole halfway up his calf.

A dog barked wildly.

"Easy boy," Schultz whispered, "Oh Christ, this is bad."

The dog was inside a chain-link fence and could not attack. Schultz worked his leg to free it from the mud. "I hear you. Good doggy. Oh God, that hurts."

Buried in the weeds and darkness Schultz wrenched on his wounded leg.

"Oh God, let me die here," Schultz whimpered, looking up at the dog. "Please, please, shut the hell up."

Schultz slipped down deeper into the grass, removed his backpack, and made one last violent twist on the knee. He clinched his teeth, being careful not to bite through any more flesh.

His knee popped free of the mud.

"Oh jeez!" Tears welled in Schultz's eyes. His jaw ached.

"Good boy," Schultz whispered. He picked up the backpack. "You must be quiet." A man was disciplining the dog for barking. "Bye bye."

Crouching in the thicket of the bayou, Schultz headed home.

• • •

The door creaked as Schultz entered his house. He slipped in unnoticed. Michelle was asleep; the kids never woke up in the middle of the night. The house was cool and dry; it smelled like bread. He moved to the bathroom and flipped on the light.

Schultz cleaned his wound. It would require stitches, but he could not risk getting them tonight. The scraped arm burned with infection. He cleaned it with hydrogen peroxide.

He placed his clothes and the backpack in a garbage bag stored under the sink. Tomorrow, he would throw them from the drawbridge.

He showered and redressed the wound with fresh gauze. Falling into bed, exhausted, he prayed.

"God, have mercy. Lord, have mercy. Christ, have mercy, and please, please, please don't let them catch me."

CHAPTER 6

Pastor Dupree sat bolt upright in bed and yelled toward his backyard window. A digital clock, reading 3:13 a.m., illuminated the room.

"Red!" He screamed, throwing off his sheet.

Grabbing the pair of gym shorts on the floor at his feet, he took off in a dead run toward the kitchen. On tiptoes, in the pitch dark, his hands waved wildly, striking door jambs, as he navigated the path to the back door.

"Red!"

On the second night that he had let Red spend the night outside, a squirrel or raccoon threatened to ruin the whole experiment.

Dupree flipped on the back porch light and fiddled with the lock on the sliding glass door. Releasing the latch, he slid open the door. A herd of roaches, who had been planning an all-out assault on his house, scattered for the shadows.

"Red," he yelled, in an exaggerated whisper. "Get here, right now!" He stepped out onto the porch.

Red quieted instantly, crouching low as he walked up toward his owner. Dupree studied the woods beyond the backyard.

"Come here boy," he said. He pulled on the gym shorts and sat crossed-legged on the back porch. Red started licking his face. "What did you see? You've got to be quiet."

Dupree stared into the darkness, focusing on a distant light, scanning through the brush and trees that lined his property.

"Was it a raccoon?"

He rubbed Red's neck. The night was thick and quiet; humidity masked the stars.

Suddenly, Red leapt forward, barking madly. Dupree jumped. "Listen! Sit!"

Listening, staring, stretching his eyes to pick up the slightest amount of light, he let Red snort and claw at the ground.

Standing, Dupree inched forward on bare feet. His eyes flashed to movement at a house with a large, inflatable moonwalk in the backyard.

"Huh," he said, taking Red by the collar. "Let's go boy. Looks like you're going inside for the rest of the night."

• • •

The curtain in the temple had torn, and the skies darkened. Pastor Dupree heard it rip. He saw its frayed ends. He felt the earthquake, and he saw the ground open beneath his feet as he moved through Jerusalem. He was rushing through people that he had met but did not know by name. He wore sandals; Dupree hated his feet. He kept moving, shoved through a marketplace with towers of melons, gourds, and dates. Baskets were stacked along the stone road. Looking up, he saw Christ, dead, on the cross. Spikes were wrenched from his hands and feet with large crowbars. He heard the popping and cracking of the wood; he wanted to help, but Mrs. Brewer stopped him. She was out of her deathbed, shouting at him to leave. Dupree fought her; he didn't want to go back to the market.

His cellphone rang.

"Mrs. Brewer, I have to leave."

The phone rang again.

"Mrs. Brewer!"

Dupree was jerked from sleep, gasping for air; he grabbed his phone from the nightstand.

The room was dark except for a faint glow from the weak back porch light that slipped past the slats in the mini-blinds.

"Hello," he said, rolling on to one elbow.

"Pastor Dupree?"

"Yes."

"This is Detective Lucille Campbell." The voice suddenly familiar.

"Oh, hey Detective," he said, waking quickly. "What's up?"

"I was wondering if you could look at a crime scene and give us your take."

"Really? Sure. Uh…" Dupree sat up, placing his feet on the floor. The clock read 5:45 a.m.

"If it's okay, I can pick you up. I would prefer it."

"Sure, can you give me a few minutes?"

"I'll be there in ten," Detective Campbell said.

• • •

Dupree dressed quickly. Professional attire was paramount with Lucille Campbell.

Her promotion to Detective First Class was a big day for her family and a bigger day for the Pascagoula Police Department. At the ceremony, the governor, himself, presented her with her new badge. Detective Campbell was the first African American woman to make detective in all of Jackson County. She took the distinction very seriously.

Dupree picked through the clothes he wore last night—black pants, short-sleeved black shirt, and the stiff ring of white around his throat. Stepping off his front porch, coffee spilled over his hand onto his favorite running shoes. Dupree uttered light expletives, as he stepped over the dewy grass toward the unmarked squad car.

The sky overhead was waking with iridescent colors of orange and blue. The air was thick and humid, making the front yard feel like a sauna.

"Hey, Detective. What's up?"

Dupree took a seat, cradling his coffee in both hands.

"There's been a murder."

Detective Campbell wore jeans and a golf shirt with a PPD emblem on the sleeve. She had a big, beautiful smile. Her dark eyes were warm yet intimidating. Dupree pitied anyone facing her in an interrogation.

"We're heading to 608 Beach Boulevard."

"Okay."

"Do you always wear a collar?" Detective Campbell asked, dropping the car into gear.

"Pretty much. In the summer I'm tempted to buy a T-shirt that looks like one. You know, like one of those tuxedo T-shirts."

"Yeah, real classy. Buckle up."

"Is it bad?" Dupree asked. He reached for the blue light that rested on the dash. "Can I put this on the roof?"

"Don't touch that."

"Yes ma'am." He grabbed his coffee with both hands.

"I really don't want to say much," Detective Campbell said. "I prefer that you look at the scene without me giving you any of my thoughts. All I'm going to say is that, yes. It's pretty gruesome."

"As bad as the Capdepon crime scene?"

Detective Campbell's face turned solemn. "Much, much worse."

• • •

Blare Capdepon was a starting guard for the Pascagoula High School basketball team and the first freshman to make the varsity team in thirteen years. Just shy of five and a half feet tall, she was small alongside her teammates. She was even smaller in a crumbled mound in the girls' locker room.

Detective Campbell made the call to Pastor Cooper Dupree. His success helping track and arrest a George County deviant, who had burned three African American churches, made him a valuable resource.

Dupree inspected the destroyed churches. He interviewed parishioners. He tirelessly combed through reams of historical data on arsonists and neo-Nazis throughout the region. However, it took one of Dupree's "experiences" to crack the case.

During a session of prayer and meditation, a pattern in the burnings surfaced. Based on a biblical passage found in the Acts of the Apostles, Dupree confidently stated that the next church to be targeted would be the Antioch Primitive Baptist Church on Hwy 63 in Lucedale.

Three nights into the stakeout of the fourth church, an arrest was made, and a church was saved.

The Mississippi Press Register ran a two column article on the twenty-eight-year-old preacher. A human-interest story, it touched on Dupree's troubled youth, his incarcerated father, and his call to minister to the imprisoned. The article detailed Sarah's missing persons case. It concluded with Dupree's call to Christ Church in Pascagoula.

Dupree's first "experience" occurred defending himself against the onslaught of a politically driven district attorney in Mobile. Following the disappearance of his wife, Dupree was the prime suspect because it made good television. Reporters hounded the young, attractive assistant pastor. Police interrogated him for hours. Polygraphs could not be trusted. So, the detectives brought in FBI profilers to pick Duprees brain and scrutinize his parents.

No one cared that Dupree had an alibi or that he had no motive. No one cared that he was totally devoted to his wife and that he worked tirelessly to find her.

Two months into the investigation, during an intense session of prayer, Dupree's groin caught fire. An electric shock ran up his spine into the base of his skull. He was moved toward the story of the Apostle Paul, charged with rebellion, on trial in front of Judge Felix. Over and over again, Dupree's mind flashed with the single name, Tertullus.

Tertullus had lodged false accusations against Paul…Tertullus the lawyer.

Dupree began researching cases involving the disappearance or murder of a lawyer. When he discovered similarities between Sarah's case and the unsolved disappearance of a tax attorney in Mobile, detectives reopened the three-year-old missing lawyer case. Dupree was dropped as a suspect.

Six months later, someone was burning churches.

Detective Campbell was aware of Dupree's work on Sarah's case. She took a leap of faith and invited him to help with the case.

When Blare Capdepon was found dead, Pastor Cooper Dupree was one of the first calls she made.

Scrawled across the locker room mirror was a scripture passage. The words were written in fake blood, and on the floor laid the apparent perpetrator. With fake blood covering her hand, Blare collapsed at the scene of the crime, struck down by an asthma attack while vandalizing the school.

"God helps those who help themselves?" Dupree asked Detective Campbell. He shook his head in disgust. "That's not in the Bible. It's not even Bible-ish."

Dupree's initial investigation discovered that the Capdepons were active members of the local Catholic church. Blare excelled as a student throughout her catechism.

For three days Dupree worked tirelessly trying to figure out the motive for writing the phrase. It wasn't until he stepped into the sanctuary at Christ Church that the "experience" happened and an inspired hunch came to light.

Dupree's mind rested on Aaron holding up Moses' hands.

When Moses' hands grew tired, they took a stone and put it under him and he sat on it. Aaron and Hur held his hands up one on one side, one on the other–so that his hands remained steady till sunset.

Exodus 17:12

Blare Capdepon was not a vandal; she was a victim. Dupree and Detective Campbell returned to the crime scene, and Dupree showed how the writing on the mirror was done. The real vandal or vandals dipped Blare's limp, dead hand in a bucket of fake blood and used it like a paint brush. Further investigation determined that the pH level of Blare's blood clearly showed that respiratory acidosis, the lethal rise of acid levels attributable to a severe asthmatic attack, was not the cause of death. Someone suffocated Blare. In the end, the Capdepon case had one innocent victim, five high school basketball players on trial for manslaughter, and one girls' basketball coach facing a heavy civil lawsuit for squashing what he knew about the practice of hazing.

• • •

The oaks lining Pascagoula Street whizzed by at speeds never attempted by Dupree.

"This thing is really nice," he said, looking at the interior of the police cruiser. A laptop sat between him and Detective Campbell in the seat. "Is it just yours?"

"Yes." Detective Campbell smiled. "But I let others use it if they need to," she said, breaking hard as they approached Beach Boulevard. Dupree grabbed the dash.

"When we get there, don't touch anything. You've been to crime scenes. I know that. But this is my crime scene, and I'm really particular about it, okay?"

"Got it," Dupree said. Turning onto Beach Boulevard, he saw the entire Pascagoula Police Department parked along the seawall. Pulling into the middle of the pack, Detective Campbell parked the cruiser.

"Let's go."

Sharing pleasantries with the cops, who were loitering in front of the house, Dupree and Detective Campbell walked up the front steps of the Hargood residence. They placed latex gloves on their hands.

Ducking under the yellow crime scene tape, Dupree scanned the front porch.

"You need to step to the side," Detective Campbell said. "Those are his footprints. Look down here."

"Who's?"

"That's why you're here."

Moving to the side and squatting down, Dupree observed the set of muddy footprints heading to the front door.

"They match the ones in the…uh…inside. You'll see."

As they approached the front door, Detective Campbell pointed at the security chain, dangling from the door. Dupree nodded, as he ran his hand over the shattered door jamb.

"I'm going to let you look by yourself. I really want fresh eyes, so I'm just going to stay out here, okay?"

"Fine," Dupree said, pushing the door open with the back of his hand.

To his right was a shattered mirror with blood streaks running down the wall. Glass littered the entire foyer. He took a mental inventory—a syringe, a spray can, an elastic band, a roll of duct tape. In the pool of blood below the mirror, footprints and smeared lines made images, like a child's fingerpaint of fire.

Dupree turned his eyes to the left; on the stairs to the left was a man. Dupree froze. Closing his eyes, he drew a deep breath. He stood perfectly still, praying for strength, guidance, and insight.

The man looked familiar. His hands were bound at the wrist; his feet were bound at the ankles. Moving along the blood streaks that ran through the foyer to the stairs, Dupree took a closer look at the victim. He was ashen with eyes sunk deep into his head. The only clothing he wore was a pair of blue gym shorts streaked with varying hues of brown. The man's feet had a spike driven through them into a step. His hands were stretched over his head, also with a single spike through both hands into a step.

"Detective!" Dupree yelled, toward the front door. "Detective Campbell?"

"Yes?"

"Is there any more?"

"No. It all took place right here. Nothing stolen; nothing else disturbed."

"Who found the body?" Dupree asked from inside.

"The paper boy saw the door was open and called 911. The officers actually found the body. Did you see the blood?"

"Yeah, it's pretty bad."

"No. Behind you, behind the door."

In the corner was a gallon jug, filled with what was apparently blood. Beside it was an open Bible.

Dupree stepped softly toward it. A single passage was highlighted in bright yellow.

"Revelation 12:16?" Dupree asked himself.

He read it aloud, before yelling out to Detective Campbell.

"Detective."

"Yeah."

"This is bad."

Then from his mouth the serpent spewed water like a river, to overtake the woman and sweep her away with the torrent. But the earth helped the woman by opening its mouth and swallowing the river that the dragon had spewed out of his mouth.

Revelation 12:16

CHAPTER 7

A cellphone ringtone, set on max level, woke Janna Sandler in a panic.

"Katie!"

Fighting and kicking her way out of the sheets, she grabbed the phone before the second ring. Panic quickly changed to relief when she saw the caller ID. Her boss, not her parents, was calling.

"Hello?" The clock on her nightstand read six-thirty a.m.

"Janna, sorry to bother you. But I've got a favor to ask."

"Sure Dave, what is it?"

A little morning sun filtered through the blinds, lighting the bedroom with a soft, comfortable tone.

"Mr. Proctor, you know, down at the end of Beach Boulevard…"

Janna opened the blinds to allow more light into the dark-paneled bedroom. With deep, blue shag wall-to-wall carpeting and track lighting over the bed, the room resembled the set of a 1970s porno.

"…it's the new house with the dormers?"

"Dave, they're all new and have dormers," Janna said, taking a seat on the end of the bed. In eighteen months, Janna remodeled the kitchen, den, Katie's room, and the main bathroom. The hideous bedroom was next.

"Yeah, it's at 410 Beach Blvd. Anyway, Mr. Proctor called, mad as hell. He saw a roach in his bathroom, and I asked if it was dead, and he said it was still wiggling and…"

"Dave, is this the one on the corner of Eleventh Street?"

"What? Yes, it's the white one, anyway. He said that he wanted someone out there immediately because he paid to have no roaches, and his wife was freaking out because they have that new grandbaby coming over and…"

"Dave, I can go. I can be there in twenty minutes."

"Really Janna? Can you be there by seven because I've got to run Ellen up to her mother's house so that she can…"

"I can do it," Janna said.

"Great. I really appreciate that. Let me know if you run into any problems."

"Sure thing. Have a great weekend."

• • •

Janna showered quickly. Making time-and-a-half, for working Saturday, warranted wearing a fresh uniform shirt. With no time to dry her hair, she wore a ball cap with the green and white Bay Pest logo. The wet pony tail pulled through the back of the cap was cold against her neck.

In the kitchen, she texted her mother.

"How's the munchkin?"

Sitting at the kitchen counter, sipping a homemade iced coffee, she searched Facebook.

"Franky Stevens Pascagoula". No result.

Her mother responded.

"She's fine. Just got up a few minutes ago, and she's with your dad. How did it go last night?"

"Good," Janna typed with one thumb. She grabbed her keys and turned off the lights in the kitchen. "I think he was expecting it. BTW guess who…" Janna stopped typing. Her mom wouldn't remember Franky; her mom didn't even *like* Franky.

She backspaced over "BTW guess who" and sent the message.

Once seated in her work truck, she dialed her mom.

"Yes?"

"Hey Mom, I got a call. I'm going to run by and check on it, then I'll come straight over. I just wanted to give you the heads up, in case it goes long."

"That's fine," her mom said. "We'll be here."

"Thanks Mom."

• • •

Janna walked up the driveway to the front of the Proctor's house. Police cars lined Beach Boulevard a quarter mile away—lights flashing, sirens off. Before the storm, the house in front of her was two stories. Reconstructed, after being reduced to kindling by a twenty-four foot storm surge, the house was now three stories. The bottom floor was a blowout floor used for parking and utilities.

Having ascended thirty stairs, Janna rang the doorbell. The front porch, extended the entire width of the house. Fresh young ferns, saturated with water from drip irrigators, hung around the perimeter. The aroma of fresh paint mixed with the salty, marine odor of the Mississippi Sound.

"Hello, I'm Janna. I'm here to re-spray." A man, about her father's age, answered the door.

"Is that really what you have to do?" He flew into a rage instantly. "I have guests coming, and I don't want the place to smell like poison."

"Well, I don't know, sir. Perhaps we don't need to spray," Janna said, stepping inside. "Can you show me where the problem is?"

She was ushered through the house.

"Your home is wonderful. I really love the ceilings, and it's so bright. I love it."

Before the storm, the houses on Beach Boulevard were huge, opulent, and cold. Uninviting, wonderful homes inhabited by some of the hardest people in the community. Janna tried not to judge. But, her experience, servicing many homes along the boulevard, found few exceptions. The houses, like their occupants, were prettier from the outside than from within.

The furniture was old and ornate. The uplifting reflections off the gulf hid behind thick window dressings. They smelled like libraries and the tired scent of money.

But the hurricane took care of that. Of the sixty homes lining the seawall, one remained standing, and it had to be demolished.

"It's in here," Mr. Proctor said, leading Janna into the guest bathroom.

"Yes sir. It's one of those big wood roaches. Some call them a palmetto bug."

Janna grabbed a wad of toilet paper and picked up the roach, pinching through the tissue to make sure he was dead. She threw it in the toilet and flushed.

"You see Mr. Proctor, these big guys come from outside. They actually live in the trees out back, probably in that big Canary Island date palm right there." Janna pointed toward the backyard. "They don't actually nest inside the house." She pulled a spray can from her work bag and sprayed around the parameter of the bathroom window. "They're really hard to keep out. This should help. The good news is that he was dying. The poison dehydrates them, so you will most often find them in the tub or sinks. This spray is odorless." She held up the can for Mr. Proctor.

"Fine, just make sure it doesn't happen again."

"I'll try."

• • •

As Janna's white, Bay Pest, truck pulled away from the curb, she studied the scene behind her in the rearview mirror. With a quick U-turn, she could roll past a crime scene that required the attention of the entire Pascagoula Police Department.

She turned right onto Market Street instead. Approaching a new Starbucks, she flipped on her turn signal and then quickly turned it off. Five dollars for a grande mocha vanilla frost, or some equally delicious liquid, was better spent on gasoline. Hitting the accelerator, she headed for Gautier.

When her phone rang, she reached in her purse and read the caller ID.

She shook her head and frowned. Her ex-husband, D.L. called only when he needed a favor.

"Hello?"

"Hey, it's me. What's up?"

"Nothing," she said, trying to figure out why he would call so early on a Saturday. "Are you at work?"

"Nah, I actually got back last night, and I'm over at Mom and Dad's." D.L.'s voice was thick. "I was wondering if I could get Katie tomorrow afternoon, after you guys get out of church. Maybe, I could keep her for the night."

"Sure, she would like that. Are you going to be at your folks?" D.L. had a trailer in George County. He and his new wife had been renting it since they moved out of his parent's house. The place was clean. Katie had plenty of room to run around and enjoy the outdoors. But, Janna was suspicious of D.L.'s spouse and any number of his friends who might stop in.

"Yeah, we'll just stay here. Mom wants to have a little party or something for her. I don't know. You know how Mom is."

Janna knew how "Mom was". Mom was a spoiler. Mom spoiled D.L. to the point that he couldn't function in society without a caretaker. Mom spoiled Katie so thoroughly that a three-day stint with "Meme" required a total reprogramming of the child.

"I thought I'd pick her up from church and take her to daycare on Monday morning," D.L. said. "If that's okay with you?"

Janna made the turn onto Highway 90 and drove toward the drawbridge.

"That's fine. So Cindy's actually going to stay at your parents? How is that going to go?"

"She ain't going," D.L. said. "She kicked me out last time I left for the rig. We ain't really spoken since I got back. So, I don't know. I don't think she would come."

"I'm sorry to hear that Dee," Janna said.

"Yeah, well, I believe I'm just going to stay here with Mom for a little while." There was a long, awkward pause. "You know Janna, if you want to come to the party, I'm sure…I mean…I'd think that would be nice and all."

Janna navigated the Bay Pest Nissan over the drawbridge.

"I don't think so, D.L. But thanks anyway."

CHAPTER 8

Willard Franklin "Franky" Stevens III opened his eyes to a world blurred in grey; everything was in fluid motion, throbbing to the beat of his elevated heart rate. He couldn't breathe; he clutched a pillow around his raging temples. Pain shot through his brain like a spear through his left eye. The point of the spear stuck in his brain stem.

"Oh…my…God," he moaned slowly. His voice twisted the spear, generating tears.

Loss of depth perception caused nausea. He covered his face with the pillow, gradually adjusting to the overload of sensory input. He let out a relieved sigh.

Franky was in his own room.

It's Saturday. It's got to be Saturday.

He couldn't be late for work again.

Rolling to the side of the bed, his stomach knotted; he wanted to vomit. Sitting up, he allowed time for his blood to reposition itself in his organs. He pressed his palms into his eyes.

Standing, a stinging pain ran from his lower back down his hamstring to his Achilles' tendon.

"What the…?"

The arch of his left foot burned like fire. He limped out of his bedroom.

"It's still morning all right," Franky said, in a cracked voice. "It's definitely Saturday."

In the kitchen he rinsed out a glass that was in the sink and poured a half glass of tomato juice. The drink was thick and tasted plain without salt or vodka.

"Yeah," he said, his throat coated with the liquid, "Thursday playing cards and…then Friday afternoon, yesterday. Right? You went to the casinos, about six, I guess, or it must have been later. It had to be later because we ate dinner…at…the El…"

He sat at the table drinking juice and putting the pieces together. The nail by the front door was empty. He patted his pants pocket. His car keys were missing.

"Dale's got the car."

Or did I leave it at Tres Rancheros?

"I must have had them to get into the apartment."

Franky walked to the front door and slowly opened it. Heat and blinding sunlight assaulted him, as he checked the outside lock for his keys. Falling back into the apartment, he slammed the door behind him.

"These are the pants I was wearing." He inspected his pants, by patting down the length of the legs. "Yeah, these are my pants."

Grabbing his glass, Franky chugged the last of his juice. The cold, thick liquid froze his brain. Sitting, he rested his elbows on the table and pressed his temples with his palms.

"Maybe, it's at the casino." He spoke to the table. "We definitely took my car, because we left his at Tres Rancheros."

Walking to the window in the den, he stuck his finger between the mini-blinds. His car was parked near the pool.

"So, I valet parked…and…"

Franky double checked that the car by the pool was actually his.

"Dale drove my car back here."

So how did he get home?

Dale didn't walk home.

Oh my God. Rosie is going to kill me.

Dale's wife was not fond of Franky.

And she doesn't even know about the money.

Inflicting marital trauma on Dale was compounded by the very real $500 Franky borrowed and lost last night.

You've got to get that back to him today.

Stepping back into the kitchen, he found his phone and listened to a voice mail message. As the message played, he grabbed a saltshaker from the center of the table and licked his index finger.

"This is an important message for a Mr. Willard Stevens, we see that your car warranty has…"

Franky hit the delete button.

He ate a few fingers of salt; he scanned his text messages.

"Where you at?" Sent from Dale yesterday afternoon. Delete.

"Are you out? Let's hang. Peach emoji." Sent from Jolynda Redhead, a girl Franky had met a month ago. Delete.

The last message he deleted was from his mom.

Franky walked toward the bathroom and tossed his shirt into the spare bedroom.

In the bathroom, he let out a gut-wrenching yell as he fell to the floor. His still tender left foot, swollen and sensitive, stepped on his keys. "Mystery solved," he said, sitting on the floor and rubbing his arch.

He took his time showering. The water washed away more than his rank smell. Bending to wash his feet, the pain in his lower back bit hard when he was at a forty-five degree angle. With the hot water spraying directly on his lower back, the pain was worse at the exact height of a craps table.

"Another mystery solved."

He shaved and brushed his teeth. Taking a handful of Vitamin I (sold generically as ibuprofen), he walked to the kitchen wearing nothing but a towel. The apartment smelled like Franky's designer cologne and toothpaste.

He pulled a bottle of gin from the freezer and took a swig. He cringed in reaction to the mixture of gin and toothpaste. He dressed in gym shorts and a polo shirt.

The shot of booze kick-started his battle. Moving into the den, Franky collapsed into his couch. A comatose-like rest was needed to defeat the peak of his hangover.

CHAPTER 9

Kenneth Schultz was in despair. Frantic, on edge, he raced down aisle after aisle looking for one last item.

Toothpicks? Where in Christ's name would they put toothpicks? He refused to ask for assistance.

The temperature in the grocery store was subarctic, the lights blinding. Schultz had contracted a fever. Although the knee was not infected yet, germs nested in the wound infected something else in his body. Schultz was convinced he would die in the relish aisle, under a shelf of olives, where the toothpicks should be displayed.

Rounding the aisle cap, he faced a row of freezers.

Toothpicks would not be in frozen food. What are you thinking? Are you delirious?

Among the groceries stacked to the rafters, Schultz searched through aisles of dog food and cereal. The smell of fried chicken from the deli and laundry detergent filled his sinuses.

Although Schultz was physically weak, the pain made him stronger, spiritually. Brother Hargood knew physical pain— genuine pain. But, he died both physically and spiritually. He fought the pain; he fought his savior. Schultz would never fight the pain. Pain was salvation.

A stock boy passed Schultz for the third time. "Can I help you find something?"

"Toothpicks."

"They're with the paper products, right above the paper plates on aisle thirteen."

Two days ago, Schultz would have refused to speak to the boy, pretending not to hear him. Today, however, things were different. Schultz connected with the boy. The pain, the nausea, the fever created a real person, worthy of Schultz's response.

Brother Hargood really did suffer.

Schultz was finally alive through his bold actions and the torture of poor Hargood.

Yes, alive, but chilled to the bone. His body shook. He hurried to aisle thirteen and was immediately faced with a dilemma. Colored or plain toothpicks? Square or round? His wife had not specified.

Schultz made a decision. He was a man of action. Two days ago, he would have bought all four kinds and not risked making a mistake.

He chose a register away from the frozen foods. His hands were tight from the chill; his fever made his eyes feel swollen. Schultz watched his hands as he loaded groceries onto the conveyor. Thin and white, the fingernails took a bluish hue. It hurt to pick cold items out of his cart.

He needed to hurry.

Move lady, move.

The lady ahead of him in line was a coupon clipper.

"Manager to lane three," the cashier said into the loudspeaker.

Neither lady cared that Schultz needed to get home. The party was starting soon, and Michelle needed her damned toothpicks.

"Paper or plastic?" the girl asked, without looking up. She scanned Schultz's items, rudely throwing them toward the bagging end.

"Plastic."

She tossed the potato chips. She slid a can of baked beans into them.

"Do you know how much this is?" she asked, holding up a small bag of cilantro.

"No, uh, I think it was two dollars."

"Are you sure?" She smacked gum as she spoke.

"No. I mean, yes. Yes, I'm sure it was two dollars," Schultz said.

"If you say so."

She began scanning the items even more carelessly. She slid the gallon of milk into the cilantro, crushing the bag.

Uh, could you…be…a little more careful?

"Uh, could you…be…a little…"

"Did you say something?" The toothpicks hit the beans with such force they flew off the counter. "Oh crap. Can you grab that?"

Schultz limped to the end of the checkout, picked up the round, multi-colored, toothpick container, and placed it gently on the counter.

Be careful, dammit!

This girl was ambivalent to the items beeping in front of her. Customers filed non-stop through her line all day. At shift's end, she was unable to identify a single item purchased. She didn't care what people bought. To her, keeping track was a waste of brainpower.

Schultz, however, was different. If he worked the line, he would study the customer, and he would analyze each item that they purchased. He would know the size of their family—the gender and age of the children. He would know the part of town where they lived and their annual income.

If the boss moved him to the express lane, he would analyze what they purchased and identify the particular item that motivated the customer to go to the grocery.

"Mr. Smith?" Schultz would have asked. "I saw him in here yesterday. He came through my express lane and purchased beer, Drano, a box of cereal, and a bag of apples. Why did he make the trip to the store? Most would say to purchase the Drano; however, most people are idiots, and they don't care. I would have guessed differently. I study Smith. I watch him and keep a running database on him in my mind. I would say that he came for the beer. He comes every day at different times, and he always goes to different registers, and he never purchases just beer. There's always an item that would be the focus of someone playing this game. One day it would be toilet paper, fruit, and beer. Another day it would be laundry detergent, bread, lunchmeat, and beer. He would always purchase something to pull the eye away from his true motive. He tries to trick me or give me a false sense of security."

"Fifty-eight dollars and forty-seven cents." The cashier said to Schultz after destroying all of his groceries.

Schultz scanned his credit card; he studied the cashier out of the corner of his eye. Attractive in a young girl way, her complexion was a little pocked, but smooth on the apples of her cheeks, where it was most important. Her eye make-up, although applied generously, accentuated her clear blue eyes. They were fresh from the lack of witnessing trauma.

Well, sweetheart, you should have been with me last night, hee hee.

Her store uniform, an apron with "Jerry Lee's" written across the front, hid her figure. She was perhaps a little skinny. She wore sandals. Her feet were unattractive, and if Schultz were her father, he would tell her to wear closed-toe shoes.

Schultz waited for her to finish the transaction.

"Is something wrong?"

"It didn't go through."

Schultz scanned his credit card again.

"It's not working," she said without making eye-contact. "Do you have another card?'

"What? No! Of course not. I just used this card."

"Well, it's not going through."

"Is there a problem?" an adolescent manager asked, stepping up behind the cashier.

"His card doesn't work."

"My card works for Christ's sake!" Schultz said, shoving the card back into his wallet.

Schultz's face turned red as the manager examined him in front of everyone. The junior college dropout looked him up and down to see if Schultz was the credit-card-thief type. Schultz's ears burned; his hands perspired as he reached into his wallet and removed a one-hundred-dollar bill.

The manager took the bill, examined it, then took a highlighter pen from his pocket and checked the bill for counterfeiting. Schultz's knees went weak. He inadvertently put pressure on his left knee and winced with shooting pain.

"Thank you, sir," the manager said. "Are you okay?"

"Yes, fine, thank you," Schultz said, taking his change from the cashier.

Now go to hell!

He pushed his cart through the automatic doors, limping on his left leg.

The over-powering heat that had developed outdoors destroyed the coolness of the grocery store within seconds.

A numbing pain returned to Schultz's temple.

• • •

Months earlier, Schultz realized that he would commit a murder to ensure his salvation. That's when, a deep hatred began to grow for the inhabitants of Pascagoula. The hatred was not because they treated him with disrespect and apathy (this type of hatred came later). Rather, Schultz hated them because, one day, someone would piss him off so badly, he would snap.

But who? His wife pissed him off all the time. Certainly, not her.

This murder could not be an impulse murder.

So, Schultz fought the urge to murder spontaneously. If his grocery store experience had happened two months ago, Schultz would have been tempted to go home, grab an AR-15, and open fire in Jerry Lee's. He would kill every stock boy, cashier, and manager in sight.

But Schultz learned discipline.

With time, he removed a few people off the list of potential victims. His friends and family were safe.

Schultz learned patience.

One day, he would indiscriminately choose a person—young or old, black or white, male or female. And, that person would suffer a death sentence.

• • •

Driving home, Schultz forced himself to drive past Hargood's house. With his knee cut as bad as it was, he didn't have time to ditch the evidence.

His stomach knotted, as he rolled past four police cars. He smiled.

The bag containing items soaked with Hargood's blood, the backpack, and the disgusting shoes were still in the trunk. If the police searched cars, driving by the crime scene, they would nail him.

Schultz turned on to Eastwood Street; cars were arriving for his daughter's birthday party. The yard needed mowing; Michelle would be embarrassed if the guests said anything.

It's too hot to be outside anyway.

Schultz pulled into the driveway. The ice cream was melting in the trunk.

Standing behind the car, Schultz felt a tinge of joy. On the short ride home, he no longer hated. His loathing of the residents faded away. How else could he have talked to the stock boy so easily? How could he have forgiven the cashier and manager so readily?

This is a preview, a little taste of the joy that I'm supposed to feel. It's the perfect happiness that…

"Hello."

Schultz turned to address the woman who had come up behind him.

"Hello," he said, politely.

A young mother struggled with a present, a bag, and the hand of her child. She was prettier than Michelle. Sweat formed on her upper lip.

Elizabeth?

"Let me help you with those." Schultz grabbed the gift from her hand.

It's Elizabeth reincarnate.

"Thank you. This is Katie. She's here for Amber's party. My name is Janna Sandler."

Schultz took her free hand and shook it.

"Kenneth Schultz, uh…it's around back."

Lovely and bright, Miss Sandler was fresh; her hand was warm and soft. She looked Californian, with blonde, sun-streaked hair, a slight tan, and a thin, freckled nose.

Schultz wanted to smile.

He actually wanted to smile!

Such wonderful thoughts, impossible before Hargood's sacrifice, surged through Schultz's brain. Miss Sandler was the most beautiful woman he had seen since…

Elizabeth.

Schultz was so happy he had made it back to the pier. He was so happy for Hargood.

"I'll put this with the others," Schultz said, in a softer voice. He held up the gift.

"Okay, great."

Miss Sandler and her daughter disappeared around the side of the house.

Schultz carried the groceries inside. The house was getting warm, even though the air conditioner was running full blast. Too many people were coming in and out.

Putting the groceries away, Schultz watched Miss Sandler through the kitchen window that opened toward the back porch. She made conversation; she smiled cordially at the other women. She was the prettiest one of them all.

Schultz rubbed his knee. His head no longer hurt.

Janna Sandler? I can't believe you don't remember me.

CHAPTER 10

Pastor Dupree showered until the hot water ran ice cold. His shoulders and lower back, massaged and limber, cooled slowly. When he spun to rinse his hair, water blasted his chest, taking his breath away. Washing and rinsing his legs quickly, he stepped out of the shower shivering.

He toweled off in front of the mirror. His dark hair, intentionally worn longer than most preachers, hung down over his eyes. His three-day beard was going on day five. He grabbed his razor from the shower.

Brushing his hair, he put the razor in a drawer. Tomorrow was Sunday. He would be forced to shave anyway.

With his muscles rejuvenated and a massive amount of ickiness from the crime scene washed down the drain, Dupree dressed.

Leaving the Hargood house, he was weakened to the core.

Detective Campbell wanted his initial thought of the crime. Dupree had nothing.

"Looks like a publicity stunt," Dupree said.

The murder was not the work of the occult. Although premeditated, there was no ceremony, no enjoyment of the process. The murder was quick. It took place in the foyer of Hargood's own home. Unless Hargood was a willing participant, the occult could be ruled out.

Dupree took a seat at this kitchen table and opened a large study Bible.

"So? Do we have a psychopath on our hands?" Detective Campbell had asked.

"Maybe, but psychopaths rarely have a reason behind their actions. The Bible passage tends to suggest a motive."

"And what would that be?"

"Maybe fear. It seems the whole thing was done to elevate the shock value," Dupree had told the detective. "It's like an act of terrorism. He orchestrated it to instill the maximum amount of gossip, get the rumors really flying around. Acid to the face? Crucifixion? It's just so overdone. Add to it the verse from Revelation and you really amp up the fear. It's like the scariest book in the Bible."

"And the blood?" Detective Campbell had asked.

"I know. It's like overkill."

"Definitely overkill." Dupree flipped the pages of the study Bible to Revelation. He patted Red behind the ear. He reread the passage left by Hargood's killer.

"Red, I should go by the hospital. Shouldn't I?" he said, tired of reading in Revelation. "Mrs. Brewer needs a visit. She deserves better than that visit last night."

Nurse Kelly won't be on shift this morning.

Important responsibilities buzzed around the back of his brain like a gnat, generating white-noise in his ears. He smiled and clinched his fists. His fingers tingled.

You've got a murder to investigate!

Images of the crime scene flashed through his mind.

You've got to practice your sermon.

"First things first." He closed the Bible. "Who wants to go for a walk?"

Red barked and circled the kitchen table.

"Let's go for a walk."

• • •

Dupree locked his front door; sweat instantly beaded on his forehead. The August sun had risen above the treetops and was bearing down on his front porch.

"Red!" he shouted. "Easy."

With his sermon stuffed in the back pocket of his cargo shorts and Red on the end of the leash, Dupree headed to the church to practice his sermon.

Washington Avenue was busy; people drove too fast. On the shoulder, almost in the drainage ditch, he tried not to twist his ankle. On a tightrope, one arm jutting straight out, circling, he stepped over discarded beer cans and uneven ground. The grass was dry and crinkly. Sweat ran down the side of his face, dripping onto the collar of his light blue polo shirt.

At Eastwood Street, he turned south. Red pulled on the leash in anticipation.

At Beach Boulevard Dupree sat down on the seawall and took off his flip-flops. Red panted madly, waiting for the command.

"Go! Go ahead boy."

With a bounding leap, Red went barreling into the gulf.

Dupree pulled the sermon from his back pocket and read the first line aloud.

"Have you ever heard the term 'attitude adjustment'?"

The words fell flat. A car passed behind him. Hargood's house was down the seawall one quarter of a mile away.

The passage in Revelation returned to him. In the back of his mind he saw Hargood's pale, lifeless body.

"Then from his mouth the serpent spewed water like a river," Dupree said. "Red, get back up here!"

He couldn't afford to get distracted; he had already worked twelve hours on his sermon for tomorrow morning.

"What does it mean to have an attitude adjustment?"

He verbalized his sermon a couple of times. Red played in the waist deep water. Rubbing his sweaty palms together, Dupree stood for a moment, catching a breath of the brisk southern breeze.

Looking toward the horizon, he prayed for Jerry Hargood and for guidance in the investigation. His eyes remained open, focusing on the thin blue line between sea and sky.

The horizon, the beginning and the end of each day, was exceptionally sharp.

The gulf air tasted salty and clean. Dupree bent over for a moment and placed the leash back on Red.

"Let's go, boy."

He and Red were retracing their path back north on Eastwood Street, when he stopped suddenly. He turned quickly to look back at the horizon.

Lord, our Lord, how majestic is your name in all the earth! You have set your glory in the heavens. Through the praise of children and infants you have established a stronghold against your enemies, to silence the foe and the avenger. When I consider your heavens, the work of your fingers, the moon and the stars, which you have set in place…

Psalm 8:1–3

The children's moonwalk.

Last night, when Red barked at a squirrel, Dupree saw a moonwalk.

"Let's go boy," Dupree said. Breaking into a jog, he crossed Washington Avenue, slowed to a walk, and searched the houses that ran along the opposite side of the bayou from his house.

A birthday party was getting started. Mothers unloaded their children, presents, and snacks. Dupree smiled politely at one young lady as she passed.

"Hey, got a party to go to, I see," Dupree said.

"Hey. Oh look, Simon. Look at the puppy."

Dupree continued his stride; Red could be a little rough with small children. He did, however, get a look at the house with the moonwalk.

A brick veneer home, nicely landscaped, the yard needed mowing. A welcome sign on the porch read "The Schultz's."

The Schultz's.

• • •

The sanctuary at Christ Church promoted a reverent mood, even though it smelled like wet paint. Newly renovated, from extensive hurricane damage, the white walls and grey wainscoting gave the impression that the interior designer once worked in a federal building. Color came from the burgundy carpet, banners, and altar.

Sun poured in through the plain windows and lighted the three dozen pews, divided into two rows of eighteen. The altar held an open Bible, a gold cross, and two altar candles. Above the altar was a painting of Christ surrounded by several angels. The altar structure favored the front of a crown with three diadems. On each side of the center diadem were seven carved knobs, and two candelabras with seven candles framed the outside edges.

Dupree stood to the right of the altar in the pulpit. He pretended the church was full as he practiced accentuating the main points of his sermon.

"I heard a story once of a principal who had an old, wooden paddle which he called 'the Attitude Adjuster'."

As he spoke, the only piece of stained glass in the church caught his eye. His mind wandered from his sermon as he continued to preach. During the early summer months, between four and five o'clock, the light of the sun would shine through the glass onto the altar. It was like a scene from *Raiders of the Lost Ark*. The sun directed a single beam onto one of the angels, who fluttered a wing and directed the young preacher to a hidden treasure or the whereabouts of Hargood's killer.

Or another murder mystery!

"But do you know we don't need to be paddled to learn a lesson in humility…to get our attitude adjusted? We can actually learn from example. The example of our Savior, Jesus, who humbled himself to death, even to death on a cross, and although our trials are difficult, we will never face the humiliation…" The words rolled from his lips.

Dupree moved through his sermon, almost unconscious of the words, no longer needing his notes to preach.

• • •

Dupree preached his sermon one more time, checked the communion setup, and returned to the altar rail. He knelt in prayer for the members of his congregation.

"The Carver family, Lord, I give this family to you. Bring Ed to a closer relationship with you through Jesus so that he comes to worship with Denise and the children."

Each member of the congregation flashed through Dupree's mind. For reference, he often brought a church directory with him to help keep him straight.

"Lord, I give to you the Rierson family and ask that you look upon Lisa, and help her with her struggle with…"

The training he received in seminary—Christian doctrine, church history, biblical interpretation—helped him prepare sermons and clarify the word. None of this training impacted his faith and his ministry like the thirty minutes he spent in prayer at the altar.

"Lord I lift up to you the family of Jerry Hargood."

A rough night's sleep left him with heavy, dark eyes and an aching in his lower back. His bare knees dug into the carpet as he continued to pray. He made fists with his swollen hands.

His last "experience" was three months ago, when he helped solve the Capdepon case. He desperately needed another one to lead him in the right direction for the Hargood case.

"Lord, lead me to understand Revelation 12:16…"

• • •

"Pastor?" Leslie Wixon said, stepping out of the fellowship hall. "Have you heard?"

Dupree jumped slightly, being abruptly shocked from deep thought. He was coming out of the sanctuary, rubbing his left knee as he descended the stairs. She held the door for him.

"Oh, I'm sorry. I didn't mean to startle you."

"Hey, no it's nothing. I was just, uh…heard what?" Dupree stepped inside.

Leslie was the nineteen-year-old, part-time office assistant for the church. Fair-skinned and slightly overweight, she had a wide, pretty smile that made her blotchy complexion bright and warm. She was unpretentious and diligent. Although she made only $12,000 per year, her parents were very proud.

"You haven't heard about the murder?" Leslie asked. "There was a murder on Beach Boulevard last night. I've heard it from several people already; they suspect it may be Jerry Hargood."

Dupree brushed his hair back with his hands. The bridge of his nose was a little red from the sun he had gotten when walking to the church.

"Yes," he said. "I've heard about it. Is Red out back?"

"Yeah, I put him out there with some water," Leslie said, following Dupree toward his office. "Did the police call you? Because I heard it was like a Satan worshipping thing, and I figured the police would call you."

"Did you know Jerry Hargood?" Dupree asked, dodging the question. Passing his office, he headed for the back of the building.

"Oh sure, practically everyone in town knows him. He owns the Ace Hardware store on Ingalls Avenue. He and Dad are really good friends from way back."

"I'm so sorry."

Leslie leaned closer and whispered. "I had lunch with Cleave, and well, he's the one that told me it was a satanic ritual or something. I'm sure they are going to get you involved."

"I don't know. Come here boy." Dupree stepped out of the set of sliding glass doors leading to the children's play area. He reached down and placed a leash on Red. "What did Cleave say?"

"Well, Don McKay was called to the scene, and him and Cleave are really good friends, and they met for breakfast. Cleave said there were some very strange things about the crime scene."

"Like what?"

"Well for one thing, all Mr. Hargood's blood had been drained out of him into a gallon jug."

Dupree cringed. So much for not releasing details of the crime scene.

"And the body was positioned like it was hanging from a cross."

"That's awful," Dupree said, shaking his head in disbelief.

They started to walk back toward the sanctuary. Red was in the lead.

"Do they have any suspects? Did Cleave know of anything like that?"

"They don't know," Leslie said, following close behind. "I guess maybe they can get fingerprints or something. Cleave thinks it was Satan worshippers because Mr. Hargood was big into that New Rock Church they're building, and they got a really good youth ministry and all. Cleave said it's probably teenagers, maybe even from George County."

The three entered Fellowship Hall together.

Dupree unlocked the door to his office. "Let's add the family to our prayer list and…don't get too worried. I'm sure they'll find out who did this," he said, flashing a weak, comforting smile.

CHAPTER 11

Janna Sandler offered her left hand as a greeting to Amber's dad. Mr. Schultz carried groceries in his right hand and she wanted the greeting to be unintrusive as possible. The opposite hand handshake was an awkward exchange. To be kind, she squeezed lightly in response to his limp, clammy grip. The second she released, she wiped her hand on the back of Katie's dress, by guiding her toward the birthday party. When Janna cleared the corner of the house, she shook her left hand, violently discarding a massive batch of cooties.

The August heat was sweltering; yet, this man's hand was ice cold.

His expression matched the handshake.

Mr. Schultz had deep blue-grey eyes and an unattractive smile. His speech was matter-of-fact. Even the child could tell that he was not the party type. The crying fit that Katie had started when they left their house ended the moment Mr. Schultz spoke.

"Are you ready to party?" Janna asked Katie. They rounded the corner that led to the back porch.

Katie did not reply to her mother. Her eyes fixed on the moonwalk in the backyard.

• • •

The party was in full swing with children running crazy, sugared-up on soda. The moonwalk was pumping. Children climbed in and out, saturated with sweat. The mothers overheated from chasing kids and yelling.

"It was a marvelous idea to have the party outside," one of the mothers said. The ladies collected in the shade of an oak tree. The discharge of an enormous fan blew across their conversation.

"Well, it would have been impossible if Kenny had not rented the fans with the moonwalk," Mrs. Schultz replied.

Janna walked toward the circle of ladies; none of them noticed her. She turned short of the tight-knit ring, pretending to admire the birthday cake and presents. She wanted to place Katie's gift on the table but Mr. Schultz had taken it inside. Glancing back over her shoulder, every so often, she waited patiently for an invite to share in the gossip.

Katie sat on the ground at the entrance to the moonwalk and took off her shoes.

"Just put them to the side," Janna mouthed, pointing her instructions to the child. "Yes, right there." Janna nodded and smiled.

Removing the hair that clung to the side of her face, she reworked her ponytail. She moved a little closer to the discharge of the giant fan and eavesdropped on the conversation behind her.

"He works at Biotech Labs, I believe in soybean research," Mrs. Schultz said, adding to a conversation started on her husband. She spoke in short sentences, making only brief statements.

"Did you hear?" Mrs. Schultz asked, successfully taking control of the conversation. "There was a murder last night on Beach Boulevard? Not six blocks away from here."

"My God! No!" one of the mothers said, exaggerating her concern. "Who was it?"

"I heard it was Jerry Hargood."

"No, my God, Brother Jerry, I just saw him…"

"It was Jerry," another mother added, nodding and catching the eyes of all the others in the conversation. Janna expressed concern and sadness from afar. With a furrowed brow and pursed lips, she let the others know that she knew Mr. Hargood and that she was upset. No one looked at her.

"It's just a shame, I mean. Amber! Sweetie, stop that!" Mrs. Schultz said, looking past the others. "We need to get them over here for the cake and ice cream." She gave a quick inquisitive stare toward Janna, who smiled politely.

"Is that your boy?" Mrs. Schultz asked.

"No," Janna said, stepping toward the other mothers. "Mine is Katie. The little girl right there."

"Well whose boy is that?" Mrs. Schultz asked. "He needs to take his shoes off in the moonwalk. I thought we made that perfectly clear."

One of the ladies exited the circle and started yelling toward the shoe offender, leaving a space for Janna to enter the clique.

She opted to spin toward the house and continue her study of the cake.

• • •

"Katie, please honey, get out of that."

Janna carried a laundry basket into the house. Stepping in from the back porch, she slammed the door closed with her foot.

The utility room was located outside in an addition someone had built to the house. The water heater, washer and dryer, and yard tools were located in a room that swarmed with lint from an improperly installed dryer exhaust.

Janna dumped the laundry on her bed and moved to the bathroom. She pulled Katie away from a shelf that held towels and her blue, plastic tackle box containing make-up. In the three minutes Janna spent retrieving the laundry, Katie had pulled the folded towels on the floor and unlatched the make-up kit.

"Sweetheart, that's Mommy's." She pried the box from Katie's tiny hands.

"That's Mommy's," she parroted.

"Yes, sweetie, now come on. Let's go get you some lunch. We can't eat only cake and ice cream today. Okay?"

Janna hoisted the child onto her hip. Grabbing a fresh dishtowel off the bed, she headed to the front of the house.

"Did you have fun at the birthday party?"

Katie climbed into her high chair. Janna placed the tray in front of her.

"Katie's a little party girl." She talked in a sing-song voice. "She's a little party girl."

Janna squatted over with her hands, patting her thighs as she sang. She inched closer and closer to the child with each verse. The party song ended with a kiss on Katie's tiny nose.

"Now what does my little party girl want for lunch? We can't just eat cake. No. No. No. Mac and cheese? Okay, and some fruit?"

Janna put a pot of water on to boil.

As Katie ate a sliced banana, Janna studied the bubbles starting to form in the pot of nearly boiling water.

Amber Schultz takes after her father.

Amber's mother was a large, attractive woman with an intimidating stature. But, poor Amber was a mousy little child. She didn't smile or giggle. When she opened her gifts, she acted like it was a chore.

"But that's okay," Janna said, toward the pot. "There's someone for everyone." Katie didn't hear. The face of Franky flashed in the bubbling water.

Oh Janna!

"He's not your type. He's not the 'someone' for you."

Katie looked at her mom with a curious face.

"Oh never mind, sweetheart."

Franky stood her up on the only date they ever planned. She forgave him because he was a little drunk when he had asked her out.

Janna dumped the box of noodles into the boiling water.

Franky was clever and outspoken. The faculty loved him and rewarded him with speaking at award night, emceeing the talent show, and hosting Congressmen on Law Day—a function Janna watched Franky perform with distant admiration. They had a class together, and they spoke often in a friendly manner.

But Franky always had a girlfriend or was working on a girlfriend. Once, he even confided in Janna about a new girl he had met—a sophomore who was exceptionally friendly in the back of a church bus. Janna warned against starting anything with a girl that was so young and religious.

Franky took the advice, but not the hint.

"Here you go sweetie," Janna said, handing the macaroni and cheese to her daughter.

Janna sat on the counter opposite the stove and the child.

"You want to go to Grandma's for your nap?"

"Grandma's."

"We'll go for naptime. Okay?"

Katie ate. Janna relived the night she and Franky shared at the party at Wilson's.

Maybe he is a pig.

Janna smiled at the thought.

"But he's a really cute pig."

• • •

"Here we go sweetie. We're at Grandma's house. Can you wake up a little bit?"

Katie was dressed in a cool, summer dress. Janna unlatched the belt and pulled her from the child seat in the back of the cab.

"I do it," Katie said, sliding down into the floorboard. Her blonde hair was wet along the temples. Placing the back of her hand on the child's forehead, Janna checked Katie's temperature.

Janna took Katie's hand as she stumbled along the backseat floorboard. The truck was cluttered with old work orders, receipts, diet Coke cans, and Cheerios. Although Janna kept the front of the cab spotless, the tiny backseat was a different story all together.

"Okay, let's go." Katie jumped from the truck onto her grandparents' driveway. Janna closed the backdoor with her hip.

"Let's go see what Grandma's doing."

"Where's Gramma?"

"Here, this is her house."

"This is Gramma's house."

"That's right sweetie."

"Where's Grandpa?"

"He's with Grandma."

"Grampas with Gramma."

"That's right. Very good sweetie."

The conversation ended when Janna's mom answered the door.

"Hey Mom." Her mother stepped outside.

"Hey honey," she replied, without looking up at her daughter. Her mom's eyes were set on the child.

"And who is this that has come to visit her grandma in the middle of the afternoon?"

"This is Katie. She's a little party girl." Janna ushered Katie into the house.

"I a paw-ty guwl."

"You are a paw-ty guwl," Janna's mom said, lifting the child into her arms.

"I bet I know someone who would like to see you." Janna's mom turned toward the back of the house. "Earl! Grandpa! Someone's here to see you."

The three ladies went into the kitchen, not waiting for Grandpa.

"Have you eaten?" Janna's mom asked.

"Kind of. We went to a birthday party and, well, no. I fixed Katie something." Janna walked to the pantry. She shopped for something to eat.

"Hello there punkin' pie!"

Janna's dad entered the room and picked up Katie. He lifted her above his head, repeatedly "flying" her down to his face for a kiss.

"Earl, put on one of her shows?"

"I think she needs to finish her nap," Janna said. Her voice rattled around in the pantry. "Dad, could you maybe just read her a book? I think she'll go back to sleep."

Janna's dad obliged without comment. All his attention was directed at the child.

"You want me to make you an omelet? I have some good ham. How about a western omelet?" Janna's mom asked.

"I don't know. I'm really not that hungry. I had cake." Janna's head was buried in the refrigerator.

"An omelet it is."

Janna sat at her parents' breakfast nook. Behind her in the den, dad read to the two-year-old. Mom chopped and whisked, preparing the omelet. Her stomach growled with the scent of ham, onion, and bell pepper in the air.

She thought about Franky.

He shouldn't have played that joke.

• • •

"Hey Janna, me and a bunch of guys are going to New Orleans for the Saints' game. My uncle got us all these tickets," Franky said, coming up behind Janna and putting his arm around her shoulders as she walked to class. He flashed the tickets like a hand of cards. "Pick one."

"Really?" Janna plucked a ticket from the hand. "Who all's going?"

"Everyone! The whole damn school, if I can convince them."

Franky's eyes flashed with mischief. His jet-black hair was clipper cut; he was a total preppy in his green Izod pullover, straight-legged jeans, and Sperry topsiders.

"Sure, if my parents will let me go," Janna said.

Her parents would not let her go. It was a huge fight.

"Mom, I have to go! I'm not the most popular girl in school!"

The fight ended when Mrs. Sandler called Willard Stevens II, Franky's dad, and confirmed that his son was not going either.

Janna found out later that the tickets were bogus; a practical joke that Franky had concocted to get the entire senior class to New Orleans for the day. Apparently, Janna was the only one that wasn't in on the gag.

• • •

Katie Sandler fell asleep on a little pallet that Grandpa had made on the floor in front of the television. Janna moved her carefully. The light from the bedroom window threw large shadows around the room. Janna stood at the door and made sure Katie did not wake up.

Walking back into the den, she took a seat on the sofa. Her dad was watching a re-run of *Saturday Night Live* on the *E* channel.

"Did she wake up?" Janna's mom asked, looking up from a magazine.

"No. She's exhausted. I think the little party girl overindulged."

"Really? She had a good time then?"

"Oh yeah, all her daycare friends were there. She ran in the moonwalk for a half hour. I practically had to climb in the darn thing to get her out."

"The party was outside?"

"Yeah, can you believe it? It was hotter than all get out."

"I imagine so."

Her dad started laughing and pointing at the television. The *SNL* cast was doing a parody that had President Clinton and Hillary Clinton hanging out at Clinton's retirement beach house. Young girls in bikinis were filing in and out of "party central."

"Is that Monica Lewinsky? Can you believe it? That's really her." He couldn't control his laughter.

"Easy Earl, you'll wake the baby."

"Can you believe that? That has got to be the funniest thing I have ever seen," he said, slightly above a whisper. He was wiping tears from his eyes.

"Where was the party?" Janna's mom asked, attempting to keep the conversation from degrading to talk of the ex-president.

"At the house of a girl in her daycare, Amber Schultz. Do you know Michelle Schultz? I think she works at the hospital."

"She's a nurse?"

"No, administration, maybe. I don't really know. She might not even work at the hospital."

"No, I don't know her," Janna's mom said. Her attention was being pulled away by the host, Christopher Walken. "Now that's a good-looking man. Most people wouldn't say that, but I think he really is good looking."

"I think Monica Lewinsky is a good-looking woman."

"Oh, give me a break Earl. You only like her because…"

"Mom! Please don't," Janna said, quickly reestablishing a more suitable conversation. The thought of her folks talking about sex stuff made her skin crawl. "You don't know Kenneth Schultz, do you?"

"I don't think so."

"Kenneth Schultz? That name sounds so familiar," Janna said, rolling 'Kenneth', 'Ken', and 'Kenny around in her mind. "Do you think Gary knows him?"

"I don't know. What are they doing now Earl?"

"It's a commercial for a disposable toilet."

"I don't get it," Janna's mom said.

"Mom, do you have one of Gary's old high school annuals?" Janna asked.

"Check the middle bedroom on the shelves in the closet."

Janna left, returning moments later with her older brother Gary's junior annual.

"I'll be doggone," Janna said, moments later. "This was his senior year. He's a year older than Gary. Kenneth Schultz. Right there."

"That was your freshman year. And, you didn't know him?" Janna's mom asked.

"Look how big the school was. I didn't know everyone."

"That's right dear," her dad added. "We know you weren't the most popular girl in school."

Janna's parents shared a laugh at her expense. The harmless joke poked fun at one of Janna's favorite statements from high school.

"Very funny, you two. Laugh it up. I'm trying to think. Was he the one that…" She flipped to the index in the back of the annual to find more pictures of Kenneth Schultz.

"What?"

"The guy from Pascagoula that got in trouble…at State…"

Kenneth Schultz's only other appearance in the annual was the chess club photo.

CHAPTER 12

Franky Stevens completed his plans for the evening while showering for the second time that day.

He would go with plan B.

This alternative, chosen only when he was at his most desperate, consisted of drinking heavily and attending the festivities at Johnny Joe's Country Palace. The drinking heavily part of plan B was not actually unique to this plan; all other plans started the same way. It was, however, the highlight of this particular plan.

Franky shaved and splashed on cologne. The bloodshot whites of his eyes had cleared to a slight yellow hue. His nose and cheeks were a little puffy. Stepping onto the bathroom scale, he registered in at 180 pounds—down fifteen pounds from his healthy college weight of ten years ago. He slicked his hair back and threw on a pair of khaki shorts and a T-shirt with "America the Beautiful" on the front. Leaving the apartment complex, he headed for the grocery store.

Along the seawall at Beach Boulevard, the water was brown from a lack of deep-water circulation. On certain days, however, the brown water was so calm and flat that it picked up the color of the sky. On those clear days of low humidity, the barrier islands, that blocked the tides, floated atop a tub of blue, like little fuzzy rafts.

Franky turned north on Market Street. He passed Thunder's tavern. A wave of nostalgia hit as he remembered his first drinking experience.

"Miller beer, in those clear bottles."

He flipped on the radio.

In Jerry Lee's, thanks to his ability to forget traumatic experiences, he purchased a twelve pack of Miller High Life.

• • •

At the Longfellow Apartments, Franky hung on the fence that surrounded his back porch. A young couple stopped a hundred feet from the pool to let their child catch up.

"Mommy looks pretty good there, daddy."

Franky whispered an imaginary conversation. His lips touched the condensation on the outside of his beer bottle. His arms crossed in front of his face, blocking his mouth from view.

Mommy's thighs were a little thick. To hide them from prying eyes like Franky's, she wore shorts over her bikini bottoms. Her "new mom" breasts, however, were proudly displayed in a red string bikini top. Daddy wore a bathing suit that hung below the knees.

"Harry go ahead and get us a good spot," Franky whispered, in the imaginary, high-pitched, whiney voice of the mother.

Daddy struggled to carry pool toys, towels, a cooler, and a beach bag. Mommy carried the floppy hat, that she took off while waiting for the child.

Franky winced at the sight.

"Yes honey! Oh, you forgot the floaties?" Franky whispered, mocking the daddy. "I'll go get them! No, I promise only one beer at the pool. She's so cute in that suit."

"Harry, no drinking at the pool."

Franky tossed the empty beer bottle into a trashcan and checked the grill. The coals burned white hot.

Walking inside, he opened the microwave. The pack of hamburger meat passed thaw and was partially cooked around the edges. Franky took the plate to the sink. Grabbing the wad of meat, he kneaded the raw and browned hamburger meat into four-inch balls. Red juice flowed through his fingers into the sink when he pressed the balls into patties. After washing his hands, he took the platter of burgers to the grill.

Flames shot a foot above the grate when he plopped the burgers on the grill.

Covering the grill, he took up his position at the fence.

Mommy, Daddy, and daughter were at the pool.

Franky was alone with his burgers and beer.

"Harry, remember no drinking," he said toasting toward the pool.

• • •

Franky drove down Beach Boulevard deliberately slow, but not too slow. The water to his left favored the desert—flat, dark, vast. A desert, however, does not reflect. The lights of the jack-up oil rigs bounced off the calm sound.

Franky watched his hands as he drove. He tried not to correct the direction of the tires too often or too quickly. As he continued toward Market Street, the lights of the shipyard acted as a beacon; the reflections off the water grew larger and larger. The lights began to blend together on the water and in the sky. There was no one walking along the seawall. Franky rolled the window down to smoke.

Grabbing a lighter, a red flicker flashed brightly in his eyes. The flame heated the tip of his nose. Readjusting his crossed eyes, he lost his vision for a second. The tires crossed the centerline. Franky, regaining his sight, smoothly returned the car back to the right side of the double yellow line. Smoke filled his lungs and mouth with an earthy flavor that complemented the taste from a beer. He watched himself smoke in the rearview mirror. He carefully navigated the streets, past Thunder's and Jerry Lee's.

Soon, Franky sat in the parking lot of Johnny Joe's as dimly lit couples swaggered and strutted toward the thumping sounds of bass. His hand rested on the keys in the ignition.

One quick turn and the car starts.

Three ladies passed in front of him. The prettiest one wore a shirt with tassels.

Ten minutes, you're home.

His hand pulled the keys from the ignition. He reached below the seat and pulled a small bottle from underneath. Taking a long draught, he winced at the taste.

•••

Ashtrays caked with ash, containing no butts, cluttered the bar. Men occupied all the stools. They cared nothing for dancing or talking. Sitting with their elbows on the padded front of the bar, they clasped their hands, almost looking prayerful, with a cigarette cradled between two or more of their fingers. Each looked at the glass in front of him, or the burning cigarette, and remained silent. They ordered beer by tapping their empty glasses. Two wore cowboy hats; the others wore ball caps with heavy equipment logos.

An uneaten bowl of peanuts sat in front of Franky. Thirty feet down the bar, the bartender tipped a pint glass at an angle and jerked on the tap. Franky and one other man kept their eyes on her as she poured; the others just looked at their hands.

On the quarter-acre sized dance floor behind Franky, a single couple held each other tightly beneath a giant disco ball. The beau was seven feet tall, the lady five. In their dance, he hunched over her with both hands resting on her behind. Her arms wrapped around his waist. Little round indentations marked her face from the snaps that ran up his western shirt. They both wore boots. They danced slowly in an offbeat rhythm, occasionally talking, never kissing.

A young girl requested a song from the bearded DJ, who wore sunglasses in his dark cage.

Franky followed her with his eyes as she took a seat with two girlfriends. The three ladies wore heavy eye make-up. Their hair was piled high on top of their heads. They drank identical drinks and smoked from the same pack of cigarettes.

Franky spun toward the bar when one of the ladies caught him staring.

"We have a request from a pretty little…"

The DJ spun a line dance. The paths to the parquet filled with slippery people, walking hand in hand, looking for a tiny space in the middle of the enormous dance floor.

•••

The bartender leaned over the bar to take an order; Franky played the voyeur as her uniform crept up the back of her thigh, exposing a tiny line between her leg and buttocks. She wore Daisy Dukes shorts that were tight on her frame. Franky got her attention and tapped his glass. He decided to make a move. When ordering his drink, he lost his nerve. He caught a glimpse of his reflection in the mirror behind the bar.

He spoke from the side of his mouth, slurring his speech. His face was distorted. Deep creases cut across his forehead and off the edges of his eyes. The blue from a nearby neon light combined with his yellow skin to give him a sick green complexion. As soon as the bartender placed the double scotch in front of him, he wanted her to leave.

In the mirror, he watched himself drink. Changing his expression, he smiled, he frowned. He took a large drink, observing his Adam's apple rise over the lump of warm liquid. Nothing took the dead, lifeless stare away from his eyes.

Franky's face was haggard, his eyes gaunt with large circles under them from lack of sound sleep. The alcohol-induced body shutdown didn't provide the dream sleep needed for mental health.

A hand touched his shoulder. "You want to dance?"

He turned slowly and responded automatically. "Yeah sure, but, I don't know those line ones."

"We can just slow dance."

"Sure," Franky downed his scotch and left to dance with one of the three girls he had observed earlier.

Halfway through the song, the new couple shared their first kiss. This special moment, to be remembered forever, ended quickly when Franky needed to suppress a gag reflex, triggered by the force of her tongue being shoved into his mouth. Franky looked for an escape.

"Want a drink?" He shouted above the song.

"Sure, Red Bull and Vodka."

"I'll meet you at your table," he shouted, pointing toward her girlfriends.

Moments later, carrying her drink and another double scotch, Franky took a seat beside his new date.

"Franky." He shouted, as he took a seat at the table.

"Yeah Franky." She nodded. She yelled her name, which Franky heard as Shiela, or Shelly, or Sh-something.

He sat with her and the two friends in an awkward, non-communicative way. He smiled or nodded, and they averted their eyes, scanning the room for prospects.

His date was the prettiest of the three. She had dark eyes and a tan, country girl face with freckles across the bridge of her nose. Her lips were full and well glossed, and her dark hair extended eight inches from her head. She wore a white western shirt with tassels that ran down the sleeves and along the collarbone.

"Franky?" his date shouted. "What kind of car do you drive?"

"A Buick, Buoo-ick," he mouthed.

"You want to show me your Buoo-ick?" she asked, finally smiling and giving a wink.

"Yeah, sure." Franky shrugged. It was still early, and generally he had to buy at least three drinks to get her out to his Buick.

Standing and taking his date by the hand, Franky nodded toward the others at the table. They frowned in disgust. Franky pushed their chairs under the table.

He kept his head down as he walked through the bar.

After tossing back what was left in his tumbler, he set his glass on the sticky bar near the stool where he sat earlier. The surface reflected patterns of light from the disco ball.

"Yeah, okay good night," Franky said to the bouncer. The bouncer responded with a comment that addressed Franky as "cowboy."

They kept silent, holding hands until they exited the front entrance. Once outside, she moved her arm around his waist and kissed his neck. In the parking lot, they moved quickly toward his car. Franky fixated on the lights above him. Rings of rainbows surrounded them. The ground moved underfoot much faster than he was walking. Franky staggered, not smiling, not laughing. Seeing double, his vision bounced with his footsteps. At the passenger side of the car, he fumbled for his keys. He opened her side first. Walking around the back of the car, he took small cautious steps as he kept one hand on the car at all times.

In one choreographed move, she unlocked his door and removed her top. As Franky climbed in the driver's seat, she unsnapped her bra from the back.

Franky panicked. He avoided leaning toward her. She shifted quickly toward him, grabbed his crotch, and kissed his neck violently.

Oh, God. Don't think. Don't think..

She grabbed the side of his head with one hand and kissed him. With her other hand, she grabbed his left hand and placed it on her breast. With his eyes wide open, Franky caught his reflection in the rearview mirror. He was hideous and sad. He moaned in response to his anxiety.

"You like that baby?" she said, jerking on his belt.

Franky closed his eyes and fell back into his seat, as she worked the button and fly of his pants with both hands. His arms dropped to his side. In the darkness, he saw the guy at the pool. He saw the guy's wife, holding the hand of the child. Certainly, by this time, the guy was sleeping next to his wife, his hand resting on her slightly large thighs. The guy could smell her clean, soft hair. He could walk to the kitchen and eat a bowl of cereal or drink juice. He could walk to the baby's room and watch her sleep. He would sleep in comfort, in a warm bed, in an apartment that was cold from air conditioning, in a land that was stifling hot.

"You okay?" she asked, with her hands inside Franky's underwear.

Franky had that life at one time, briefly. He had an apartment and a girlfriend, and he slept next to her, and her body was warm at night. Her breath was smooth, her voice wasn't raspy. She didn't smell like cigarette smoke and hairspray.

"Franky?"

He and Renee always had food in the refrigerator and fresh milk.

He slept well. He ate well. He hated that it was gone. Opening his eyes, he turned his head toward his date with a blank, dead stare.

"I just don't understand you. Don't you want me to give you a…"

"No!" His voice raised, it reverberated throughout the car. "I mean no," he said, much softer. "Not just right now, I…it's just that…I just don't feel comfortable here in the car, you know, where someone might…"

"Wow baby, that's the first time I've ever…"

"I want to, don't get me wrong, but not right now. Maybe later, okay?"

"Can we go back in?" she asked, looking noticeably disappointed. "I mean, can we go back and dance and stuff?"

"Yeah sure, whatever you want," he said, fastening his pants.

"I know it's weird, but every time I go out and meet a great guy, all they want to do is leave as soon as they can and go have sex or something. So I like to go out to the car and get that out of the way, and then maybe we can spend time with my girlfriends and dance and stuff, you know?" she explained.

"Yeah sure," he said.

Once they got back to the table, Franky talked little and drank a lot.

CHAPTER 13

The sector of Biotech Labs, where Kenneth Schultz worked, was not sterile. The soy beans he tested were often covered in dirt, when they arrived in his inbox. Schultz wore his full length lab coat, anyway. The lab was cool and deserted. No one worked weekend nights at Biotech Laboratories.

A germ free environment would have helped Schultz's infected wounds. But, with filthy soybeans strewn all over his desk, he was glad that he had disinfected and redressed his injured knee and arm.

When Schultz entered the lab, he flipped on every light. He tuned the radio to a local NPR station.

As he studied the samples in front of him, Beethoven's third symphony played. The aspirin kicked in during the scherzo. Schultz lost his chills.

After placing a new slide in his microscope, he stretched his back and grabbed his phone.

"I'm at work. Are you at home?" He texted Michelle, his wife.

She was supposed to watch the kids. But often when Schultz worked evenings, the kids wound up at his in-laws for the night.

Michelle never questioned why he worked late on the weekend. She didn't care.

"No. At my folks house." She replied.

"Are you staying at your mom's with the kids?"

He didn't expect a reply.

Schultz smiled. He pressed his eye to the microscope. A pattern was developing. Another twenty slides and he would be complete with his first sample population.

"Why do you always work late?" He imagined Michelle getting angry about his work habits.

Maybe I am having an affair with another woman.

Schultz laughed. He needed to concentrate.

Brad was expecting a report on Tuesday.

Schultz's illness last Thursday and Friday had put him behind. He had lied and told his team leader that he had a sinus infection. Brad would have never understood Schultz's sickness.

You could have an affair with her.

Schultz's mind wandered as he worked. His infatuation with a younger coworker, a chemical engineer in sulfur products surfaced. She had beautiful, dark hair. Short and anorexic, she was the opposite of his wife. If Schultz made love to her, he could throw her all over the bed. He would never feel small.

She once teased Schultz with a wink.

She was just messing with you.

She was too pretty; Schultz was too weird and introverted. Besides, his coworkers at Biotech Labs talked too much. They probably told her about the crazy ideas he shared in the lunchroom.

Janna Sandler. I could have an affair with her.

Schultz looked up from his microscope. The first of three sets were complete. He studied the notes he had written.

"Michelle wouldn't like you talking to her again," Schultz said, aloud into the empty lab. He placed another slide into the microscope and started his study of the second population.

· · ·

Schultz took a break after the third set of specimens. When he returned to his station and began his study, the microscope lens was cold. The bench needed to be a little higher; his lower back was strained.

"You knew Janna when she was Elizabeth," he said, into the room.

In the late evening hours, Schultz's mind was becoming scrambled from exertion and lack of sleep.

Elizabeth had the same eyes. You can't change your eyes.

Janna's blue eyes and smile flashed in the sample he studied.

"I see you, Miss Janna," Schultz said. "Only then you were a little younger. It was cool outside, was it not? You wore a sweater with…with…Greek letters on the front. Yes. I never thought I would see you again. I would like to see you again, Miss Elizabeth Sandler…perhaps in another sweatshirt."

· · ·

To: Brad Philagen
      Team Leader
      Grain Research, Biotech Labs

A report on the four strands of grain from the Greene County Extension office, sample tracking numbers 2314 A-D, by Kenneth R. Schultz, Chief Engineer.

Introduction:

Brad, I must be honest, in my twelve years of analyzing soybeans, I have never found a seed worth planting. I may have endorsed certain seeds in the past. But you forced me!

Remember that day you yelled at me? I gave you an answer. But, personally, I didn't like a single one. I found them all flawed to some degree. I always have.

That is until today!

In the batch that I have analyzed from the Greene County extension office, I have discovered perfection. In its variations, I found the evolution of the perfect seed.

In an effort to explain my findings in the clearest manner possible, I've decided to use the "Parable of the Sower" as a backdrop to my discoveries. I hope you're familiar with it.

A farmer went out to sow his seed. As he was scattering the seed, some fell along the path, and the birds came and ate it up. Some fell on rocky places, where it did not have much soil. It sprang up quickly, because the soil was shallow. But when the sun came up, the plants were scorched, and they withered because they had no root. Other seed fell among thorns, which grew up and choked the plants. Still other seed fell on good soil, where it produced a crop—a hundred, sixty or thirty times what was sown.

Matthew 13:3–8

Unlike Jesus, who seems to be concerned with the field where the seeds are sown, I've been tasked to analyze the seeds themselves, and I too find that they can be separated into four separate and ever-evolving samples.

Set "A" are plump, ripe seeds with thin shells. Vulnerable and tasty, they are scooped up by the world, never getting a chance to set roots. This seed represents youth. By the handfuls, they are tossed into a cruel mix and swallowed whole.

I was this seed once—fat, happy, ignorant. But I evolved!

Oh, Elizabeth, like all the others, we had to evolve.

Mind your own business, Brad! Or I'll yell at you this time!

Back to my report.

Set "B" is perfect in symmetry and color. It appears perfect.

I was this seed once; I think most people are. A nice home in the suburbs, a respectable car, and a country club membership were the façade. I donned my career as the overcoat to my fashionable clothes. My wife was well kept. My children wore expensive tennis shoes. I was making plans to purchase a boat.

But I had no depth, no inner strength. I withered in the scorching heat of vanity. Finding no purpose in my hubris, I was forced to evolve once again.

Set "C" is a seed that is lean and hearty. It's a strong seed, hard working—a taskmaster. Indeed, it wills itself to grow, even on rocky soil. It grows out of a sense of duty, even when choked by weeds.

I became this seed. I never missed work or church. I took my kids to soccer and dance classes; my yard was immaculate. To look at me was to look at one who was totally committed to duty.

Alas, this was a failure as well. For duty served no other purpose that to convince me that I had evolved into my own little god.

And who would worship me? Certainly not my wife or kids. You've always hated me; don't think I haven't noticed.

I can't believe you thought you could yell at me like that!

Well, good news, Brad. The fourth grain is perfect. Call them up in Greene County. Tell them to start planting.

Set "D" is a seed that is ugly and stout. It will feed from the earth with the best absorption rate. It will become one with its provider.

Yes Brad, I have evolved into set "D." My little crime has made me the good seed. I'm not a god; I was insane to think I was. I'm the seed of God. Contrite, forgiven, alive—my action will produce a crop a hundred, sixty, or thirty times what was sown.

As will this ugly, little soybean from Greene County.

Respectfully submitted,
Kenneth Schultz

• • •

Schultz dragged the report into the trash can on his desktop. Monday he would write it properly. The lab was too bright; his knee began to throb.

It had to be a crucifixion. There was no other way.

He exited the lab. His actions last night weighed heavy on his mind.

Crucifixion, Schultz. Pleasure, duty, and will did nothing.

Schultz struggled to carry his briefcase.

CHAPTER 14

Standing at the locked sliding glass back door, staring into the backyard, Pastor Dupree ate an apple, trying to see past his reflection. The crunching sound rattled around in his head and muffled the television newscast, blaring in the adjacent room.

After a few minutes of standing perfectly still, he tossed the apple core into the sink, flipped off the back porch light, unlocked the door, and stepped outside onto the back porch with his Bible in hand.

The night was hot, saturated, identical to the night before. The bayou was dark and silent. A light breeze from the gulf pushed branches of trees and thicket into spooky apparitions that moved stealthily through the canal. Several, with large horns like rams, appeared in the back lighting from Eastwood Street. Dupree held his Bible out toward them, as he took a seat on the edge of the porch. Red sat beside him. He studied the canal, staring, straining his eyes for light, identifying the ghosts and specters that flew in circles around his backyard.

Satan worship?

"There was no worship." Dupree spoke into the night air. He wiped his forehead with the back of his hand that held the Bible.

Leslie Wixon, the church secretary, heard exactly what the killer wanted the public to hear. The scene was perfectly orchestrated.

"Right down to the Bible passage."

Dupree flipped the pages of the Bible to the bookmarked page. In the pitch dark, he held the open Bible toward the Bayou and recited the passage from Revelation Chapter 12 from memory.

"When the dragon saw that he had been hurled to the earth, he pursued the woman who had given birth to the male child. The woman was given the two wings of a great eagle, so that she might fly to the place prepared for her in the wilderness, where she would be taken care of for a time, times and half a time, out of the serpent's reach. Then from his mouth the serpent spewed water like a river, to overtake the woman and sweep her away with the torrent. But the earth helped the woman by opening its mouth and swallowing the river that the dragon had spewed out of his mouth."

"Okay Red. To start off, you've got to get the characters straight." Dupree said, confusing the dog.

"The dragon/serpent is the devil—hurled to the earth—cast away from God's presence." Dupree crossed his legs underneath him and used the tail of his shirt to wipe sweat from his forehead.

"The woman with child represents the believers in Christ, the invisible church, pursued by the devil." He tapped the pages of the Bible with his index finger.

"The only question is…who or what is the 'earth.'"

Dupree closed his eyes and began to pray.

"Does the earth represent those who are not saved?" Red placed his head in Dupree's lap. "The earth after all is Satan's realm. Is it not?"

The passage repeated over and over in his mind.

"The earth comes to help the woman? The non-believers come to save the believers?"

It doesn't make sense.

Dupree placed the open Bible on top of his head, pushing the words into his brain. He rubbed the back of his neck and pain ran up the back of his legs into his groin.

"Of course! That's exactly what he's thinking."

He closed the Bible. Kissing the front cover, he pointed it toward the heavens.

"Let's go, Red," he said, standing. He headed toward the back door. "That sicko thinks his crime will actually save people," Dupree said. "That's why the crucifixion."

• • •

Dupree's den was dark, illuminated only by the television screen. He reclined, watching *Sports Center*. On his shirtless torso, a bag of Cheetos rested on his stomach. He reached into the bag without thinking, without hunger. Munching Cheetos, allowing the crumbs to fall on his chest and neck, he licked his fingers in an attempt to keep them from being permanently stained orange. Reaching to the side of his lounge chair, he grabbed a twenty-ounce Mountain Dew, drinking through a straw by tilting his head slightly forward.

His love of heavily salted snack treats and carbonated beverages was a vice. It had to be a vice; only a vice could bring on such a euphoric feeling.

Tired of thinking about Revelation, tired of thinking about a substandard sermon written for tomorrow's church service, he relaxed with a few simple pleasures. He checked his watch.

Nurse Kelly gets off shift in twenty minutes.

His visit with Mrs. Brewer, earlier in the day, went well. She was breathing. He read to her from Psalm 139, verse 5.

"You hem me in—behind and before; you have laid your hand upon me."

Dupree reassured her that even unconscious, God was in control and had secured her a place in eternity. He held her hand, cold and lifeless as it was, and brought warmth to her fingers. He left her with a prayer and a promise to return.

At the nurse's station, he talked to Nurse Kelly. During their brief conversation, Dupree learned that she worked until ten thirty. He didn't think it was right to ask for her phone number.

Sitting forward, he brushed Cheetos crumbs from his chest onto the floor. He flipped through the channels, stopping on the late local news program. A handsome, middle-aged anchorman read flawlessly from a teleprompter.

"The murder occurred at a home on Beach Boulevard in Pascagoula around three o'clock a.m."

Dupree sat upright.

"It's just a real shock." The newscast had moved to a recording made earlier in the day. A lady from the community was being interviewed. "We just all thought the world of Mr. Jerry. He's going to be missed."

Dupree moved closer to the screen.

"The scene was very disturbing," Police Chief Tillman said. "We don't have a lot of details to share. However, we can say we are looking for a white male."

Forensics has been processed.

"He is between five-feet-ten and six feet tall."

They've analyzed the foot prints.

"Surveillance video is still being processed, but we know the perpetrator walked some distance to the crime scene. He wore shorts and a black T-shirt."

No car was seen in the video.

The newscast moved forward. A video shot from the pier of Beach Boulevard was being shown with a voiceover from the reporter.

"Police are encouraging anyone who may have seen anything suspicious in this area to call Crime Stoppers. A reward for any information leading to an arrest has been offered."

Dupree didn't hear about the reward. He sat in a numb silence for several minutes, his heart rate elevated, his ears pumping with blood.

They must have some DNA by now.

He stood. In the utility room, he grabbed a small vacuum cleaner. Flipping on the lights in the den, he cleaned around the lounge chair, before vacuuming the rest of the den.

The day had been hot; the air conditioner struggled to keep up. Replacing the vacuum cleaner, he moved to the back door to make sure it was locked.

Hargood was killed six blocks from his house, and just a moment afterward, Dupree had been sitting on his back porch looking for a raccoon.

"It wouldn't hurt to investigate," he said, returning to his seat in the den. Pulling his legs in as tight as his stomach would allow, he wrapped his arms around his knees.

"The Ross's live over there, and then there's…what was that name? The moonwalkers." Dupree talked to himself.

It was probably an animal.

The phone on the floor beside him rang, nearly giving him a heart attack.

"Jeez!" he said, laughing.

"Hello."

"Hello, is this Pastor Dupree?" The female voice sounded familiar.

"Yes."

"Hey, this is Kelly Mitchell…from the hospital. I hope you don't mind that I called so late."

"Uh, no. Of course not. Is everything alright?"

"Yeah, everything's great. I just got off work and…wanted to talk. You know, when we're not on the clock."

Dupree pumped his fist and fell back into his lounge chair.

CHAPTER 15

Janna Sandler opened her eyes and awoke entombed in a time capsule buried on her last day of high school.

Posters of the Twilight Saga, Justin Timberlake, and the US women's soccer team dominated the wall above her desk. Each poster was intentionally skewed and enhanced with pictures from high school. Although her dad was forced to change the paint in every single room at least once per year, Janna's room remained the bright, sickeningly happy yellow. Her collection of preppy headbands and costume jewelry cluttered the top of the chest-of-drawers.

The baby crib in the corner ruined the high school time capsule. Also, pictures of Katie dominated the giant cork board, covering prom photos, concert tickets and ribbons from football games. There were no photos taken of Janna during her short college career or even shorter marriage to D.L.

The forgotten years.

Janna stretched and smiled. She rolled to her side and grabbed the picture on the nightstand. Her date was smiling; her wrist corsage was ornate. Barry wore a tuxedo with a ruffled shirt dyed to match her dress. Janna settled. No matter how many hints she dropped, Franky wouldn't ask her to prom.

Katie was waking; she kicked her foot against a crib slat. Rolled tight in her blanket, she struggled to free her right arm. Her blonde hair was tossed, wet against her temples. She squinted and yawned. All the functions of her body pulled themselves from sleep. Katie wet her diaper giving her mother a morning smile.

"Momma," she said.

"Here I am, sweetie."

They got up quietly making the beds and straightening the room behind them as they left. It was seven o'clock, and her parents wouldn't be up for another half hour.

Janna's mom had a philosophy for decorating rather than a style. Each room had a theme. Janna's old bedroom was the I-never-want-my-kid-to-grow-up theme; the formal living room was nautical, complete with a painting of a whale and coffee table made from the helm of a sailboat. The kitchen, with its collection of Norwegian plates and window dressings, was a flashback to the old country—Minnesota.

Janna pulled a frying pan from the pantry, noticing that her mother had changed the contact paper on the shelves. Her sheets had been the same for twenty years; the pantry contact paper had a six-month life cycle.

She made scrambled eggs for Katie and sat at the kitchen counter reading her phone and drinking coffee. A Facebook post reminded her of the murder that was mentioned at Amber Schultz's party. She read an article detailing the story on the Mississippi Press website.

"Hey, honey," her dad said, walking into the kitchen wearing a T-shirt screen printed with "Super Dad". "Hey, Katie, sweetie, how's my precious little boo-boo baby?" The giant man was reduced to a babbling lunatic in front of his granddaughter.

"Ga-pa."

"Good morning, Dad. You want a cup of coffee?"

"Sure, I'll get it."

"No, no, I got it." Janna pulled a mug from the cupboard. "Did you hear about the murder in Pascagoula?"

"No."

"It's headline news. His last name is Hargood. Do you know him?"

"Hargood? I know a Martin Hargood out at the yard in the fifty-four department. It wasn't Martin Hargood, was it?"

"No, Jerry Hargood." She poured the coffee. "Do you still take Splenda?"

"No, black is fine," he said, bending to a knee in front of the high chair. "Jerry Hargood?" He picked up scrambled eggs from the floor and threw them into the sink.

"It says in the paper that he ran the hardware store on Ingalls Ave in Pascagoula. Here you go."

"Thanks." Taking a sip from the coffee, the light seemed to go on. "Oh yeah, I think I've met him. He runs the rental part. Now, jeez, that's a shame. Do they know who did it?"

"Nope," she said, pushing more eggs in front of Katie.

The morning fell into a routine that brought a great deal of comfort to Janna. The rebellious youth was long gone, and she was happy to spend a Saturday night with her parents. Her mother came in after showering; she wore an ancient terrycloth robe tied at the waist, and her hair was in a towel. They ate breakfast together.

"Guess who I saw Friday night," Janna said, starting the conversation.

"Lawrence. You told me you broke up with him."

"Yeah, I know, I just saw someone else." Janna paused; she wanted to take back her words. "Franky Stevens," she blurted out. "You never would have guessed; I don't know why I even asked." She shook her head, turning a little red from mentioning the name.

"Uh, oh," her mom said, lightly patting her husband on the shoulders. "You're not getting goofy again, are you?"

"Stop it. I was never 'getting goofy,'" she said, raising her voice to cover her mother's. "I just saw him and well, that's that. I didn't talk to him; I mean he didn't even see me."

"Where did you see him?"

"On the drawbridge. He was looking at the ships while the bridge was up."

"Uh huh."

"And 'uh huh' nothing, that's it, end of story. I hate that I even brought it up."

"I'm sorry." Janna could tell her mom was trying not to laugh. "Really? I know you hate it when I do that," her mom said. "Sweetheart, you're a grown woman. You don't have to play games anymore."

"I just mentioned it, Mom. It wasn't a big deal."

"Did you breakup with Lawrence before or after you saw him?"

"After," she said, quickly. Her mind was addled. "No, wait, it was after the movie. I saw him after I broke up with Lawrence. But before he dropped me off. It was while he was…what difference does that make anyway?"

"I was just playing with you." Her mom smiled, placing her arm around Janna's shoulder. "Is he back in town?"

"I don't know," Janna scooped up the remaining eggs from the high chair and ate them quickly.

"Call him up."

"You've got to be kidding me, Mom. There is no way I'm going to do that."

"Look him up. If you want to talk to him, call him. Tell him you saw him and invite him over for dinner or something. Your dad and I would love to see him again."

"I don't know." She washed her hands in the sink.

"We love you, honey. He'd be lucky to go out with you," she said, moving toward her and giving her a kiss on the forehead. "We've got to get going, okay? Will you be here when we get back?"

"I doubt it."

"Well, you know you're welcome."

"I know. I'll think about it."

Her thoughts raced. Her hands went numb, picturing herself calling him.

There was no way she could ever make a call like that.

CHAPTER 16

Waking from a deathlike sleep, pain raged in Franky's temple. His eyelids, matted and swollen, fought against the impulse to open. He couldn't block the pain in his abdomen, his bladder was bursting. Wetting the bed was an option, but without opening his eyes, he didn't know which bed he was in. Doubled over in pain, he rolled back and forth, brushing up and down the sheets, searching for someone, anyone, who get help him to the bathroom.

Opening his eyes slowly, he rolled onto the floor, landing with a thud. Grasping his knees tight to his abdomen, he saw the top of his dresser. The picture of him and his brother at his sister's wedding caught an early morning sunbeam, moving through a slit in the blinds.

Franky crawled toward the bathroom, slowly regaining consciousness. The smell of perfume and cigarettes escaped his shirt. His pants were missing. The hard tiled floor was cold on his knees and hands. Standing, steadying himself with one hand on the bathroom sink and one on the wall, he finally straightened, as he relieved the pressure on his bladder.

In front of the bathroom mirror, he splashed cold water on his face. Throwing his shirt into the hall, he examined his chest for hickies. He drank a handful of water. It hit his empty, acidic stomach and boiled immediately. Franky grabbed his abdomen in reaction.

Looking deep into his eyes, Franky vowed that he would give up one of two things: drinking or hillbilly dance joints.

Closing the commode, he took a seat and fell forward with his head between his knees.

His arms hung limp along his side. His knuckles rested on the floor. He let the pain increase in his temples until they were numb. Surviving the pain of a hangover was often his one reason for living—his Everest. But this one hurt. His lungs were tight, his fingers numb; he needed oxygen. He was staring into a frozen crevasse, and he was losing his footing.

"Why do you…," he said, slowly and deliberately, not allowing himself to finish his sentence.

Franky's life was in decline; every action was convoluted and twisted. Phone calls and lies, promises and apologies had become the daily routine of a man who lived for drink.

"This is killing you."

• • •

Franky awoke suddenly; his head and the back of his neck ached from the pressure of resting against the bathroom wall for God knows how long.

He massaged his temples.

Composing himself, he went to the refrigerator. His first dilemma on whether to give up on honky-tonk's or drinking was quickly answered. He drank down the remainder of a frozen bottle of gin and tossed the bottle in the trashcan.

Grabbing a Budweiser from the refrigerator, he found his phone and took a seat at the kitchen table.

He had a text message from Shiela.

"Made it home. Call me tomorrow."

Checking his Uber app, he saw a charge at 1:35 a.m..

Lighting a cigarette, he thought briefly about showering. He grabbed another beer instead.

• • •

Franky exited the Uber, without talking to the driver. The asphalt parking lot of Johnny Joe's Country Palace was the temperature of the sun. At his car, the oppressive heat cooked a garbage can, overflowing with nearly empty beer bottles, and created a toxic atmosphere that made Franky gag. He briefly held the door of the Uber, thinking he might jump back into the air conditioning and abandon his idea to go into work altogether.

He rushed into his car instead.

Franky lit a cigarette. Driving through the middle of Pascagoula on Highway 90, he passed the tandem of stores that made Pascagoula look like every other city in the USA.

Walmart was on his right, flaunting its Sunday morning packed parking lot. The hurricane spared it from flooding. When it opened, three days after power was restored, it sold out of everything. Spam, Vienna Sausages, and deviled ham were the only items left on the store shelves. The Red Cross supplied enough potted meat to cause sales of these items to plummet.

On both sides of the highway sat a McDonalds, Taco Bell, Burger King and eight other lesser franchises, that provided dollar menu items of calories wrapped in salt to an ever-fatter clientele. Chipotle, Chick-Fil-A, and Five Guys offered the same quality fare, disguised in more expensive prices to appear healthier.

Pizza joints, auto part stores, car dealerships, and at least twelve pharmacies cluttered the thoroughfare. Of all the streets in Pascagoula, Highway 90 was the most dismal. Void of character and charisma, defined by function, Highway 90 was the "all" street. The one that everyone had seen a thousand times, assuming they had been in a thousand cities. Billboards crowded the view; trees were a past memory. A person couldn't swing a dead cat without hitting a gas station, vape shop, or cellphone outlet.

Franky hated Highway 90, not because it carried the burden of being the busiest street in Pascagoula, but because it had no life. Even the projects had personality.

His frown broke when he turned south off this sad slice of Americana onto Pascagoula Street.

Pascagoula Street, with its oak trees, palmettos, manicured lawns and churches, was a perfect little lady. It was a homecoming queen with a bright white smile at the south end near the beach, long flaxen hair of moss-covered oaks, and a friendly, warm demeanor.

Unlike real homecoming queens, she was not snobbish. Every socio-ethnic group, every level of affluence or lack thereof, could be found in her court.

• • •

"Does that guy ever take a day off?" Franky whispered, as he stepped into the front entrance of Fineburg, Fineburg, and Fineburg.

He tucked his newspaper under his arm and tip-toed down the hallway. Closing the door to his office softly, he engaged the lock and rested with his back against the door.

The office was paneled with leather-bound law books along the interior wall to his left. Franky decorated the wall to his right with his diplomas and a painting of a sailboat. A baseball bat and an unused gym bag were the only items in the room that he owned.

Franky tested his breath by breathing into his cupped hand. He sniffed his shirt.

Opposite the office door was a glass wall that faced Downtown Plaza—an outdoor mall built in the seventies. Constructed along both sides of a narrow street, its grand opening was a throwback to simpler times when people stayed outside more often. The mall became unprofitable with the innovation of large industrial air conditioners and on-line shopping.

In 1975 the venue housed several great shops offering shoes, food, athletic equipment, and just about anything. Now, however, it was home to the law office of the Fineburgs and little else.

Stepping to the window, Franky searched the walkways. No one. The residents of Pascagoula were either in bed or in church, there were few in-betweens. Pascagoula was chock-full of Bible thumpers and drunkards, Sunday school teachers and the damned.

Taking a seat, he spun around to face his desk. His hangover would return in a couple of hours. The beers and the high level of alcohol, still waiting to be processed through his circulatory system, allowed him to sit, coherent, free of most pain, and read the paper.

"Murder in South Pascagoula."

Franky closed his eyes and placed his forehead on the paper. His arms went weak. Looking into the darkness of his eyelids, he saw visions. Memories flashed through his mind—disco balls and cowboy hats, pool toys and tacos. Jigsaw puzzle pieces crushed together in a wavy distorted pattern. Pogy boats, craps tables, his bedroom blinds, and five-hundred dollars in twenties were shadowy images almost too fuzzy to identify.

A snapshot of the Pascagoula drawbridge, so far above the earth that the water was invisible, flashed across his eyes. A chill ran up his spine.

The bridge?

Lifting his head, he slowly read the first paragraph of the news article.

"Police have reported the murder of Jerry Hargood of 608 Beach Boulevard. Investigators believe the assault took place between midnight and the early morning hours Saturday. Hargood, a small business owner from…"

Franky wanted to call Dale and ask him about Friday night. Did they go out on the bridge?

I didn't jump from the bridge.

His clothes weren't wet when he woke up Saturday.

"No one could survive that jump."

His blood turned to ice. He was instantly chilled, stricken with a fever.

What happened last night?

Memories of Renee were strong.

He needed a cup of coffee.

CHAPTER 17

"Michael, settle down!" Kenneth Schultz yelled into the rear-view mirror at his five-year-old son. "Sit back!" The child pulled the shoulder strap over his head and climbed in the front seat.

The boy looked exactly like Schultz. He had jet-black hair and cool, blue eyes. His eyelashes and brows were long, giving him slightly effeminate features. His smile was a perfect set of baby teeth.

"Did you hear me? I said sit back. You're going to step on your sister." Schultz accelerated, swerving into the on-coming lane. The child grabbed the sunglasses off Schultz's face.

"Mine!"

The sun bounced off the hood, under the visor, instantly blinding Schultz. The glare baked his eyeballs. He swerved back into his lane, running the tires onto the curb.

"I said sit back!" Schultz screamed. Braking hard, he swatted at the boy, who had expertly timed the swing and plopped down into the floorboard of the backseat. His foot struck his sister across the forehead.

Amber Schultz let out a blood-curdling scream.

Schultz lost it, screaming and ranting as the entire family, less one, headed to church.

• • •

The air conditioner cooled the car to a comfortable temperature. Schultz's voice was hoarse from screaming. The children were silent, sullen, their ears still ringing from daddy's tirade.

They would never make the ten o'clock service at the Methodist Church on Ingalls Avenue. However, Christ Church started service at ten thirty. Schultz decided to drive around for another thirty minutes.

"I'm sorry, kids."

They didn't respond.

"It's just that, you can't be doing that when I'm driving. So, let's just relax and have a good time, okay. Okay?" He turned onto Polk Street.

Janna Sandler lived on Polk Street.

Schultz played the pseudo-stalker before leaving the house. He acted like a silly schoolboy. Typing her name into Google, finding her address, her work location, with every key stroke his face burned red with embarrassment. He marked her Facebook page. Michelle came up behind him, when he was reading a church's website that outlined her involvement with the youth group. He quickly minimized the screen. She didn't even ask what he was doing. Schultz wanted the opportunity to lie.

It's the new girl in my class.

Ideas, fresh and uplifting, came to his mind. He would have enjoyed sitting and talking with Miss Sandler.

"I have a son and a daughter, but you already knew I had a daughter. I noticed that you live alone. How? The Internet of course. Your daughter is cute. Has her father abandoned her? What a coincidence! Your daughter and I have something in common."

There it is!

No cars were in the driveway.

"She must be an early riser, or she has spent the night elsewhere," Schultz said aloud. His voice was covered by road noise and the hum of the air conditioner.

"Sit back and look out the window, son."

"Your son is sweet," Miss Sandler said. Schultz pictured her sitting in the seat beside him.

"Children? Michelle insisted on them. I never wanted any," Schultz covered his mouth as he spoke.

"You don't like children?"

"As a class of humans? No, I don't really like children. Why? Because they're spoiled rotten. Well, when they turn three or so. I mean, they can't be spoiled until they understand right from wrong, until they start communicating. That's the beginning of the spoiled rotten phase of a child's life. Parents these days have no clue about proper parenting skills. Most act like monkeys or dogs in the way they treat their kids. They lavish attention on them until they reach puberty, and then they stop talking to them and they send them off to be raised by the internet."

"I don't like you, Kenneth Schultz."

"Miss Sandler, it takes time to like me."

Schultz drove past her house. An empty garbage can was by the curb. Garbage pick-up was Friday. If she had left this morning, she would have walked right by it.

No one could be that lazy.

• • •

Schultz was driven to murder, a murder that would scream for repentance. A murder jerked him back into grace.

But what? Murder, really? Even murderers lose faith. This sin had to be more than just a crime; it needed purpose, meaning.

Schultz was cured the day he realized that murder was more than murder when it drove people to God.

"Most people are ignorant and incapable of comprehending the importance of sin." Schultz wrote in his journal. "These are the ones the Lord has sent to me."

Everyone in Pascagoula knew about Jesus. They just didn't care. They turned away, and they acted rude and hypocritical. For these people, the crucifixion of the Sinless One was not enough.

Therefore, Schultz had to sacrifice the sinful one. He had to crucify one who was exactly like them.

"That is me on that cross," they would say. "And I must be saved before I die like that."

Despair would drive them to the sinless Christ.

Schultz fretted for a month on how to commit the crucifixion.

The blood was the tough part.

Schultz wished he could go Old Testament with the sacrifice, throwing buckets of blood all over the place. He could have gone in just slashing and flinging blood without a second thought.

But this sacrificing was a New Testament kind of thing.

Priests had to be careful; they couldn't spill the consecrated blood, not even a single drop.

Within a few months, the plan was perfected. Schultz would simply knock and wait. When the victim answered, Schultz would immobilize him, bleed him, and crucify him.

When Schultz understood this, it was just a matter of finding the perfect victim.

• • •

The altar at Christ Church was decorated in green. The cup and the host were covered with a white linen, embroidered with a cross, and sat beneath a large painting of Christ ascending into heaven.

It was the season of Pentecost. Hidden behind a banner displaying a rose in the desert, the organist played a lilting, intricate prelude composed by Bach.

The acolytes wore white. Their tennis shoes showed beneath their robes. They bowed to the altar in respect.

No one had taken a seat in front of the Schultz family. Schultz was tempted to look behind him to see if anyone else had come to church. A family took a seat in the pew adjacent to his; he saw them out of the corner of his eye.

The candles were lit; the choir entered singing "A Mighty Fortress Is Our God." Their robes matched the burgundy carpet, which clashed with the colors of the altar.

The pastor walked to the front, bowed to the altar, and turned to start the service.

"We begin in the name of the Father, the…"

Oh my God! It's him!

Schultz recognized the preacher instantly as the one from the newspaper—the Capdepon Case.

Schultz flipped to the front of the bulletin.

Reverend Cooper Dupree. He's Pastor Dupree—the police preacher!

Schultz sat back, staring at the preacher who he had marveled at from afar—his notoriety for ministering to the incarcerated and aiding in investigations was well documented.

I wish I still had the article.

"I'd like to take a moment to review something that I've been studying." Dupree started his sermon. "Revelation 12."

A chill ran up Schultz's spine.

"It's a vision in the Bible that appears to contradict the rest of biblical teaching."

Sweat formed on Schultz's lip, and his infected knee shook uncontrollably.

"Daddy, can I…"

"Hush!"

"…where we have a serpent and a woman and the earth."

With every word uttered by the preacher, Schultz's anger rose. It was obvious the Pascagoula Police Department had already involved Dupree in the investigation of Hargood's murder.

And now he thinks he understands the motive? How arrogant!

"It appears that the earth, or those outside of the body of Christ, actually comes to the aid of the Church," the pastor continued. "However, looking at the Greek manuscripts, in this verse the Greek word *katesthio* refers to God, to an 'earthly' God or to the human-ness of Christ, and no one else."

Schultz wanted to place his fingers in his ears and start humming. The line of dribble spewing from the preacher was damning for all who listened. He wasn't preaching salvation; he was paving the way to hell for the Schultz's and anyone else who stumbled into Christ Church at ten thirty.

"The 'earth' in this passage is not those who do not believe coming to help those who do believe," Dupree said. "The 'earth' refers to the Messiah, the true man and true God, who saves his Church. It says that only Christ has redemptive power. His passion alone saved mankind."

And with this Schultz let out an audible grunt. He covered it immediately by faking a sneeze.

. . .

Schultz had a passion. Schultz's passion was unlike that of Christ's or man's.

Jesus's passion was to die so that man could find God. God suffered and died physically so that man could live, spiritually.

Conversely, there was the passion of man. Man would suffer and die, so that God could live. This was not to be a natural death, but a spiritual one, because "God does not live among the dead."

Neither of these passions were Schultz's. His passion was the third in the perfect trinity of passion. His was the passion of a madman—the passion of immense pain—the implementation of which resulted in Hargood's death.

Hargood's suffering would certainly drive people to a spiritual renewal.

. . .

Schultz waited for a response from the squawk box. He placed his order; it was customary and polite for the cashier to repeat it.

"So that's two chicken nugget happy meals with Cokes and a Big Mac meal with water," the voice said. The man in the car behind them crept even closer. "That's $15.45. Please drive around."

"But…that's not…" Schultz let off the brake. He had ordered only the Big Mac sandwich and not the meal. He didn't normally eat french fries.

"Sit back, Michael. You don't want to make daddy mad again, do you?"

Pulling up to the window, he paid in cash.

"So, Amber, what did you think about the pastor's sermon this morning?" Schultz spoke with a cold, unfeeling voice. The two-year-old strapped in the car seat in the back had fallen asleep.

"I thought it was rather awful, and I have a good mind to tell him."

"Here you go, sir," the lady said, leaning out of the window. She reached out to Schultz. "Here are your drinks and…here are your meals. Have a nice day."

"Thanks."

The fries filled the air with an irresistible odor that made his stomach growl.

"No, Michael. I said you need to wait until we get home."

Schultz smiled.

"You know, Amber, maybe I should visit the young pastor. He might need a little insight into the true meaning of that passage in Revelation. What do you think, sweetie?"

Schultz turned onto Market Street and headed south. Waves of heat rolled off the road in front of him.

"Sit back, Michael."

"Daddy, can I have the toy?"

"Sit back, I said, or I'll toss it out the window."

CHAPTER 18

Janna was a member of the only mega church in Pascagoula. With a sanctuary that held more than the Panther football stadium, the First Baptist church was a pillar of the community and the only structure of the skyline that wasn't a gantry crane or distillation tower. The three thousand members attended one of the four services on Sunday, and many headed for the local restaurants and diners for lunch afterward. Such a force was the First Baptist church gang of locusts that all other churches changed their worship time so that they could get a table.

Janna held Katie's hand. They stood in the parking lot waiting for D.L.

"Oh, isn't she darling," an elderly lady said, bending at the waist to pat Katie on the head.

"Thank you."

Katie wore a little sundress and bright white shoes. Janna was attractive in a light green skirt that hung just above the knee and a wildly patterned blouse. Her muscular calves were accentuated with a pair of espadrilles. The sun was bright and the humidity high. The only shade available was a dot next to one of the light poles.

"Hey there, girl!" A voice said from behind Janna.

"Hey you." Janna saw her best friend, Kelly Mitchell. They hugged.

Kelly bent down to pick up Katie.

"I didn't see you in there. Where were you?" Janna asked.

"How's my precious? How's my little precious," Kelly said to Katie. "Oh, I was late. I overslept. I stayed up way too late."

"Really? What did you have going on?"

Kelly was holding Katie on her hip. "Oh, nothing," she flashed a mischievous smile. "Just a phone call."

"Really…and with who? Don't tell me it was…"

"No! Heavens no. It was a new friend. A guy I met at work." She smiled, flashing a brilliant set of teeth. Her green eyes reflected the brightness of the day. "We're going on a date. What do you think of that, Katie?" She pursed her lips when she talked to Katie to make it sound like baby-talk.

"That's terrific. Who is it? Someone at work? Is he a doctor?"

"No, actually, he's a preacher. And Janna, he is gorgeous!"

"You've got to be kidding me."

"No, he has these dark eyes and this dark hair that's kind of wavy, and he's tall, and cute. He wears a collar; it's just so adorable."

"Wow, so when are you…"

"Hey," D.L. said, walking up behind them.

"Daddy!"

"Hey there, punkin'. Are you ready to go to Meme's?"

"Meme's!"

"Thanks," he said to Kelly, who handed Katie to her dad.

"Hey," Janna said. "So you're taking her to daycare tomorrow morning?"

"Yeah, around nine I guess."

Janna reached in the bed of her work truck and grabbed Katie's overnight bag.

"All right, well you two have a great time. Mommy loves you," Janna said, giving Katie a kiss. "Bye, bye."

She turned to Kelly. "Do you want to do lunch?"

"Oh, sweetie, I can't. I've got to work this afternoon, but call me later and I'll tell you all about my new friend," Kelly said, as she headed out across the parking lot.

And with a final quick exchange, Janna had the afternoon to herself.

CHAPTER 19

The Sunday morning air was humid, stifling. Pastor Dupree stood by the back door of the sanctuary donning layers of pastoral robes, trying to maintain a position in the shade. The Pentecostal green sash that fell over his shoulders made his eyes darker. His cheeks hurt from smiling.

The congregation filed past the preacher on their way to coffee and pastries. Dupree made small talk as he ushered them out the door, shaking hands and patting children on the head.

"Good morning, I'm Pastor Dupree," he said, taking the hand of a visitor. "I'm so glad you came to worship with us this morning."

"Thank you," the man said. "I'm Kenneth."

"Awesome. It's really good to meet you. And who is this pretty young lady?" Dupree brushed the hair out of the eyes of the two-year-old Schultz was carrying. "You're looking a little tired. Huh? Are you a little sleepy?"

"This is my daughter, Amber, and this is Michael," Schultz said, looking down at his son.

"Well it's really nice to meet you, Michael," Dupree bent at the waist and shook the five-year-old's hand. "Are you traveling through Pascagoula or just visiting with us this morning?" Dupree returned his attention back to Schultz.

"No, we live here."

"Outstanding, well we are really glad you came this morning. You're always welcome. We have coffee and a few refreshments next door if you would like to go over. I can introduce you to some of our families. Michael, I'm sure there are a couple of boys your age over there."

"I don't think so, pastor. Not today." Schultz spoke coldly.

"Okay, then." Dupree smiled. "Perhaps another time."

"Pastor," Schultz said, as he stepped toward the street. "When are your office hours?"

"Uh well, I don't have any set time. I'm almost always available—by appointment, but I'm usually here every day of the week between eight and noon."

"Thanks."

"Sure."

Schultz descended the stairs one at a time, protecting an injured knee, holding his daughter on one hip, while holding his son's hand.

"Can I help you with them?" Dupree stepped down to help Michael down a step.

"No thanks, I'm fine," Schultz said. "This way, Michael."

"Okay, well come see us again soon." Dupree turned to address the next person leaving the church.

• • •

Dupree rarely ran in the heat of the day. But church was long, and his mind buzzed with thoughts he couldn't align logically. Exhaustion normally cleared his mind. Running down a paved Mississippi road in the middle of August usually proved more than effective.

When he hit Beach Boulevard at a quarter after one, the Sunday afternoon air was hot and thin. Dupree forced himself to breathe; he could taste the heat. The sun was blistering down from above his head and cooked everything it contacted. Only the constant sea breeze made exercising bearable. With the warm-up jog from his house to the seawall completed, he picked up his pace to a seven-minute mile and headed for the Coast Guard point.

To his left, whitecaps kicked up from a brisk southern wind. A little dot of a shadow followed beneath him. His eyes burned as he focused on a distant barrier island. He tasted the sweat dripping off the tip of his nose; the liquid was much saltier from running along the gulf. Past the whitecaps to the brown water, past the island floating on the horizon, the water was blue and clear.

Dupree fixed his sight on the perfect line where the sky converged on the sea, a screen of pastels that separated the heavens from the earth. Wind cut his face; waves crashed into the seawall. Mist was everywhere, burning his unblinking eyes.

A penitent mood arose as he tortured himself with exercise, cleansing him with sweat and physical exertion. Dupree was a sinner. He had been rude to Mrs. Brewer. He had lustful thoughts about Nurse Kelly. He was self-centered and cocky.

He laughed at words like *cocky*.

Dupree dropped his head and picked up the pace.

He cursed the breeze that seemed to cut him in half.

It was at the turn when he stopped running away and started running toward home, exactly two miles into his run, that his penitence turned to relief. Sinner? Yes. But, he had a Savior in Jesus, who was much greater.

"Thank you, Lord Jesus," he said, raising his hands to the heavens, squinting toward the sky as he continued to run. "Thank you."

Ten minutes later he finally stopped in the shade of the pier, exhausted and saturated with sweat. He removed his shirt and laid it across his shoulders. A large wave splashed up onto his leg, inducing a cramp. The water was cooler than the air, and for an instant Dupree was cold. Now wet, the leg knotted even tighter. The pain was growing in both directions, moving to both his foot and lower back.

He stood and limped along the seawall. Crossing Beach Boulevard, Dupree took a different path home.

● ● ●

One block east of Eastwood Street, Dupree jumped into the canal that ran between his backyard and the backyards of those who lived on Eastwood.

The sky in front of him was decorated with thin, high clouds.

His heart rate rose again, but not from physical exertion. His leg cramped severely, warning him not to proceed. He stiffened the leg and rocked heavily on the toe, stretching the calf with every other step. He wiped sweat from his forehead using the shirt on his shoulders.

The canal was nearly dry. He stepped cautiously down the banks as he crept forward. Several sets of footprints were visible; none were barefoot. The terrain was filled with sticker plants, broken glass, and razor-sharp weeds. A set of bicycle tire tracks weaved back and forth ahead of him. The wind whistled through the tall grass and provided relief from the putrid smell of decaying swamp mud and garbage.

When Dupree's leg relaxed, he stepped up the canal, crossing back and forth, leaping to dryer, higher patches of ground. He was nearly home when the leg cramped suddenly, forcing him to stand erect, jutting it straight out. Grimacing from the pain, he massaged his thigh vigorously as he studied his back yard through the brush.

He had to get home, but the weeds and briars engulfed him, forcing him to backtrack and take another path. After a few strides, his steps fell exactly on another person's footprints. A normal footprint, about the size of his, was followed by a line from a foot being dragged.

"Step, then drag the other foot. Step, then drag the other foot."

He placed his own feet in the same pattern, playing a game as he progressed up the canal.

"Oh jeez…"

Dupree froze when a large hole, made by the previous walker, opened deep into the mud. Beside the hole were a set of handprints, twisted like angels in a bank of grey snow. On one edge of the hole was blood. Dark, brown, and streaked against the pale mud, a great deal of blood was lost.

Taking a step forward, he fell to his knees to examine the hole. Lifting his eyes, he followed the footprints as they continued down the narrow path, disappearing into the thicket. Beyond the bayou, the moonwalk was gone.

As he turned to look at his house, his heart sank. The scene from the other night was displayed in reverse. Through a clearing in the weeds and brush, his own back door was in perfect frame. Red was sleeping underneath the lawn chair. The back porch light was still on.

Dupree stood for a moment, collecting his thoughts, wiping his arms and head with his saturated shirt. Locusts and crickets filled his ears; the bayou smelled of decay. The hole with the blood-soaked edges grew larger, as Dupree fixed his stair in the center.

"That was no raccoon."

Dupree instinctively reacted by patting the pockets of his shorts for a cellphone, that was charging on the kitchen counter.

• • •

Once inside his house, Dupree immediately went to the back door and turned off the porch light. Grabbing his cellphone, he dialed Detective Campbell and headed for the shower.

"Hello, pastor. What can I do for you?" Detective Campbell asked, answering the phone.

"Hey, Detective. I was wondering if I could take another look at the crime scene," he said, undressing with one hand. He kicked his running shorts into the clothes hamper.

"Of course. Do you need me to go with you?"

"If you want to." He turned on the hot water to the shower. "You don't have to though." He removed his socks with his toes.

"I think I'll pass. I'm working on some stuff from the crime scene. We've got the blood work back, and I'm…"

"Let me guess. There are two types of blood at the scene."

"How…"

"I think maybe Hargood injured the perpetrator," Dupree said. "That's why I want to revisit the scene."

"What makes you think that?"

"I was walking behind my house, in the bayou, and I found a significant amount of blood by a set of tracks. Also, I swear I saw something back there the night of the murder."

"Seriously?" Detective Campbell asked. "Why didn't you mention this earlier?"

"I don't know. I actually forgot about it. I thought it was a racoon." Standing naked, he checked the shower water, perfect. Another call popped up on his phone. It was Kelly Mitchell.

"Okay. I'll send someone over to check it out," Detective Campbell said. "Let me know what you find at Hargood's. I'll get a black and white to meet you."

"Thanks, Detective. Gotta go."

Dupree pushed the button to receive the other call.

"Hey Kelly."

"Hey Cooper, it's Kelly…I mean, uh…sorry…"

"No problem. What's up? I thought you were working today," he said. He turned the water off to the shower and took a seat on the commode.

"I am. I'm calling from the hospital. It's Mrs. Brewer; the doctors say she's probably not going to make it through the night. I just thought I'd let you know."

"Oh really? I probably should go up there," Dupree said, covering himself with a towel. "What time are you working to?"

"I'm on till midnight."

"All right. I've got one thing to do and then I'll head that way. I should be there in an hour or so. Thanks, Kelly. I appreciate you calling."

"Sure, you're welcome. I'll see you soon."

He pushed the end call button on the phone.

"Sweet."

CHAPTER 20

Curled in a fetal position, Franky reached over the back of the couch and pulled a blanket over his torso. Kicking, squirming, he covered his bare feet. His hangover officially kicked in.

The New Orleans Saints pre-season game played on the television. Reflections from the windows crisscrossed the room, throwing a checkerboard pattern across his sparsely decorated apartment. The starving artist painting of a seascape, the framed photo of Franky skiing Breckenridge, and the dozen empty schnapps bottles glistening atop undusted surfaces caught glints of sunlight. He smacked his lips, rubbed his eyes with the back of his hands, clutching tightly to his cover. He curled tighter into a ball.

The apartment was arctic cold, with the thermostat set at seventy-five. Franky's fever hadn't broken; his hands shook uncontrollably.

Franky jumped when his phone rang. Rolling off the couch, he wrapped the blanket around him like a cocoon and walked to the kitchen. The shakes moved to his chest, making him stagger.

Dale was calling. Franky dove back onto the couch before answering. "Hello?" He held the phone to the one ear, pressing the other deep into the sofa.

"Hey, it's Dale, what's going on?"

"Not a lot, just trying to shake the cobwebs out from last night." Franky shuddered. The air conditioner kicked on.

"Did you go out?"

"Yeah, I went over to Johnny Joe's." Franky rose holding the blanket around his shoulders. He walked to the thermostat and turned it up to eighty.

"Jeez, man you must have been hard up. Country music? What were you thinking?" Dale commented. "So did you get lucky?"

"Nah, not really. I met a nice girl, and…I don't know…I might call her." He walked toward the back door.

"What are you doing later?" Dale asked. "I need to come by and talk to you about something."

The five hundred dollars.

Franky stepped onto the back porch. "Well, uh…I don't have any plans. I guess I need to do some laundry, but that's about it."

"All right, I'll be over in an hour or so. I've got to wait for my kids to get back from the river, okay?"

"Yeah, great, whatever, just come on over."

Taking a seat on the back porch, he ended the call.

The afternoon sun was on the other side of his apartment. The heat from the day was still scorching. Franky dropped the blanket on the back of a plastic lounge chair. He brushed off his tender bare feet, that picked up grains of sand and grit from the brushed concrete porch.

You've got to go to an ATM.

Franky planned to make it a quiet night. Watching television, drinking just enough to help him sleep, he wanted to be on time for work.

That means you've got to run to Gautier.

The main branch was the only bank that distributed more than two-hundred dollars at a time.

I'm not paying $15 in ATM fees.

The trip to Gautier and back, crossing the drawbridge and the Pascagoula River delta, would take forty-five minutes. Franky didn't have enough booze in the apartment to cover the road trip.

So, a quick stop by Shorty's for a handle.

With the thought of driving with a bottle of Irish whiskey between his thighs, Franky's hangover began to subside quickly. He stood at the back fence of his patio and stretched his arms over his head.

Moving quickly to the kitchen, he grabbed an icy bottle of Bombay Gin from the freezer and returned to the porch.

Watching the pool, Franky followed the shadows as they rose into the treetops. He took a large swig. The darkening leaves on the trees above his head fluttered in the breeze. A kid, he used to know, waved at him from the parking lot.

He waved back.

You need a nice road trip.

• • •

The storm blew through with such ferocity, that the oaks at the Longfellow Apartments were stripped of every single leaf. Days later, the mighty trees began to sprout fresh, tender sprigs. They thought it was spring.

Electricity was a commodity for those who could get gas, and no one could get gas. It would not return to Longfellow Apartments for thirteen days. The smell of grills, wood chips, chainsaws, and diesel generators filled the air. Streets teemed with concerned neighbors—helping, pulling, working. Nights were black as pitch, and the silence was deafening. Debris of soaked mattresses, sheetrock, and carpeting was stacked on both sides of every road leaving only a single lane of traffic. Drivers stopped, waving others through.

Ice was scarce. Beds were hot. Pascagoulians slept with sticky sheets. They learned to drink warm Cokes and beer. Meals at first were huge—steaks, pizzas, chicken, and beef. The freezers were thawing, and the food had to be eaten. With each passing day the meals got worse, the meat was potted, the bread stale, and everything was lukewarm.

For thirteen nights the apartment complex had no lights, television, or air conditioning. Residents went outside and sat on their porches. They talked to every person who walked by. Franky made conversation with several kids.

"You miss school? No? Ha ha. Have you guys been exploring out in the woods? Really? Wow, that's a nice red fish. You caught that off the seawall? Good job!"

Once, he had actually thrown the Frisbee with one of them. The night when Mississippi Power and Light flipped the switch to Longfellow was the last night that Franky saw any of them.

He no longer remembered their names.

• • •

When the doorbell to Franky's apartment finally rang, it was nearly dark.

"It's about time." Franky caught his balance as he rose from the couch. "There's no way those kids were out this late."

Franky stopped at the freezer and threw a couple of cups of ice in his glass of Jamison. Grabbing his wallet from the kitchen table, he walked gingerly to the front door.

He opened the door slowly

"Hey, man, sorry I'm late." In a flash, Dale walked in, mumbled something about his kids being stranded, and took a seat on the arm of the sofa.

"Hey, no problem." Franky raised his glass in a cheer and took a large drink. Coming up beside Dale, he pulled the five hundred dollars from his wallet and handed to Dale. "Hey man, thanks for the loan."

"Yeah, no problem, you didn't have to…"

The doorbell rang.

Franky spun toward the door.

"Now what?"

Dale shrugged.

"What the…? Hey, what are you doing here?" Franky asked, when the door opened.

Franky ushered his sister, Sandra, into the apartment. She looked at Dale, who was staring down at his feet.

A cold chill ran up Franky's spine.

"What, uh, what are you doing here? Where's Petey?" Franky followed Sandra across the room. She didn't speak. She didn't make eye contact. "Is everything all right? Dale, you remember Sandra. She…"

The doorbell rang again.

"Hold on, let me get that. It's like a party in here," Franky said, as he opened the door.

The party ended.

It was his folks, Linda and Willard II. Suddenly, Franky was incredibly intoxicated, trapped.

"Hey guys, jeez, it's good to see you." Franky covered his breath by trying to speak by breathing in. He stumbled backwards, taking refuge behind the door, and placed the glass of whiskey on the windowsill.

His folks walked across the room and hugged Sandra, who was crying. Franky pushed on the door. A foot obstructed the door from outside. As Franky pushed harder on the door, knocking deafened him.

It was Eddie, his brother.

The look in Eddie's eye cut through Franky like a knife.

Franky's stomach knotted. He backed behind the door once again as Eddie's wife followed him into the apartment.

Franky grabbed his drink from the windowsill and downed it quickly.

"Is this all? I mean I've only got six chairs in the whole place. Seven, if I pull in the lawn chair."

No one laughed; no one smiled. They stood there without saying a word.

The silence was unbearable.

"Hey, can I interest anyone in a drink?" Franky asked, laughing. His ears burned with embarrassment. He reached behind Eddie to grab the bottle of whiskey. Eddie grabbed his wrist.

"Well? What? What are you going to do, Eddie, break my arm? What? Let go!"

"The drinking is over, bud! It's over," Eddie said, throwing Franky's arm back at him. "It's over!"

"Who do you think…you…"

Franky's little brother was ready to back up his threat. The shock and awe of the intervention hit him square in the chest. No one said a thing.

He was intoxicated, miserable. Franky sat down on the couch with his head in his hands. He looked down at the floor; he couldn't remember when he had eaten last. His stomach hurt; his liver diseased. An arm went around his shoulder.

Franky started to laugh. His laughter turned to tears as waves of remorse surged through his body. When it flashed in his mind that he was sick, seriously sick, the tears turned to sobs—big, man-size sobs erupting from his chest. His whole body heaved. Every pang of despair stabbed him in the side. His feelings vacillated between guilt and shame and a sense that he had let everyone down.

Franky lifted his head, but kept his face covered with his hands. Eddie, his little brother, had his arm on Franky's shoulder. His little brother was the first to sit next to him. Franky choked back more sobbing as Eddie pulled his brother closer.

Eddie's entire life was lived behind the lead of his big brother. Now Franky was ashamed, hurt; Eddie was watching him make a total fool of himself.

"Franky, we love you," Sandra said. "We're here to help you." She was crying.

"I have a friend who runs a terrific…"

Sandra explained their plan. They had made all the arrangements. Franky was to come home with her so that she could take him to the hospital tomorrow. Everyone was nodding. They were all in on it. They had made a vow not to leave him alone until he was in a treatment facility.

Franky could do nothing.

"I'm sorry, guys. I mean you really don't have to do this. I'll go get some help or, you know, I'll just stop drinking. I mean, that's all there is to it. I've stopped."

They didn't listen.

"But my job. What about my job? I need this job, and I know those guys aren't going to keep me on. They hate me. They're not going to throw me a rope. Seriously, they hate me. I know it."

"I'll talk to Mr. Fineburg. He'll understand," Sandra said.

Franky made eye contact with his parents.

He dropped his head.

"Okay."

Franky stood and walked out the door with the help of his dad. His mom picked out a sack of dirty clothes for Sandra to wash overnight.

Sitting in the passenger side of Sandra's car, Franky watched the activity in his apartment.

Dale was talking to Eddie. Sandra was hugging their dad. His mom answered a cellphone.

"I need my phone," Franky said, when Sandra walked up to the car.

CHAPTER 21

Kenneth Schultz pushed his luck watching for so long—sitting, sweating, constantly adjusting the focus on the binoculars. If the police ever came into the Polk Street neighborhood, they would ruin his stealth with their flashing blue lights.

Parked in front of an abandoned house, 100 yards down the street from Janna Sandler's, Schultz checked his rearview mirrors constantly. Car-jackers were lying in wait, camped out behind the dilapidated pier and beam house. They sat patiently, timing their attack, on the late model BMW and the spooky little man inside.

The houses in Janna's neighborhood were small, rundown, with scraggly lawns and wild, mad dogs caged in backyards encircled in chain link fences. Void of landscaped flower beds and plush Saint Augustine lawns, like in Schultz's neighborhood, there was a very real threat of a rat jumping through the open window of his car.

Schultz wanted to roll up the window, but the heat was unbearable. His shirt was saturated; closing the window would only add to his misery. Although he could protect himself from a rat, he would be trapped in the car with his own smelly breath and body odor.

I can't sit with the windows up. Besides, where would I rest my hands?

The day was rough for Schultz.

The church service practically killed him.

Schultz cranked up the car and adjusted the interior lights to the lowest setting. Even without the headlights on, the BMW knew it was dark enough to engage the dash lights.

"Technology has outsmarted itself," he said, adjusting the air conditioning vents and raising the binoculars into position.

Yes, Schultz was exhausted from the trauma of the day—church, McDonald's, dinner with the in-laws, and two hours of babysitting while Michelle "visited a friend."

Michelle had spent a lot of time visiting her friend.

"It's amazing she can't find the energy to get dressed up and go to church, but she'll spend an hour getting ready to visit a sick friend," Schultz said to no one. He smiled. "It'll be great when her friend finally kicks the bucket."

The cool from the air conditioner was fogging up the lens of his binoculars. Schultz stuck his forehead in the vent. His greasy hair was blown around in clumps.

Janna had disappeared into the kitchen; Schultz enjoyed the role of peeping Tom.

His face flushed thinking of his trial for peering in people's windows.

Can you physically die from embarrassment?

No! That was proven earlier in the day when he refused communion. The usher waved and prodded and practically pulled Schultz into the aisle, before realizing that the visitor and his two children would not be taking communion.

Parishioners stared as they made their way to the altar, shaking their heads and saying things like, "Tsk, tsk, poor lost soul."

Schultz wanted to drag his kids down the side aisle and out the back door, but that would only justify their judging him to be a heathen.

Schultz could not take communion from a hypocrite.

"There, Miss Sandler, I see you now," Schultz said, into his cupped hands. His voice bounced off the bottom of the binoculars. "Where is your daughter? You told me you didn't want children. Yes, I remember that conversation well."

• • •

Kenny Schultz ejected the CD from his four-year-old, 2002 Honda Accord. Reaching above his head, he slid it into an empty slot in the organizer above the sun visor.

"Do you like Modest Mouse?"

"Sure."

He turned off Highway 25 in rural Oktibbeha County, Mississippi, onto a dirt road. Elizabeth Hastings rested her hand on his thigh as he drove down the lone, dark farm road. The lights of campus had disappeared behind them, allowing a milky glow to illuminate the sleeping cows and dewy hay bales. The November moon was full and hazy.

"I'm never going to have kids. I think I'm way too selfish," Elizabeth said. "Do you know where we are?"

"Yeah," Schultz said. "I've got a lab out this way for one of my forestry classes."

"It's pretty out here."

"You're pretty." Schultz saw Elizabeth's reflection in the rearview mirror. Her eyes flickered with light from the dash. To-night, at the exact right time, Schultz would find the strength to finally tell her he loved her.

"Do you want another beer?" Elizabeth asked. She finished hers and reached into the backseat to get another. Schultz followed her tight, round backside in the mirror as she wrestled with the lid of the cooler. He fidgeted in his seat, adjusting his pants.

"I'm good."

Returning to the front seat, she leaned over and kissed Schultz on the neck. He braked and made a turn onto a tighter dirt road.

"What's this?" Elizabeth dropped her hand into Schultz's lap and began to rub him lightly.

In the dark of the car she could not see Schultz blush. He made another turn onto a thin, single lane road that was leading to a voluminous structure rising from the field.

"Look at that," Elizabeth said. "What is it?"

"It's a barn," Schultz said. "It's just a really big barn. It's owned by the university."

"There're no lights."

"I know."

Elizabeth took another drink of beer. Schultz pulled the car behind the barn. They were hidden from the road. The moonlight shined in through the windshield.

Throwing the car into park, he killed the ignition, rolled down his window, and changed out the CD.

The musty smell of the farm, coupled with the soft balladry of John Mayer, heightened the level of romance to an unbearable pitch. Schultz loosened his belt and moved next to his date.

Elizabeth moved forward and turned with her back to the dash to make room for his advances.

Schultz's hand moved under her sweatshirt; she grabbed him beneath his drawers. Kissing, caressing, jockeying for more comfortable positions and more freedom of movement; the two lovers took advantage of their newfound privacy and freedom.

Schultz moved his hands down to Elizabeth's waist and began to work the button and zipper on her jeans. She slithered from her Levi's in awkward gyrations, until eventually she was able to pull them off completely and throw them in the back seat. She continued to caress him with her free hand.

When he touched her, she let out a long exhale and suddenly became rigid. She pulled her hand from his pants.

"Kenneth, you know we can't go all the way." Her voice was soft and unconvincing.

Schultz grabbed the back of her panties and pulled violently, trying to get them over her hips.

"Kenneth! Did you hear me? We can do some stuff but we can't…stop it!"

With one quick violent tug downward, he tore the stitching from the side of the cotton panty at a seam.

"Ouch! Kenneth, now stop that!"

"Dammit!" Schultz screamed. In a dazed, hormone-induced rage, he jerked his hand from behind Elizabeth, twisting her violently in the front seat. Her temple slammed against the column stick shift, knocking her out cold.

"What the hell?"

Elizabeth fell face down into Schultz's lap.

"Elizabeth? God, Elizabeth! Why did you do that?"

He wanted to beat the back of her head.

She should have never stopped him. It would only have taken a few seconds, and then it would have been all over. Now there would be apologies and break-ups. The police would get involved, and then what? A registered sex offender?

"But we didn't even have sex," Schultz said.

What happens to my scholarship?

Certainly his mom would find out, and that meant his stepdad would find out.

"No. Absolutely not!" Schultz yelled. His mother would not pay the price for another one of his screw-ups.

"Elizabeth? Why won't you wake up?"

• • •

A horsefly bumped against the windshield inside the car. Dropping the binoculars in the seat, he chased the horsefly into the corner of the dash and smashed it against the window.

"We were talking, and you told me you were too self-centered to have kids."

He flicked the bug out the window and wiped his hand on the floorboard. He returned to his watch and steadied the binoculars.

Janna returned from the back of the house.

"Ah, there you are," Schultz whispered. "You've taken a shower. Marvelous hips. Who are you calling?"

He dropped the idling car into reverse. The air conditioner blew colder when the engine revved. He turned the headlights on after clearing the driveway.

At Ingalls Avenue, near Jerry Lee's, Schultz turned right.

"I want to kiss you, Miss Sandler," he said, his voice weakening with each word. "But on my terms. I saw you in your short pants yesterday. You looked awfully pretty in your robe. Do you like complements? I could almost see the form of your breast."

Schultz imagined that Janna would be too shocked to even respond.

"I want to enjoy sex with you. Don't make me be the aggressor again."

He pulled into his driveway; the lights were on in the kitchen.

"Does she ever go to bed?" Schultz shoved the gearshift into park. "Seriously, why does she constantly hound me? Janna Sandler would never do that; she's not one of those manipulative women."

CHAPTER 22

"Hello, Franky? This is Janna Sandler…from high school…and I thought well, crap!" She hung up her phone.

He'll see the missed call.

There was no way that she could make this work. With every attempt she sounded more desperate and pathetic. Her voice quivered with nerves, and if she actually made the call, she was sure that her tongue would swell and go totally numb.

"Heado, Fray-ney, dith ib Dana San-ner."

"What? Who is this? Stop calling me, you freak!"

"Impossible!"

She stared at the phone. Katie was with her dad, and Janna was left alone with her thoughts and an ill-devised plan for calling Franky.

"This is ridiculous!" Janna said, as her finger hovered over the top display on the 'recent' call list.

She walked to the kitchen and poured a glass of juice.

You're a basket case!

She looked at her reflection in the window. Her eyes were dark. Wrinkles formed in the corners of her eyes; she had aged ten years in the last two hours.

There were times when Janna personified confidence. On stage during her act, she demanded attention, never stuttering or pausing. She handled new customers with poise.

"…and now my hands are so sweaty, I can't hold the phone in fear of electrocution!"

She looked deep into her reflection.

"Franky, this is Janna Sandler. I saw you the other day, and well, I thought I would call. I was curious to see if you would like to go out with me."

Too much.

"I was calling, well; honestly, I was calling to see how you have been. So how are you doing, Franky? How the hell are you doing?"

The rehearsing was over. Janna walked quickly across the room to the couch and sat down. Grabbing her phone, she dialed the number she had memorized since finding it on the Fineburg, Fineburg, and Fineburg website.

The phone rang twice.

Janna's hands were wet and shaking, and she cleared her throat several times. She closed her eyes tight directing her eyeballs up, searching in the deepest recesses of her brain for the perfect words.

She would not hang up; she would not hang up.

"Hello, Franky's phone," the female voice said on the other end of the line.

Janna's heart sank. It was a female, but something was odd. With her eyes closed and her brain firing on every neuron, she recognized the voice from years ago. Deep in the confines of her long-term memory, in her ability to identify sounds and old music tunes, Janna definitely recognized the voice. She hung up the phone.

It was his mother.

CHAPTER 23

Pastor Dupree parked in his designated spot at Christ Church. His backpack swung from one shoulder. Wearing a saturated T-shirt and running shorts, he jogged toward Memorial Hall with the sun, low in the sky, blinding him. Entering the shade of an awning, he punched the code for entry and stepped into a cool air conditioned hallway.

The expensive, spotless BMW, in the visitor's reserved parking, went unnoticed.

Earlier, the young preacher prayed and meditated at his kitchen table. Eating a protein bar and drinking coffee, the bayou behind his house came to life. The image of a bigfoot or sasquatch, arms swinging out of rhythm with his stride, moved across the bushes and trees. A sniper, invisible in a ghillie suit, directed the end of his rifle at Dupree's forehead. A murderer, injured during his attack, escaped the scene of his crime camouflaged in thicket and swamp grass.

Red had definitely heard something early Saturday morning, and it wasn't a raccoon. The streaks by the hole were blood.

Yesterday afternoon, when Dupree reviewed the crime scene, he found a shard of mirror with dried flesh, adhering to a razor sharp point. Perhaps, Hargood put up a fight. Perhaps, he attacked his assailant. In addition, Dupree noticed that the duct tape had been used for a makeshift bandage. Blood was caked on the inside of the roll.

Dupree pulled on the door to the offices. The secretary's office was a tiny foyer for his own. It lacked the aroma of Leslie's normally strong perfume. Coffee had not been brewed. Stepping into his office, he set the backpack down, flipped on the light, and spun toward his desk.

He let out a girlish squeak of panic in an involuntary reaction to a masked man sitting at his desk.

"Uhh—uhh! Wha!" Dupree's voice was high pitched. Pins and needles shot up the back of his legs and his spine.

"Shut it!" The man commanded in a deep, fake, guttural tone. "Hands up! Now!"

Dupree's stomach lifted into his throat when the gun came into focus. It was pointed at his chest; his knees buckled under him.

"Stand up, and don't drop those hands!"

Realizing he wasn't actually shot, Dupree regained a bit of composure.

"What…where's Leslie?"

"No one's here."

"How did you get in? What do you want? I don't have any money in the—"

"Shut the door with your foot."

At first sight of the intruder, Dupree's face drained of blood; now he was flushed. He clinched his fists to work blood into them.

The man stood, keeping his hands in front of him. Moving slowly, he limped around the desk and motioned with the gun for the preacher to take his seat. Thin, almost emaciated, with a thin, fragile neck, the intruder stood slightly shorter than the preacher, although he was hunched over at the waist. Dupree focused on the gun and the man's unclipped fingernails.

Dupree remained standing; the man took a seat across from the desk. He moved slowly, painfully, as if every joint in his body ached. He was gaunt. His eyes were deep blue, but unattractive. He didn't blink.

"Sit, pastor."

"I'd rather not."

"I said sit."

"Please allow me the dignity to stand," Dupree said. "Please."

A long pause followed. "You know you don't need that," Dupree said, looking toward the gun. He slowed his breathing. His hands remained above his head.

"Maybe."

"I'll give you whatever you want. What do you want?"

The man leaned forward and in a low, angry voice said, "I want your undivided attention."

It was then that Dupree realized that he was in the presence of Satan himself.

• • •

The office was hot, made hellish by the madman's presence. Dupree listened as the man described the murder of Jerry Hargood.

"I never anticipated the noise. Hargood's screams were much greater than I expected, and did you know that bones make a high-pitched, popping sound when cracked?"

Dupree wanted to lay his head on the desk. He wanted to place his hands over his ears. Needles stabbed his back as images of the crime scene flashed through his mind. His hands were numb. He clinched his fists in reaction.

"Then there's the motive. Curious? Well, you see, I'm a psycho-path, Pastor Dupree. I have no conscience. Nothing I've done has ever driven me to feeling apologetic. Nothing has ever driven me to seek a savior. That is until now. And to be honest, it's wonderful."

The madman let out a little laugh.

"You were off target with your Revelation 12:16 interpretations. Yes, my friend told me all about it. Ridiculous. To think that my motive was to make myself God! I don't want to be God; I want to seek God. The whole thing really pissed me off."

"I'm sorry."

"You see, that's exactly what it's about!" he said, smiling through the mask. "If I could get to the point where I say 'I'm sorry' about something, anything, well then even a psychopath like me could actually be transformed into a man of God...a veritable 'fisher of men' so to speak."

"And that's what you want?" Dupree asked.

"Don't we all?"

The two stared at each other for a few minutes. Dupree could tell the man was planning his next step.

"I heard from a friend that you are investigating my little sacrifice," the man said, his voice sounding suddenly familiar. "So…what did you think?"

"Can I drop my hands?"

"No."

"Because my hands are going numb."

"I said no."

"Well, then, I didn't think much of it, your sacrifice," Dupree said. "Is that what you called it? It looked a little overdone."

"You're a fool."

"Now, can I drop my hands? Please."

"Jesus Pete!" The gun began to shake. "Place them on the desk in front of you! Never in my life…you're worse than a kid! I've sat here and explained the greatest murder in history, a justifiable murder…one life for another…outlined perfectly…and all you can do is think about your comfort!"

Dupree placed his hands on the desk and started drumming his fingers. For a few moments, the only sound in the room was the constant tapping.

"So you thought it was overdone. Camp comedy in your book I suppose," the madman said. "Stop that!"

"Aren't you hot in that thing?" Dupree asked, pointing at the mask by nodding his head. "You can take that off if you like."

"I don't think so."

Dupree continued to drum his fingers on the desk.

"I said stop that," the man said, rising to his feet. The gun was steady in his hand.

"What do you want from me?" Dupree asked. "You know I can't…"

The room suddenly exploded in noise as the gun discharged. The force of the first bullet knocked Dupree against the bookshelf behind him. The second shot, fired into his abdomen, dropped him to his side.

"Oh, poor preacher." The madman turned toward the door. "The only thing I want from you is to accept my apology." He laughed. "I'm truly sorry."

• • •

Dupree was numb, disoriented, sweating. He wanted to cry, but he couldn't. Crawling under the desk to hide, he wrapped his arms around himself tightly, rocking and bleeding and banging his head against the desk drawers. He wanted darkness, a cave, solitude. But the room was so hot.

Rolling on the floor, the preacher pulled his knees to his chest and began to pray as his hands became hot and wet with blood.

The weight of the matter, the events of the past two days, the safety of his little hideaway hole under the desk, and an overpowering sense of calmness hit him. Dupree was going to die. He was going home to be with his best friend, Jesus.

"And maybe even…Sarah," he said in a weak whisper.

With the thought of Sarah, the idea that she may still be out there, the numbness suddenly left and pain shot through his spine to the back of his head. Like a lightning strike, Dupree convulsed as an electric charge rocked every muscle in his body.

His mind cleared.

Placing his face down on the floor of his office, he pushed his nose into the carpet and groaned. He curled into a ball. From a fetal position, stretching his legs out only inches, he reached into his pocket and grabbed his cellphone. Looking into Jesus's face, with an overpowering feeling of love and protection, he touched a recently dialed number, redialing a random person who had called him.

"Yo, Cooper, what's up?" It was Gregor Thomson.

"Gregor, help me."

"Coop, where are you?"

"Help…me."

"Cooper!"

Dupree listened to his friend Gregor scream into the phone as the lights of his office slowly dimmed to black.

CHAPTER 24

Sunlight was not allowed into Room 1043 of the Charter Rehabilitation Clinic; the windows were painted grey to match the walls. Franky sat in his first group therapy session, battered by the pulse of the dim fluorescent lights overhead.

The grey window worked its depressing magic outside as well. In a sweltering Mobile, Alabama, morning, a pile of dead birds lie on the barren ground beneath the window—dying instantly as they mistakenly flew by.

A heavyset nurse had rousted Franky out of bed at six o'clock to start his first hour of recovery. Battling his "last" hangover was different at Charter Hospital. There was no tomato juice and the nurse dispensed drugs exactly as directed on the label. Franky choked down apple juice as he took only two aspirin and the rest of his new meds.

The psychological effects of less aspirin and being force-fed unknown drugs corresponded to an instant loathing of the nursing staff. Every joint and organ in his body hurt. Overnight he had swollen like a balloon. The "vitamins" made his face flushed, and the redness forced the yellow, sickly color from his cheeks and eyes.

The physical addiction, actually detox, was a short, painful process. Franky needed re-hydration; minerals and vitamins would be consumed and absorbed into the cells at an alarming pace. Within three days, the physical dependency on alcohol would be conquered. However, the work of removing the addiction from his mind would take a lifetime.

This process started when Franky stepped inside the lifeless walls of Room 1043 and heard the first war cry of alcoholism recovery—one day at a time.

He rejected it immediately.

Franky could do anything for one day. It was the "rest of your life" trip that he needed help with.

Sweat formed on his upper lip as he the thought about speaking. His throat was dry, and his leg started shaking uncontrollably.

"Just keep coming back," the leader said, verbalizing the second war cry of the alcoholic. Uneasiness filled Franky's limbs.

"Thank you for sharing." The leader turned his attention to Franky. "You, sir, would you like to share?"

"Me?"

"Yes, what's your name? And maybe you could share a few words about yourself."

"I don't think so. I don't share," Franky said. His face was flushed. "What am I supposed to share? My experiences?"

"Anything. Your thoughts," the leader responded, "anything you want to talk about."

"I'm not sure my comments would be welcome."

"Try us out."

"Well, my problem is alcohol," Franky said. His voice was cracking as he spoke. His stomach was knotted. "I drink too much, and I think about drinking too much, and I plan my day around drinking, and I am essentially miserable when I do not drink. This coupled with the fact that I'm miserable when I *do* drink, makes me in general, a miserable person. And I'm having a hard time figuring out how listening to all of you is going to help."

No one said anything. No one was even listening.

"I mean, I'm not like you guys. I haven't been locked up or rolled a car or had kids taken from me," he continued. "It's just that I drink, and I enjoy drinking, and to be honest with you, I really wish I didn't have to quit. But I guess I've got to, I mean…what? What else do you want me to say?"

"Nothing. Are you done?"

"Yeah, I'm done."

"Thanks for sharing."

Franky sat embarrassed by his comments. Of all the crap spewed from the mouths of the participants, his was the most insincere. He wanted pity, and there was none coming.

The people surrounding him in group therapy were the biggest collection of self-centered egomaniacs ever assembled in one room. Franky would never say another word.

• • •

Dr. Charles was tall and looked like a member of academia. Franky pegged him as a man that had no life experiences other than plowing through dusty books and getting off on other people's misery.

The focus of the first three days of Franky's "outpatient" program attacked the physical addiction with pain relievers and water in a hospital setting. During this time, he would be introduced to intense group therapy, individual work with a counselor, a few trips to an AA meeting, and visits with the staff psychotherapist, Dr. Charles.

After three days the patient was allowed to return to work and a normal life, except that normal life consisted of six weeks of nightly AA meetings, random alcohol tests, a handful of prescriptions, and weekly visits with Dr. Charles.

In their first session, they talked about alcoholism, its genetics, its control, and its relentlessness. Franky paid attention to the parts that interested him, namely those that gave a hope that he may one day drink again. Dr. Charles left Franky with a strong recommendation to take his AA meetings very seriously.

• • •

Sandra signed the register at the front desk; she would be responsible for Franky for the afternoon. Although it was difficult for her to get approval to take him for a few hours, she was a trusted member of the Mobile medical community.

"His liver has been pickled since high school," she said. Sandra was convinced that Franky would go into renal failure by going cold turkey.

"We have doctors on staff."

"I want him to see our family doctor in Pascagoula."

"I don't think that's a good idea."

"Please, doctor, I'll take full responsibility. I won't let him out of my sight."

Dr. Charles approved the leave. Sandra and Franky walked toward the entrance.

"You know you'll have some blood work done."

"Whatever," Franky said. He would have endured surgery to escape an afternoon session of group therapy.

"Oh, I talked to Mr. Fineburg."

"Uh huh."

"He said that you can come in on Thursday, no problem. But, I think you've got to take three days of vacation. It sounded like he didn't want to consider this sick time."

"Really?" Franky asked, somewhat shocked. "So he was good with this? I go back on Thursday…no questions asked."

"Yup."

The first step outside of the hospital was like walking into a blast furnace.

"Jeez, Louise, what is it, 300 degrees out here?" Franky held his hands over his eyes to block the direct sunlight. He immediately started sweating, sending Sandra into a panic.

"You won't make it halfway to Pascagoula."

They fought the heat as they made it to the car.

"I talked to Dr. Charles. He wants you to go to an AA meeting in Pascagoula this afternoon," Sandra said, waiting for the car to cool down.

"Why over there?"

"I guess to get you used to it."

She spoke like she wanted to add, "So maybe you'll go." But she held back.

"Thanks. Where is it?"

"At Communy Street. Do you know where that is?"

"Yeah, it's near the office."

• • •

Communy Street was exactly what Franky expected from AA. The once white room was now yellow with layers of cigarette tar and nicotine. Walls were covered with posters curled at the edges, stained and askew. The room smelled like a wet ashtray. Couches, tattered and threadbare, were pulled from dumpsters. New drunks showed up at Communy Street every day. Franky was the drunk du jour.

Franky sat forward on the edge of the couch, elbows on his knees, to limit contact with the upholstery.

He had been asked to "share."

"I guess…I expected to sit and learn from others on how to deal with resentment," Franky said, looking into his hands. "I mean, everyone else can drink, but I can't. It's really working on me." He rubbed his hands. "I know I can't drink again my whole life and… well, that seems too long. I don't know anything I will or won't do for the rest of my entire life."

Franky looked up. "And this one-day-at-a-time stuff really doesn't help."

Stuttering as he spoke, he wanted to just shut up, but there was no good transition. He collected his thoughts and started down a new path.

"I guess…I don't want to go back out there and drink. I know it'll get worse." He paused, taking a deep breath. "I'm struggling. I can't see myself not drinking forever, and yet I can't drink today. So, I think I'll just sit and listen to see if maybe I can figure out a way to not jerk my insides out or throw myself in front of a train… anyway, that's all I've got."

The words fell from his mouth like he was chewing marbles.

He stared at George, the middle-aged man who had asked him to share.

Jerk!

Picking up the newspaper that was lying on the coffee table, the Hargood murder still topped the local news. In the three days since the murder, the only suspect was a member of a local skinhead clan.

"Just keep coming back."

Franky snorted.

The morning had been full of little nuggets of advice. Franky instantly devalued all of them, except for one. Dr. Charles recommended that Franky not date anyone he met in AA meetings. With this single remark, Franky had elevated the doctor to the level of genius.

Directly across from him sat a ninety-pound waif. Her blouse favored a burlap sack, giving her the appearance of a bag of antlers. She was biting her fingernails. From the corner of his eyes, he watched in freakish, morbid curiosity.

One part of her anatomy drew most of Franky's attention. It wasn't her skin—leathery, overly tan, and stretched tight over her hallowed cheeks, or her stringy, bleached hair. Franky was completely freaked out by her feet. Her heals were covered with scales, like a snake or armadillo. The flip flops she wore were paper-thin, and she flipped them against her tiny, dry ankles in some sort of sick, nervous habit.

She was ignorant of the nauseous affect her disgusting feet had on Franky. She was totally blind to her faults.

Then it hit him. Franky came to a dangerous realization.

Ignorance kept her from being miserable. She had no idea how repugnant Franky found her feet. What was even worse—if she did know, she didn't care. Those feet, coupled with her obvious drinking problem, made Franky want to take a gun and put her out of her misery.

But Franky was the miserable one. Which direction should he turn the gun?

Someone was "sharing" about how wonderful life was now that she had lost the desire to drink. Sunshine was coming from her behind. She wanted to get up every morning and give the world a great big hug.

Franky snapped.

Certain synapses connected with different neurons, and the chemical and electrical impulses were collected to create a deadly reaction. Franky was ill, and his recovery took a new direction. He would now accept the inevitable, the futility. What they wanted from him was never going to happen; he had no desire whatsoever to live the way she was describing.

His head throbbed; his throat tightened. He couldn't speak. His hands twitched with nervous energy, as he focused on this woman.

The heat, the smoke, the ugliness of his life and those things that surrounded him were closing in, creating a darkness, a sense that he was not only ready to die, but already dead.

He wanted to "share" what was raging in his mind.

"There isn't one single activity I could think of that I would want to do so badly that it would be worth not drinking for the rest of my life. Ah ha! I found it! I actually found it. The meaning of life! It's all about finding the one thing you love and then spending the rest of your life in a constant search for something that will take its place."

Franky rose and stormed toward the bathroom.

As he washed his face, everything became crystal clear.

• • •

Franky crawled out of the Communy Street bathroom window into a camouflage of dried, wilted azalea bushes. The parking lot, where Sandra waited patiently for Franky's meeting to end was on the other side of the building. The sun was high; thunderclouds were forming; it was a good day to drink.

He sat for a moment realizing that it was time to pledge his eternal love—till death do they part. Death was pointless when it came at the expense of being separated from the one he loved, alcohol.

Franky walked from behind the bushes and jogged slowly toward Pascagoula Street.

Castaways, an obscure bar that catered to the shipyard lunch crowd, was built on stilts and was surrounded by an oyster shell parking lot. Franky walked with his hands under his eyes, blocking the reflection from the white glare below. He ascended the flight of stairs, stepped inside, and waited a few seconds for his eyes to adjust to the darkness of the bar.

He ordered a pitcher of beer and a double scotch and took a table near the restrooms. Franky stared at the two containers of liquid, one so large and the other so small.

Booze had ruined every good thing in his life.

Franky was thirty-three years old and had nothing. He had no savings, no health, no relationships, nothing except his dear friend Mr. Pitcher and Mr. Tumbler.

Mr. Pitcher was a friend when he needed to talk. Mr. Tumbler was a friend when he needed to escape. Combined, they impacted his life in every way imaginable. He sat for a moment before asking who wanted to be first.

CHAPTER 25

Kenneth Schultz grabbed the mask, ripped off his head in the parking lot of Christ Church, and stuffed it under the driver's side seat of his BMW. The gun was gently placed in the glove box.

If Schultz came home for lunch, he would pull into his driveway at twelve-fifteen sharp. Michelle was always home and always hungry. God forbid she would actually make him lunch. No, she just sat on the sofa and waited for Schultz to make a couple of sandwiches, or heat up leftovers. All the while, nagging him for not stopping by Wendy's and getting something decent to eat.

But today he was early. Schultz checked his watch—10:45a.m.

"Maybe her friend is over; they both can sit begging with their little mouths open."

Schultz entered the house, slamming the door behind him.

"Michelle!" he yelled through the house. "Where the hell are you?"

She didn't respond. Her car was gone. Schultz stormed into the kitchen. Cereal bowls sat out from breakfast; the sink was full of dishes.

"This is unacceptable."

Schultz grabbed a bowl and threw it into the sink. Milk and soggy Cocoa Krispies sloshed onto the counter, spilling down the cabinet onto the floor.

"What the…"

Wiping the counter and cabinet with paper towels, he made large swipes, capturing the milk but grinding cereal into the crevices of an inlaid cabinet door. Grabbing another wad of paper towels, he bent at the waist and scrubbed the tight grooves with the very edge of the paper towel. The pain in his lower back forced him to drop to a knee, as he rolled up little pieces of paper towel to get deep in the crevices.

"This is total bullshit!" Schultz yelled as he ripped the cabinet door off its hinges and threw it across the kitchen.

He sat cross-legged on the floor, huffing.

Minutes later, he collected the dirty paper towels and stuffed them deep into the garbage can. He leaned the cabinet door against the counter where it was hung.

Collapsing into a chair at the kitchen table, he dropped his hands beside him. He made so many mistakes when he confronted the preacher. His stomach cramped at the thought.

One half-hour after leaving Pastor Dupree's office, Schultz made a U-turn at the entrance to Biotech Laboratories. He couldn't face Brad and the task of rewriting his stupid report.

You didn't explain the motive well enough. He just never got it.

From the kitchen table, Schultz pulled the phone from his pocket and dialed his wife.

"Hello," she answered on the third ring.

"Hey, where are you?" Schultz's voice was stern.

"At home, why?"

"Because I'm at home, and I don't see you."

"Well, I meant I'm on my way home! Don't get smart with me. Why are you not at work?"

"I don't feel well. I've got a stomachache."

"Great, another sick day. I've really got to go. I'll be there in about a half hour."

"I thought you said you're on your way home?" Schultz smiled.

"I am. I've got to stop by the grocery, don't I? I'm sure you didn't bring anything home to eat. Am I right?"

"Yes dear," Schultz said. "Pick me up some chicken soup. Oh, by the way, you need to call in your friend the handyman. Something is wrong with one of the cabinet doors."

Schultz dropped his phone onto the floor.

You never even mentioned Janna.

Last night, leaving Janna Sandler's, Schultz was hit with a flash of insight. He had planned to tell the preacher that not only was he sorry for crucifying Hargood, but he was sorry for Elizabeth.

"You were sidetracked, man."

Janna Sandler messed with his mind.

"She's messing with your mind. Janna is not Elizabeth! Janna Sandler is Janna Sandler. Elizabeth is Elizabeth."

• • •

Schultz peered through the back door window as Michelle pulled into the driveway.

He dialed his phone.

"Brad here."

"Yes, Brad, this is Kenneth. I won't be in today. I've got a touch of the flu."

"Schultz, it's already after lunch. You can't just call in at…"

He hung up the phone and dialed Janna Sandler's number.

Michelle burst through the back door, carrying an oversized purse. She wasn't wearing any make-up. She scowled at her husband.

"Where's my soup?"

"I didn't make it to the grocery." She went straight to the kitchen.

"Hello, Bay Pest control, this is Geena. May I help you?"

"Yes, this is Kenneth Schultz at…"

"This place is a wreck," Michelle yelled into the den. "How the hell did this happen?"

"…she's a friend of ours, and I really want her handling this account. She's a friend of my wife's."

"Who are you talking to?" Michelle stuck her head in from the kitchen. She held the cabinet door up for Schultz to see.

"The pest control people."

"Well, sir, I see she has an opening at four o'clock. Is that okay?"

"It's no wonder we don't get carried off with rats, the mess you leave this house in," Michelle said, returning to the kitchen.

"Thank you. Four o'clock will be fine."

* * *

Schultz sat beneath an awning connecting the sanctuary of the Baptist church to the Sunday school building. He found a bench in the shade. Locusts buzzed noisily. Heat rose from every surface exposed to direct sunlight.

Above the gathering hordes of mourners were large white clouds. All were collecting to pay their last respects to Mr. Jerry Hargood.

Most of the participants wore black. They were suffering from more than grief. Schultz suspected that a few would pass out from heat stroke.

The cars continued to stream in. There were hundreds. The hearse had not yet arrived with its bloodless corpse.

Did he look so young? Was it 'such' a tragedy?

He mocked those that had passed through the visitation line that morning.

At the pier three nights ago, Schultz's maddening curse, his mental sickness, was finally purged. It had shriveled and fell from his head into the pool of acid in his stomach where it would live forever. Schultz was suddenly hungry. He needed a sandwich or a hamburger from the grill on Market Street. Taste had returned; his senses were keen once again. Life was sweet, and salty, and bitter, and wonderful.

Feeling both good and bad, both physically and emotionally, returned to Schultz. He felt joy and anger. He felt the beautiful taste of a nectarine and the smell of his infected pus-filled arm. He felt the tugging warmth of his love for Elizabeth (or Janna, or whoever) and the constant, debilitating pain emanating from his swollen arm and knee.

Good mixed with bad. Good pain counterbalanced bad pain. Good joy counterbalanced bad joy.

As he adjusted his position on the bench, the pallbearers removed the casket from the hearse. Smiling, he suddenly stopped being so hard on himself. The meeting with Dupree went well enough.

Several clergy arrived.

"I thought Dupree from Christ Church was going to be here." Schultz whispered mockingly. He let out a little laugh.

A bead of sweat ran down his temple. His arm was sweating where it contacted the bench.

The long, black vehicle disappeared from Schultz's sight behind a line of parked cars. In the middle of the graveyard was an awning, providing shade for the one person at the funeral who didn't need it.

Most mourners would be distracted from their grief by the sun beating on their black suits. In the sweltering Mississippi heat, their sorrow would be replaced with simple thoughts of survival.

We never liked him enough to have to withstand torture.

Schultz knew people.

Tears of joy welled in Schultz's eyes. His sinuses drained, and he had a lump in his throat.

He was the catalyst in the salvation of many—they were crying and mourning and beating their chests and in complete sorrow and despair. Their hearts were opening to the Comforter; His peace was among those who grieved.

Schultz had never been happier in his entire life.

Wanting to beat the traffic from the parking lot, he stood and walked toward his car.

"Thank you, God," Schultz said, under his breath. "Thank you for not making me a miserable idiot like those poor souls."

CHAPTER 26

"Jeez, Franky, you look awful." Janna Sandler said, letting out a huge breath of air. Years of exterminating in public restrooms gave her the lungs of a pearl diver. She could easily hold her breath for ninety seconds.

Franky jumped. A death stare, fixed on a pitcher of beer and a tumbler of scotch, was broken by Janna's interruption. He squinted and brushed the hair out of his face.

Janna pulled a chair out from across the table, taking a seat. She had just exited the room with "Mates" stenciled across the front.

"No, I wasn't using it," Janna said, pointing back over her shoulder with her thumb.

Janna was wearing a Bay Pest ball cap, her blonde ponytail pulled through the hole in the back. She made sure that her starched white oxford uniform displayed her name tag.

Franky glanced at the name printed on the uniform, then looked up quickly to meet her eyes. Janna smiled and looked down to read her own name.

"This is where you say, 'Thanks a lot, Janna,'" she said, in a deep, manly voice. She waved her hand under her name tag as she spoke.

"I was…"

"Are you drinking lunch today?" Janna asked, interrupting. She slid the still full beer mug across the table. "Do you mind?"

"No, no, help yourself. I was just, you know, well I had a rough morning. I thought with the heat it might be nice to sit in a dark place and throw back a couple."

"And the booze?" Janna took a sip of beer and grimaced.

"Well, uh…like I was saying, it was a pretty rough morning." His face turned dark, solemn.

Castaways Bar was the last place Janna expected to see someone that she really wanted to talk to. She had never been inside the bar after dark.

Franky looked tired, disheveled. The short sleeves of his blue polo shirt were wrinkled. Sweat darkened the fabric across his abdomen and around the collar. His eyes had dark patches below them. However, Janna noticed a spark, perhaps from him finally flashing a smile, when she set the mug of beer back on the center of the table.

"I guess a sip of cold beer is the only respectable reward for spraying toxic chemicals in a men's bathroom. And you thought you had a rough morning. Tell me yours was worse than that!"

"It was pretty rough, but I don't know if I'd trade with you."

The two high school friends were content to look into one another's eyes, waiting for the other to start a conversation.

"So, what's up with men's restrooms anyway?" Janna asked, after a long awkward silence. "Do you ever wonder why they put the condom dispensers with the naked ladies right in front of the urinal?"

Franky shrugged.

"I think it's so that while you've got it out, you might think, 'Hey I think I'll put a condom on it.'"

"It's all in the marketing," Franky added.

"And another thing," Janna said, trying to get on a roll. "Men don't think twice about standing side by side holding their thingies and peeing on a wall. But these same guys won't even go out to a restaurant together for fear that people would think they sang with the Village People?"

"I was the construction worker," Franky said, grinning.

"Don't get me off track. I'm working on new material," she said, laughing.

"And the smell," Janna continued. "What's up with that? I mean is a man's pee one of those substances that can penetrate ceramic tile so that it can omit a vile odor for days later?"

"Not unlike Old Spice."

"Or Brut…by Faberge," Janna said. "I'll consider that." Janna took a notepad out of her pocket and started writing. "So, Franky, how are you? You know, I saw you the other day."

"Really, where?"

"On the bridge," Janna looked up. "You looked drunk. You know that stuff's not good for you."

Franky was silent. His dark hair flopped down over his eyes.

"Yeah, a friend of mine and I had been to the casinos and I may have been over-served."

Janna looked at him questioningly.

"Or…more likely…I over indulged."

Silence.

"Are you going to drink those?" Janna nodded toward the pitcher of beer and the tumbler of scotch.

"Yeah, well, you know, I don't think so," Franky said. "I came here to kind of forget my day and well…it's not really that bad. You want some?"

"Ah, no thanks. On duty and everything," she said, holding her hand up. "So are you here waiting for your girlfriend?"

"No, don't have one. Not married either," he said, showing his bare ring finger. "So, Janna," Franky said, stretching out her name as his eyes moved to her nametag and he pretended to be reading while he spoke. "What about you?"

"No."

Janna looked down at the nametag. "You're lucky I didn't borrow my partner's shirt again. I wouldn't like you calling me Cleophus."

Janna's eyes were bright even underneath the baseball cap. She was fresh and open.

"If you can hold on for a minute, you can walk me out to the truck," she said, smiling and getting up from the table.

"Yeah, I'd like that."

Janna excused herself. Meandering toward the bar, she looked back over her shoulder. When she made eye contact with Franky, she abruptly stopped, turned, and pointed her sprayer at him from across the room. Imitating a roach, Franky pretended to dive under the table.

Getting a signature from the bartender, she motioned for Franky to come over.

Franky grabbed the pitcher and tumbler, jumped up quickly; he stumbled across the bar, running into as many tables and chairs as possible.

"Smooth move, killer," Janna said, picking up her spray bottle.

Franky placed the drinks on the bar and threw a twenty dollar bill on the counter to cover the charge.

"Let me get that." Franky grabbed the sprayer with one hand. He hooked his other arm through Janna's.

Janna grabbed her paperwork.

"Jeez, this is heavy; I never knew killing bugs took so much strength."

"We don't actually kill any bugs. We just chase them next door," Janna said, giving a wink. "Better for business."

• • •

The sun was parked outside the door. Blinded for a moment, they descended the stairs cautiously. Holding the ancient wooden hand-rails, they avoided splinters by not sliding their hands.

"What's the big reel on the back for?" Franky pointed to the bed of her truck.

"Do you really want to know?" Janna asked. "I mean I could tell you, but I'd have to shoot you, or even worse, spray you with it."

"Well, no, I mean, I guess I really don't need to know. It's just I bet you can kill a lot of ants with that stuff," Franky said, stumbling on his words. It was obvious he was trying to make conversation. "I guess that would come in handy, you know, to clear out an entire picnic area."

"Not much call for that…a picnic in August?" Janna asked, with a clever smirk. "That's about as popular as playing in an oven while we bake cookies."

Janna grabbed the sprayer from Franky. She threw it in the bed of the truck. "But you know what I really like…even better? I have the ability to clear out any restaurant by simply lobbing in a few roach bombs."

Janna tossed up a big fat softball.

"Well, how would like to do that with me," Franky said, taking the hint. "I mean, maybe you would like to throw a roach bomb in with me, or…oh hell, would you like to go to dinner with me Thursday?"

It wasn't smooth, but it was functional.

"Not Thursday. I've got a thing. What about Friday?" Janna asked.

"Yeah, sure, Friday's great. Can I call you on Thursday? You know, to set things up?"

"Okay," she replied, climbing into the truck. She cranked the engine and rolled down the window.

"See ya," she said, backing into Ingalls Avenue.

"Hey!" Franky shouted. He walked up to the window. "What's your phone number? I mean, so I can call you."

"You've got my number." She let off the brake.

"Whoa, hey, how?" Franky asked.

"I called you Sunday," she said, smiling.

• • •

Janna walked around the back of the house; the moonwalk was gone. The grass where the moonwalk had been was flattened in a thirty-foot diameter, and the spot for the entrance was trampled and muddy. Janna continued to spray around the perimeter of the house. She needed to inspect the yard for fire ants.

Stepping onto the back porch, she sprayed under the large picture window in the kitchen. The evening sun was bright, and the window was a perfect mirror. Smiling into her reflection, her uniform was really cute. She loved the green and white ball cap, white starched shirt, green khaki slacks, and leather work boots.

But Friday, she had a date with Franky Stevens.

Franky Stevens!

She pumped her fist as she sprayed the perimeter of a landscaped bed of azaleas.

Her uniform was cute. But Friday…

Pulling her phone from her front pocket, she dialed Happy Nails.

"…Thursday at 3:00? Yes. Yes. A mani-pedi with Gwen. Thank you."

Completing the back porch, she returned to her truck to get the ant poison. Inspecting the yard was a little difficult; the yard needed mowing. When she found a bed, she kicked it and watched as thousands of ants went immediately into rebuilding mode, working frantically to fix the breach in their protection. Work mode was interrupted briefly when it became gather-and-eat mode as a shower of poisoned cornmeal was scattered across the top. Like refugees of the storm, they worked and gathered and rebuilt their lives as quickly as possible.

Janna painstakingly searched the entire yard for more colonies. Sweat ran down the back of her neck. A chill ran up her spine when Mr. Schultz stepped outside to watch her work.

"Mr. Schultz," Janna walked past him toward her truck. "Are you sure your wife is going to be okay with this?"

"Yes, of course," Schultz said. He was exceedingly pale. His legs were alabaster with dark black hair; Janna thought he should not be allowed to wear shorts.

"Dave told me that she specifically asked for me. I was here Saturday, and it sounded like she wanted to talk or something."

Janna was rolling up the hose that she had used to spray the house. The shade from an enormous oak tree was cool.

"Oh no, she's fine. She probably wanted to set up a play date with the daughters or something. She can call you." Schultz stuttered slightly. "Uh…what's your cellphone number?"

"She can just call my work number." Janna reached into the cab of her truck and grabbed a clipboard.

"I guess."

"Well, I got everything." She walked up next to Schultz. Standing shoulder to shoulder, she displayed a checklist of the services that Bay Pest provides. "The interior looked pretty good. I did see some roach droppings, but with these oak trees, that's not uncommon. I sprayed for that." She made a large circle around "interior roaches".

"If you see any, call the office anytime. They'll come back right away."

Reviewing the document, she circled items as she progressed through the checklist.

"The exterior was sprayed."

She made a big circle on the invoice.

"And I got all your fire ants," she said, circling the word *fire ants*.

Schultz was nodding.

"Now Mr. Schultz, I need to talk to you about termite control."

• • •

Janna sped away from 908 Eastwood Street. Keeping her eye on the rear-view mirror, she hoped Mr. Schultz would not run after her. She dialed her cellphone.

"Hello, Janna? What's up?"

"Dave, you are never going to guess what happened at the Schultz's," Janna said, with a quiver in her voice.

"What? What?"

"I just sold them the double gold protection." Janna flashed an enormous smile into the mirror. "The double gold!"

CHAPTER 27

Seated on the side of his bed, Pastor Dupree pushed off a pair of slippers that had logged 120 laps around the nurse's station. Stretching his arms over his head, a sharp pain stabbed his abdomen. He untied the strings from behind his neck and dropped the front of his hospital gown in his lap.

"Okay, pastor," a nurse said, stepping into the room, "the doctor is on his way over right now. How are those stitches looking?"

"Great." Dupree gently ran his fingers over the butterfly stitches that held the small bullet entry wound intact.

"Do you mind if I take a look?"

Nurse Alicia was a petite redhead, with small hands and broad hips. Bent over at the waist, with her eyes only inches from Dupree's stomach, she pushed gently on the skin on both sides of the wound.

Dupree held his breath, tightening his abdominal muscles.

"Does that hurt?"

"No.'"

Standing, she nudged Dupree's legs with her hip, indicating that she wanted to look at the exit wounds.

He rolled onto his side.

"These are looking really good." She pressed on the wounds.

Dupree bit his lip.

"Does that hurt?"

"No."

Dupree would have three scars to show for his stay at Singing River Hospital. The surgeon, who performed the surgery three days ago, stated that only a miracle saved the young preacher. Actually, the miracle was that Dupree was hunched over with his hands on his desk when the first shot entered his body. The path of the bullet entered between the last set of ribs on his left side and exited the body above his left kidney. The second bullet, a miracle in its own right, entered the body in the same location, exiting four inches above the other exit wound.

One kidney was destroyed.

"Okay, you can sit up," Nurse Alicia said. "Are you going to be here for dinner? Do I need to order you something?"

"I don't think so. I was hoping the doctor was bringing the discharge papers." Dupree placed his feet back in the slippers. He stood and walked to the window.

"Okay. Who will take you home?"

"Kelly Mitchell's here. She said she would drive me home."

"Sounds good," Nurse Alicia said, stepping toward the door. "The doctor should be here any minute. I'll be looking for those papers. I'll be here as soon as I get them."

"Thanks."

The room was cool; precipitation collected on the outside of the windows obscuring his view.

Dupree thought about going for another walk. A few days ago, his recovery was measured in steps, now on Thursday, his recovery was measured in laps and minutes.

Outside his window was a perfect view of the parking lot. His car was not in one of the clergy spaces.

I wonder if it's still at the church.

The traffic light at Hospital Road reflected in the rippling water of a duck pond. A fountain spewed water thirty feet into the air, blocking his view of the Home Depot across Highway 90. The ducks hid in the shade. It was two o'clock, and heat was frying every exposed surface.

Pascagoula had started its workday as normal. The highway was packed by six thirty with shipyard traffic. The fresh morning air was transformed into a noxious yellow haze of exhaust and moisture.

Mothers and children took to the roads afterward, adding chaos to the general order of industrial traffic.

Dupree's day started with Nurse Alicia finally removing the IV from his arm.

"Well, hello there, pastor."

Dupree broke his stare from outside. "Hey, doctor," he said. "What's the good news?"

"Well, actually, all the news is really good. I'm prepared to release you. Your blood work came back perfect, and I hear that you've been doing laps around the nurse's station, so let me take a good look at your abdomen, and we'll see about getting you home."

"Thank the Lord."

• • •

"Come in," Dupree said in response to knocking on his hospital room door. "Thank you, doctor." He stuffed a packet of information into his backpack.

"Hey man," Gregor Thomson said, entering the room.

"What's up?" Dupree asked, waving in his friend. "Hey, this is Doctor Becker. Doctor, this is Gregor Thomson, the guy that saved my life. Or should I say, the first in a cast of characters that saved my life."

The two men exchanged handshakes, as the doctor made his exit.

Gregor wore tattered cargo shorts, stained with various colors of paint, and a faded muscle shirt. He was very tan. A huge mop of sun-bleached, curly hair, that couldn't be tamed with a gallon of hair gel, obscured his eyes. He never wore shoes, even when they played softball. Although he favored a frat boy on spring break, he was responsible and hard working. Dupree held a slight crush on his coolest friend.

"Are you leaving anytime soon?" Gregor asked, falling into a chair. He propped his feet up on the end of the bed.

Dupree was surprised that Gregor managed to put on a pair of flip flops to go to the hospital.

"As soon as Kelly gets here with a wheelchair," Dupree said. He started putting on a fresh pair of socks.

"Kelly's taking you home?" Gregor made a huge smile. "The preacher and the naughty nurse."

"It's not like that."

"Uh huh. I guess it's all professional." Gregor winked, putting his hands behind his head. "I bet you haven't even asked her out. You're a total chicken."

"Actually, we're going out Saturday."

"Really? Is she bringing the wheelchair with her? Where're you going?"

"I don't know," Dupree said, looking over at Gregor. He paused for a moment; his face took a serious expression.

"Hey, man, I've got a real problem."

Gregor started picking through the leftovers on the cafeteria tray sitting on the table beside him. "I know, man. First dates can be a real bitch." Gregor looked at Dupree. "Sorry, man, my bad."

"No, it's not that." Dupree hesitated. "It's…well let's just say… this morning I started remembering things. Stuff I was investigating. I'm starting to remember details about the shooting. I've got this idea about…"

"You know who shot you! Dude, that is seriously cool. Who is it? Do you know him?"

"Maybe." Dupree returned to the window and adjusted the blinds to allow more light into the room.

"Call the police, man. Tell them what you think."

"I don't know."

Dupree took a seat on the opposite side of the bed.

"This morning I started remembering the conversation we had before he shot me. He confessed to killing Hargood."

"Seriously?"

"Yeah, I only remember snippets, but he definitely talked about killing Hargood."

"You've got to tell the police."

"I'll definitely tell them the guy who shot me confessed to killing Hargood."

"Wait a minute dude. What if that was confidential? You know, preacher confession stuff. Isn't that confidential?" Gregor ate the rest of a roll that Dupree had nibbled on.

"I think they'll make an exception if the preacher gets shot."

"You're probably right."

Dupree walked back to the window to adjust the blinds.

"But like I was saying, I have a strong feeling I know who shot me and…well…also killed Hargood."

"Tell the police and let them work it out."

"No, I need to identify the guy with evidence." Dupree took a seat back on the bed. "It's just a hunch, and I don't want to falsely accuse him. You know what I went through in Mobile."

"Totally."

"I mean, he's got a wife and kids. I don't want to put his family through a bunch of trauma, especially, since I'm not 100 percent sure."

Gregor ran his finger along the edge of a bowl of pudding. "Well, I know what you can do." He stuck his finger deep into his mouth and sucked back the remaining scraps of the chocolate dessert.

"I'm listening."

"Well, from all my years of watching *Law and Order,* whoever you suspect, you've got to get a sample of this guy's DNA. You know like a cigarette butt or a mouth swab or something?" Gregor flashed a mischievous smile.

"A mouth swab? Seriously? How the hell do I do that?"

"You said the investigators found DNA from the crime scene that wasn't Hargood's. You just give them the swab of your suspect." Gregor turned his attention to a pack of crackers. "They test it. They compare the two, and presto-bango…you've solved another one."

"Like I said, how do I get a mouth swab?"

"I don't know, man," Gregor said, flashing a perfect smile as he bit into a saltine. "I'm more of an idea guy."

• • •

Dupree finished packing while Kelly and Gregor carried loads flowers and plants to the car.

"Looks like we got it all," Dupree said, when they entered. "I really appreciate you guys carrying that down. What? What is it?" Dupree read their faces as they moved into the room. Bad news was coming.

"What is it?"

"Cooper," Kelly said, moving up next to him and placing her arm around his waist. She was directing him toward the wheelchair. "I've got some bad news for you. Mrs. Brewer passed away this morning. I just found out about it."

"Oh, jeez, that is bad," Dupree said, somewhat relieved. For a moment, he thought he wasn't being discharged.

"Also, we need to know what…" Kelly said, trying not to be callous. "We need to know the arrangements. We tried to contact her son. The people at the prison said that you would take care of it."

"Yeah, sure. I'll take care of it. Where is she?"

"They've moved her down to the morgue."

"That's on the ground floor?" Dupree asked, taking a seat in the wheelchair.

"Actually, the basement."

"Do you mind swinging by the morgue on the way out?"

"Not at all," Kelly said, pushing Dupree toward the elevator.

Along the way, Kelly and Dupree excused Gregor with the bags and with instructions to pick them up in front of the hospital in twenty minutes.

Dupree rolled into the morgue at Singing River Hospital; the smell of death was surprisingly absent. The reception area, although dark and grey like every other room in the hospital, smelled like cinnamon. Kelly moved him up to the nurse working the counter, who was eating a cinnamon bun.

"Hi, I'm Cooper Dupree. I'm here to check on the arrangements for Mrs. Brewer."

"Yes, sir," she said, dropping her snack. She wiped her hands and grabbed a folder. "Oh, hey, Kelly."

"Hey."

"Let's see, Mrs. Brewer?"

"No one's been in contact?" Dupree asked.

"Nope."

"Hold on just a second," he said, reaching for his cellphone. He dialed Fred Norton.

"Fred here."

Although Fred Norton worked at a funeral home, he was not above using levity to make a grim business a little brighter. He had a thousand politically incorrect jokes about his profession, of which Dupree laughed at anyway. He had no idea that Fred got all his material from watching reruns of *The Munsters*.

"Fred, this is Pastor Dupree."

"Yes pastor, what can I do for you?"

The news of Dupree being shot was not given to the news media. Detective Campbell was convinced that the information leaked from the Hargood investigation led to his attack. She threatened to jail (on the grounds of obstructing justice) anyone who breathed a word to the press.

"I've got a minor problem, Fred. I've been ministering to an older lady at the hospital, and well, she died, and she has no family."

"Uh huh?"

"I wanted to do something for her."

"You don't want the county to take care of it?"

"No, I really don't. I kind of grew an attachment to her, so I thought I would bury her properly. What would a respectable funeral cost, no viewing, just a graveside? What do you think that would set me back?"

"Well, since you're such a good customer, usually I don't have any repeat business, you know," he said dryly.

Dupree tried not to laugh. He pressed his hand deep into his side.

"I would think you could do it for less than $1,500."

"That sounds good. Her name is Brewer, and she's at Singing River. Can you come get her?" the pastor asked.

"Sure, sure, we'll head that way. You gonna get back with me on the details?"

"Yeah, I'll call you at home this evening if that's okay," Dupree said. "Hey, thanks a lot."

"Holder-Wells will handle it," he said, addressing the nurse at the counter. She nodded.

Dupree dialed the church office.

Leslie answered the phone. "Yes, pastor? How are you? Are they releasing you today?"

"Hey, Leslie. Yes, I'm on my way out now. I need you to send out a message to the prayer chain."

"Okay."

"A dear friend of the church has passed on, and her funeral will be Saturday."

"Oh, really. I hate to hear that. Who is it?"

"You don't know her. It was Mrs. Brewer. I need to plan a funeral and fast. If you can, see if we can get some people together. Have them call the church tomorrow morning for details."

"You got it."

"It's just a graveside service so…"

"I got it, pastor. I'm glad you're going home."

"Me too."

He hung up the phone.

"Well, I guess that's that," he said to Kelly. "You ready to go?"

"Sure."

"I can't thank you enough for taking me home," Dupree said as Kelly wheeled him toward the elevator. "Was I under anesthesia, or did you accept a date for Saturday night?"

"Of course. I'm looking forward to it," she said, leaning over and flashing a smile. "Are you sure you're up for it?"

"Sure."

"What have you got planned? What should I wear?"

"Well, since I'm really behind on preparing for Sunday and I need to make it a pretty early evening, I thought you could come by the church and I could practice my sermon on you for a couple of hours. Dress in Sunday clothes, I guess."

"Really…I…"

"I'm kidding," Dupree said. "There's a restaurant in Mobile, on the bay, that I've wanted to try. Do you like seafood?"

"Yes, I love it. That sounds great."

"Okay, Saturday it is. Pick me up at seven?" Dupree said, smiling. He pointed down at his abdomen and made a what-can-I-say face. "Sorry. Can't drive. You know, I got shot and everything."

CHAPTER 28

Franky Stevens called Janna on Thursday at six o'clock sharp. Finding her number was easy; Bay Pest called at 7:30 on Sunday evening. The odds that it was a cold call from a Bay Pest marketer were slim.

"Janna Sandler," Franky said, reading the name he typed as a "new contact" into his phone.

"Hello?" Janna answered on the second ring.

"Janna Sandler? This is Franky Stevens."

"Hey, Franky, I thought that might be you. You remembered my last name, eh?"

"Of course, although I did think it might have been Westmoreland," he said, laughing slightly. "Wasn't there a Janna Westmoreland in our class?"

"You mistook me for her? We don't look anything alike."

"Not really, I was just playing with you. I knew it was you all along."

"She's Janna Lamprey now. She married the guy that does the weekend weather on News 13, Jim Lamprey. You know the guy from the drama club?"

"I don't remember a lot of our classmates," Franky said. His memory loss was a function of time and the number of healthy brain cells he killed in ten years of heavy drinking. On the fourth day of his sobriety, memories were not any clearer.

"Speaking of classmates, did you know Kenneth Schultz?"

"No, why? Is he a friend of yours?"

"Heavens no! I sprayed his house after I left Castaways. I was just wondering if you knew him."

"I'd probably know him if I saw him."

"Probably not. He's pretty obscure. I'm not sure why I even asked. I guess, I was kind of creeped out by him and well…"

"How so?" Franky asked.

"First, his wife requested that I exterminate the house. It's not even in my territory. I have west of Market Street. Anyway, when I get there, she's nowhere to be found, and then he, like, follows me around."

"Did you tell him you were classmates?"

"No. I was going to, but there was something about him that made me want to say as little as possible."

"Really?"

"Yeah, he kept staring at me, and he called me Lizzy, I think."

"Lizzy?"

"Yeah, by mistake. But he started laughing about it, in a creepy way. Anyway, I'm boring you with all this work stuff. Tell me about your day. What did the illustrious Mr. Willard "Franky" Stevens III, esquire, do today?"

"Esquire?"

"I know you're a lawyer. That's how I got your cellphone number. I called your law office. So what kind of lawyering did you to today?"

"Wow, where do I start?" Franky said in a sing-song voice.

Should I mention I returned to work after three days of detox, or perhaps she would like to hear about the AA meeting or the time I spent with Dr. Charles?

"Well, I had a really great day," he said. He paused. "I guess because I was looking forward to talking to you."

• • •

During the visit with Dr. Charles on his last day of in-patient rehabilitation, Franky sat in an overstuffed chair, facing the window. Dr. Charles' office was cool and refreshing. Franky sipped on

162

a cup of freshly brewed coffee, with an ounce of cream. In three days, his taste buds returned. He suffered a permanent, slight headache, due to sinus problems.

"What do you mean when you say you are not going to 'screw up' this relationship?" Dr. Charles asked, looking over the top of his reading glasses. Franky spun in his chair to face him.

"Well, doctor," Franky said, looking introspective. "It's been a long time since I've seen someone who I could really like. I know I haven't even called her yet…but I'm not going to screw this up. Right from the start, I'm going into it with the intentions of doing the right thing."

"And by 'screw up,' what exactly are you referring to?"

"I guess I'm not going to cat around and stuff, you know, screw up. I'm not going to be selfish. I want to see if I can make her happy. I want to see if I can make a woman happy."

"You think that's what she would like, for you 'to make her happy'?" Dr. Charles asked.

"Sure. What else would she want from me? Or from anyone else for that matter?"

"Do you like her for the things she does?"

"Yes."

"What has she done for you? You haven't even called her yet. You're calling her tomorrow night?"

"Yes," Franky said. "Well, I've known her since high school."

"I realize that. You know what I mean."

"Well, I guess, she hasn't done anything. But she was nice to me on Monday. She was friendly. She didn't judge me, even though I was sitting in a bar about to drink myself to death."

"Okay."

"Yeah, that's it," Franky wanted to jump over the desk and see what Dr. Charles was writing so frantically on his notepad. He sat forward instead, with his elbows on his knees. "I would say she made me feel important to her…a priority."

"But you think she wants you to do more than that?"

"No, I guess not. What are you getting at?"

"I'm not getting at anything," Dr. Charles stopped writing.

"I just want to do more this time. Not screw up and stuff."

"There's that phrase again."

"What phrase? Screw up? What? What's wrong with screw up?" Franky pushed himself back and gripped the arms of the chair, squeezing so hard his forearms hurt.

"Nothing, it's just that you use it a lot."

Franky paused. Sitting forward, he brushed his hair out of his eyes. He caught his reflection in the little mirror by Dr. Charles' desk. His face had color; his cheeks were a little pink from an afternoon basketball shoot around with his friends in rehab. The whites of his eyes were clear, making his brown eyes look almost black. He smiled over at Dr. Charles, and ran his tongue over his teeth.

"I'm not going to drink, doctor," Franky said, with a grin. "I'm not going to drink until she dumps me."

• • •

Franky double knotted the laces on his running shoes. He stood against the front of his apartment, pushing on the newly power-washed siding, stretching his calves. He bent one leg over the other and groaned as he touched his toes.

As he stretched his upper body, a neighbor carried groceries in from the car. He took in a deep breath and smiled. Janna was looking forward to their date tomorrow night. She had even made plans to have her daughter stay with the grandparents.

"Meaning what, Detective Stevens?"

He started off on a fast walk.

"Answer: She wants you to spend the night."

"No!" Franky yelled out, hitting his forehead repeatedly. "You can't think like that!"

Franky picked up his pace to a very light jog.

In the late evening, the breeze off the gulf was cool. Franky turned west on Beach Boulevard and ran toward the setting sun.

On the first Thursday night that Franky would not drink alcohol since he was sixteen-years-old, he left his apartment with a purpose.

"Do not drink," he said, starting to breathe heavily. "Do not get smashed."

Perspiration formed on his temples as he forced himself to swing his arms and stretch his chest muscles. As the scenery of houses and sea moved in his peripheral view, an unchanging scene of grey asphalt with a white stripe bounced in front of him.

Flat, clear water was to his left. The wind created a light chop. Franky was forced to run through puddles made by the biggest waves. On his right were brand new homes replaced after the storm.

Within ten minutes of his exercise, he found himself concentrating only on his very next stride. Passing the half-mile mark, his legs were weak from too many hours seated on a barstool.

Nearing the Hargood house, crime scene tape covered the front door; the front yard needed mowing. There were no vehicles in the drive. Franky maintained his stare by turning his head while he ran. He envisioned the night of the murder. Many rumors had been running through town.

Decapitation?

Yesterday, Franky was told that the mortician had to sew the head back on before the funeral. The most common rumor was that poor Hargood was stabbed, and his face was burned off with acid.

Stride by stride, Franky forced himself to run. His breathing moved to the beat of his feet. He started counting his breaths; his chest was tight.

"Getting your face burned off," he said, in short breaths. Franky struggled for air. His mind raced with thoughts of the victim and the murderer.

A car passed too close to him and jolted him from his daydream.

Franky made the turn at the Coast Guard point. Throughout the loop, he studied the ships being built across the river. Two cruisers and a destroyer were parked along the west bank of the Pascagoula River.

As he completed the turn, the sun fell behind him. He slowed his pace; his legs were cramping.

"Yeah, that would be pretty cool." His mind flashed with the idea of joining the Navy. He laughed aloud.

"Not long now." He breathed heavily, holding his side; his liver was hurt, over stressed.

He took a quick glance to the left at the crime scene again and slipped into exhaustion-induced delusions. His vision was blurred and hazy.

"Maybe…I will…join the Navy!"

Another hundred yards passed.

"Come on, pier!"

Passing Beach Park, Franky nearly passed out. He had only a quarter of a mile left.

"Maybe…the Navy…maybe…the Navy."

He stopped 200 yards short of the pier.

• • •

Exhausted, Franky walked, flailing his arms, pulling in as much air as possible. His heart spiked to the point of exploding. With each step thumping heavily on the pavement, he moved closer to the pier, trying not to pass out.

He walked onto the pier. Cracks between the boards made it easy to focus on the water directly beneath. The faster he moved, the more he walked on air. With the sun setting to his right, the sky was on fire. Clouds reflected the brilliance of the late evening. Franky placed his hands on his hips and stood looking out over the Mississippi Sound.

He had a date tomorrow, an actual date, and the anticipation was more than he could stand.

Leaning over the pier, the light surf splashed on a piling below. In the three feet of water, he saw the bottom; tiny minnows darted around in schools. A blue crab bumped against the base of the piling.

As the crab picked at the barnacle encrusted piling, Franky focused on the water line. Sharp barbs caked the edges three feet above the water line. It was a kaleidoscope of white and blue and green with a light coating of…

"Blood?"

Franky focused on the piling that was directly under him. The barnacles had been disturbed. The barbs were fresh and even, and then a swath was pushed flat. Below it was a line of dark reddish-brown.

Exiting the pier, he went down for a closer look.

Jumping onto the sand, he ducked under the pier and moved toward the shoreline.

"Definitely blood," he said.

Franky looked along the beach in both directions. No one was present. He could check the paper, although he had been scouring it for days looking for a new lead on a client.

"Your Honor," he said, looking around for a container. "We have been after the city for years to protect these children from the pilings."

He found an old Ziploc back in a garbage can. Leaning over the seawall, he washed it out.

"This young boy was walking innocently enough along the seawall, and because of the neglect of the city to barricade this hazard; he was slammed into the piling by a wave and lacerated his arm."

Franky stepped over the seawall and waded out to the piling. He scraped some of the damaged barnacles into the Ziploc bag, making sure some of the bloodstained ones were captured.

"…or maybe his head or chest. Wherever, he was hurt! Oh, the pain and suffering and the infection and scarring are all too horrible for this young man…" Franky said, continuing his argument before a fictitious judge. "…or, God forbid for a young woman to endure such trauma."

Franky closed the bag. Stepping back over the seawall, his shoes squished as he made his way back to the street.

He crossed Beach Boulevard.

"Besides," Franky said, smiling. "That poor child's lawyer really needs a payday."

• • •

Franky hurried to unlock the door. His legs continued to cramp, and stiffness developed in his lower back. He answered his phone on the fourth ring.

"Hey, Janna," he said, still winded.

"Hey, Franky, I needed to call you about tomorrow night…"

His heart sank.

"I didn't tell you because I thought I had cleared it off my schedule, but I have a commitment until around eight thirty, and I really need to go or else…"

"That's fine, Janna. I'll take a rain check. We can always…"

"No! Franky, no. That's not what I meant," Janna interrupted. "I was hoping you could go with me, and we could go out afterwards, to dinner…like we had planned."

Franky pumped his fist, biting his lower lip and nodding.

"I've got this thing at the church. I sponsor the youth group, and I'm emceeing a talent show. I'm going to do some stand-up comedy while I emcee."

"You do stand-up?"

"I'm going to try. I've been working on it…like a hobby. But, if you don't want to go, I guess I can…"

"No, I'll go. It'll be fun."

"I think so. We have a lot of talented kids."

"Are you going to tell me one of your jokes?" Franky said. He kicked off his running shoes toward the front door. Opening the refrigerator, he shopped for a drink. His mom had stocked it with sports drinks and juice. "You're not planning on using the material on men's restrooms are you?"

"No, absolutely not," she said emphatically. "Besides, I don't tell jokes. It's stand-up. It's stories, observations, current events… stuff like that. A lot of it won't be funny, but I think it's funny."

"All right, then you can tell me some of your stories."

"Okay, I promise during our date I'll try some of my new stuff on you," she said.

Franky let a pause follow her statement.

"Terrific, then you could tell me a few of your stories," he said, laughing.

"You're so bad. I'll see you at six."

CHAPTER 29

The arm was infected, and Kenneth Schultz had the fever to prove it. All night he battled terrible dreams and a burning in his veins; the tips of his fingers on his right hand were permanently numb. In a painful exchange, the nurse that took him back to the examination area, removed Schultz's homemade bandages. Tears formed in the corner of his eyes, as she used tweezers to pick long strands of cotton that had been sucked into the wound.

Sitting in the waiting room in the emergency room at Singing River Hospital, he rocked back and forth, cradling the arm close to his chest. The room was nothing more than an examination table surrounded by curtains. Sitting on a protective layer of butcher paper, his right heel kicked heavily against the side of the table, making a loud, rhythmic thud.

The curtain slid to the side, and a young doctor of eastern origin entered. He held a clipboard with all of Schultz's information.

"Let's see now. It says here you have scraped your arm on a piling at the public pier. Let's take a look." Schultz was pleased with the doctor's appearance. Capable, professional, well-groomed, the doctor talked with a pleasant cadence in his speech. "Well, it is certainly infected. Are you allergic to penicillin?"

"No."

The doctor poked around the wound, moving his finger gently over the worst damaged areas.

"Okay, well, it's a good thing you came in; this was only going to get worse." The doctor patted Schultz on the knee.

Schultz grimaced and jumped.

The doctor snapped his hand back. "Oh, I'm sorry, is there something wrong with your knee?"

"No, the knee is fine. I…uh…"

"Should I look at it?"

"No!"

"Okay." The doctor wrote on the clipboard. He spun to address the nurse and gave her the instructions for the penicillin shot. Schultz looked over the doctor's shoulder but could not see what he had written about him.

"Okay, Mr. Schultz, I'm going to give you a prescription for antibiotics, and we'll get this wound cleaned up really well. You said it happened at the pier. Were you crabbing?"

"No, just playing around with the kids and slipped."

"I see. Anytime you get a scrape on barnacles and stuff like that, you have to be really careful. They are teeming with bacteria and really get infected fast. Anyway, we'll get this cleaned up. That's going to hurt a little, but we'll teach you how to bandage it, and you'll be good to go. Any questions?"

"No, sir."

"Okay then," the doctor said as he was exiting. "And make sure you get that knee checked out."

• • •

Tools were scattered around Kenneth Schultz's bedroom. So far, he used a drill, screwdriver, hammer, and putty. All were placed just out of arm's reach in different locations. The hammer rested on the top shelf of the closet; the putty was on the floor underneath the stepladder. In his work bucket, which sat next to the bed, were other supplies like wire, wire nuts, and the lens.

With each step in the progress of his little project, Schultz was getting more aggravated. He wanted to add despair into his life, but since shooting the preacher, everything in his life had gone into a tailspin.

Schultz tapped gently on a wire clip inside the closet. He needed his screwdriver.

Of course it's on the floor.

He stepped down from the ladder for the ten thousandth time and picked up the screwdriver.

"You okay in there?" Schultz yelled out to his son. The boy was entranced in a *Nick Jr.* cartoon.

"Uh huh, I'm fine." Michael's soft voice returned.

Back up on the stepladder, Schultz fished in the back of the closet for the wire clip and tightened the screw. After two turns, the screwdriver slipped from his hand, hit the top shelf, and fell to the floor, bouncing a couple of times on the padded carpet.

"Good gravy! This is going to kill me!"

Schultz stepped down from the ladder and grabbed the screwdriver.

"Did you call me?" Michael walked into the bedroom.

"Of course not. Now go watch your show!"

Back up the stepladder, he returned the tip of the screwdriver to the screw.

"Son of a…" Schultz screamed as he spun and threw the screwdriver across the room into the hallway.

On his last trip down the ladder, he mistakenly picked up the flat-head screwdriver, rather than the Phillips-head that he had dropped.

Back down the stepladder, he grabbed the correct screwdriver. Up the stepladder, he returned to the screw and tightened it. Fishing the wire through a small conduit, he directed it into the back of the digital recorder. In the darkness of the closet, his eyes shut tight, he worked using only his non-dominant hand, concentrating on getting the tiny wire in position.

"Here daddy," Michael said, from the base of the stepladder. He was holding the screwdriver that Schultz had tossed into the hall.

"I don't need it." Schultz glanced briefly at the tool, closed his eyes again, and continued with his work in the depths of the closet.

"I'm hungry."

"I'll get your lunch when I'm done here."

"How long is that?"

"Not long."

"Because I'm really hungry."

Schultz lost his grip on the wire. Spinning to address the boy, he slammed his wounded forearm into the closet door jamb. Expletives flew from his mouth as he chastised the boy and sent him away with a threat of taking his nap with no lunch at all.

The whole project was taking entirely too much time.

• • •

Schultz sat on the edge of the bed, looking up at his handiwork. The project was nearly complete.

The room was cool and fresh. The soft scent of powder or air freshener drifted in from the adjacent bathroom. Light flooded in from the backyard. Schultz picked up his phone and dialed.

"Bay Pest, this is Annette. How may I help you?"

"Yes, I would like an exterminator."

"Yes, sir, fine. Is there a specific problem?"

"No, just roaches," Schultz said.

"Okay, well, what's your address?"

"I want a specific exterminator."

"Pardon me?"

"She was here earlier in the week, and she said to call if I saw any more roaches. Well, not only have I seen one, I've seen a half dozen, and I'm none too happy about it."

"Oh, I see. Well, what's your address?"

"I live at 908 Eastwood Street."

"Okay, well, that is, let's see here, that is Mark's territory, and…"

"Yes but it was Elizabeth that came by. I think Monday, and I bought the Gold Termite Protection, and she told me…"

"Did you say you saw termites or roaches?"

"Roaches, but I bought the Gold Plan, and she said to call her if I saw any pests and she would come back out," Schultz said, getting more and more irritated.

"Well, sir, I see where we made a service call on Monday, but that was Janna Sandler. We don't have an Elizabeth."

"Yes, yes, it was Janna. That's her. I need her to come out immediately to re-spray because we are infested with roaches. They're coming out of the woodwork."

"Let me see. She is booked up today. Can she come in the morning?"

"Absolutely not!" Schultz yelled into the phone. "I have small children in the house, and my wife is a fanatic about bugs, and I'm a Gold Plan owner, so I…"

"Mr. Schultz, I will clear her schedule," the receptionist said, breaking into his tirade. "I'll clear her schedule so that she can come by. Is four okay?"

Schultz's son walked into the bedroom with a curious face. Schultz shook his head and waved him out of the room.

"Sir, is four okay with you?"

"Yes," Schultz said, his voice calm. "That would be fine."

"And you said 908 Eastwood Street. Correct?"

"Yes," Schultz said, hanging up the phone.

He wanted to laugh. Reaching into the bucket, he picked up the lens.

At four o'clock, Schultz would see Miss Sandler again. He would act surprised when she knocked on the door.

• • •

Schultz completed the installation of the lens. He stopped to catch his breath.

Michelle had decorated the bedroom, and it was always kept spotless. She minimized the pictures of the children that hung on the wall. Her dresser, however, was covered with framed snapshots of vacations past. Schultz's footprints disrupted the stripes made by the vacuum cleaner in the grain of the finely knit carpet. Small slivers of wire coating littered the floor with the wrapping from a roll of electrical tape and the three or four tools. The dust from the tiny hole that he drilled into the sheetrock littered the pristine flooring by the closet.

Schultz straightened the bed and started cleaning in the closet. A receptacle somewhere near the camera would have made the installation a lot more reliable. Instead, he would have to rely on battery power.

The motion detector was the stroke of genius. The recorder ran for five minutes when the camera was activated. If motion continued, it continued to record for another five minutes.

Schultz carried the small, wooden stepladder back into the utility room, passing Michael. He strained his back trying to navigate it through a doorway. When it struck the wall and left a mark, he cursed.

This will be the death of me.

"It's time for your nap," Schultz said, returning to the den.

"I want to watch TV?"

"I don't care what you want." Schultz picked up the five-year-old by grabbing one of his arms. He ushered him through the kitchen, ignoring the boy's pleas.

"In you go." Schultz hoisted Michael onto the bed. "You want a blanket?"

"Can I look at a book? Mommy lets me look at a book sometimes."

"Whatever."

Schultz handed him a book and covered him with a blanket. He exited the room quickly.

Returning to his own bedroom, Schultz shook his head in disgust.

Crucifying Hargood and shooting the ignorant preacher elevated Schultz's level of perception. No longer was his head stuck in the sand. He was alert. He studied bank statements. He scoured the phone bills and the corresponding list of calls. His wife had an incredible number of sick friends. The amount of undocumented time in her day was staggering.

When Schultz went on a mission to find out about his wife's extra-curricular activities, he started with aggressive interrogation. He loved watching her squirm. But Michelle was very manipulative and parried his verbal assaults expertly.

So Schultz decided to get a technological advantage.

Removing the can of flat white paint from the closet, he touched up the marks on the wall made during the installation. He returned the paint can and walked to the kitchen to clean the brush. The smell of paint was heavy as he washed the brush in the sink. White streaks swirled and fell into the disposal.

Schultz dried his hands with a paper towel. He used the damp towel to gently wipe the jagged laceration across the top of his left knee, being careful not to disturb the scab. His forearm throbbed, even though it had been cleaned and dressed by a professional. The penicillin was not working fast enough. His fever had returned.

Stepping into the bedroom, he immediately noticed the lens sticking from the wall above the closet. The tiny eye of the camera was like a beacon. The lens protruded from the wall about an inch and reflected light from the windows. Schultz had drilled the hole too large. A ridiculous amount of caulk was used to hold the lens in place.

The small digital recorder sat quietly collecting data. Schultz looked at the image on the tiny viewfinder. The display on the camera was a direct view of the bed.

• • •

Kenneth Schultz sat on his back porch in the scorching sun waiting for Janna. Fever pulsed through his mind. He cursed under his breath.

She's going to see the camera.

"It looks like it was installed by a god damned three year old."

His backyard haunted him. Suffering from tunnel vision, he scanned the canal with his eyes as if he were looking through a telescope. Every sound was magnified—the locusts, a passing car, the rustling of leaves above his head.

In the darkened brush of the canal, Schultz saw his complete ineptness. He cursed his childishness, prancing through the canal like a little schoolboy, celebrating his puny victory in a game of solitaire.

"If you would have done it right," Schultz said in a whisper. "If you just did one thing right!"

Schultz could not live with the mistakes that he had made at Hargood's. Blood was everywhere, Hargood cried like a girl, and to top it off, Schultz left the jug of blood behind.

Shooting the preacher was a colossal screw-up. Schultz failed to correctly explain the motive for killing Hargood and so he just went rogue.

"And you didn't even kill him," Schultz said, pressing his palms into his temples.

"And now this bullshit with Michelle."

It can still be done right.

A voice speaking softly in the back of Schultz's head. The sun was bearing down, sweat poured from his brow.

For a million convoluted reasons, Schultz began to believe he was no better off than before the sacrifice of Hargood.

"You're worse off, much worse," Schultz said. "Because now you're doing stupid things."

It can still be done right.

Schultz bit into an apple; it was void of taste. He spit the chewed mass onto the porch and chunked the rest into the backyard. It rolled across the space crushed by the moonwalk.

"It's much worse now."

Darkness closed in on Schultz's eyes as the heat and light rose to a blinding pitch. The canal was getting dark. Flickers of light danced off the trees, changing the images that flashed in front of him.

With the first flicker, he saw a shallow grave, the little short grave of a child. With the next, he saw a mass grave with soldiers standing beside the hole. The corpses were stacked like cordwood. In another flash, he saw the crosses and wreaths placed at a roadway intersection.

With the last flicker, a deadly thought came to his mind.

It can still be done right.

"No, Kenny, you said that would not be necessary."

Schultz pressed harder on his throbbing temples. "You promised that would not be necessary," he whispered as he stepped into his silent house.

• • •

Schultz sat on a tiny chair not designed to support his weight. He was lonely, tired, and ashamed. The crucifixion of Hargood was nothing more than a weeklong vacation from his madness.

The knife rested on his lap.

The murder of Hargood, a product of hate, did Schultz no good. It had not jumpstarted his conscience. The murder was a pleasurable experience, and the conflict, the unrelenting sorrow for the deed, was just not there.

It was love that provided conflict.

Miss Sandler proved this to Schultz. It was love, not hate, that drove people to despair—and not just any love, unconditional love. Unconditional love, directed toward something other than God, created true despair.

Schultz shifted his weight on the little chair; it creaked. The legs of the chair made a scratching noise on the hardwood floor. The afternoon light brought a warm, comforting look to the room decorated with race cars and Spiderman posters. Schultz rotated the knife slightly in his hand, watching the reflection run up and down the length of the sharpened tempered steel.

Unconditional love toward natural things drives them to despair.

The quiet, rhythmic sounds of Schultz's son's breathing drifted softly into his ears. The boy's head was buried into the pillow and small beads of sweat formed on his brow. He liked to sleep with a blanket, even in the middle of summer. Schultz watched as his eyelids fluttered and his little hand twitched.

Schultz didn't love him.

Love was spiritual, and Schultz was ignorant of spiritual things.

"Oh, son, if only I could save you from the evil in this world. I know evil. I knew evil when I was a little older than you," Schultz said softly. Tears were forming in his eyes. He was poking the tip of the knife into the side of his leg.

"No, son, you won't live long enough to see that kind of wickedness." Schultz's throat was tight. His whispering voice cracked on most of the words.

"But you don't love him." The voice said to Schultz. "And it's love that provides conflict."

It can still be done right.

Schultz stood. His buttocks hurt from sitting too long on the little stool. He looked down at the boy. He placed the knife into his line of sight. It caught a beam of sunlight when it moved between his eyes and the boy's neck.

The tip of the knife was stained with blood from Schultz's leg.

"I'm a coward." Schultz said, softly.

"You're a coward." The voice said.

The act would serve no purpose but to cause the boy's mother and sister grief. Schultz didn't love. Killing his son would be nothing more than killing Hargood.

Love is hogwash.

He stepped away from the boy and backed into the hallway.

"You are such a coward."

Walking into the kitchen, he placed the knife in its holder after rinsing it in the sink.

• • •

"Just let me know if you see anything else," Janna Sandler said, hurrying toward her truck. Her keys rattled in her hand as she waved back. "Bye-bye, Michael. It was nice meeting you." She jumped in and immediately started the engine. The truck took little time exiting Eastwood Street.

"All right, Michael," Schultz said, ushering his son into the house. "Go to your room and play until your mom gets home. Okay?"

"Okay."

Miss Sandler had given Michael a toy bug that lit up when his antennas were moved.

Schultz moved quickly to his bedroom closet and hit the rewind on the digital recorder. It had picked up something while Miss Sandler sprayed the bedroom.

The picture was perfectly clear.

The recording started with the bedroom door opening.

"Let me get around the exterior walls in here," Janna Sandler said.

Schultz's response was inaudible. Janna closed the bedroom door behind her very quickly.

"There, right there," Schultz said, as he inched closer to the television screen.

"Miss Sandler, why did you have to lock the door? You shouldn't be so scared. I think I love you."

Janna made a face of disgust.

"Did you not like my little joke, Miss Sandler?" Schultz asked as Janna sprayed the master bedroom.

"Lizzy, oh I mean Miss Sandler. I'm sorry, you look just like someone I knew named Lizzy," Schultz said, trying to mimic the exact words he had said when she was filling out the paperwork.

Schultz smiled.

"No, that's too bad that you didn't like my little joke."

Schultz punched the stop button.

Sitting back on the bed, Schultz pulled a large hunting knife from the nightstand. He examined the blade. Running his thumb along the edge, he snapped his hand back when it cut the skin. Sticking his thumb in his mouth, he tasted blood.

"Yes, Miss Sandler, I'm afraid you leave me no choice but to do something I swore I would never do."

CHAPTER 30

Janna Sandler threw her uniform into the dirty clothes and pushed them to the bottom of the hamper using a towel.

Leaving the Schultz's house, she felt violated. Mr. Schultz had intentionally bumped into her as she passed him in the hall. His hand brushed against her buttocks, forcing a reactionary swipe of her hand that carried a cannister of insect poison.

He cried out in pain when the cannister struck his knee.

Rushing into the bedroom, she quickly locked the door behind her. Janna lied to Mr. Schultz when she said it was an accident. Personal safety warranted little white lies.

In the ten-minute trip between the Schultz's house and her own, she made two phone calls: the first to her mom to make sure she had picked up Katie, and the second to her boss to tell him she was never going back to the Schultz's.

Stepping into the shower, she washed off the poisons that had collected on her throughout the day and began to feel human again. Using an excessive amount of hot water, she did the full shower routine, cutting no corners. Everything that needed washing was washed; everything needing shaving was shaved. She stepped out pink and relaxed.

On a little stool, she sat in front of a fan and groomed—plucking, drying, curling, straightening—everything got its proper attention. Lastly, wearing only her cotton panties and bra, she applied her evening, summertime make-up. Light foundation, light eye make-up, and a pink lip gloss were all that was necessary. It was five; Franky would be there in an hour.

Tonight would be a great night.

• • •

Janna watched Franky through a slot in the blinds. He made last-minute preparations in his car. He ran his finger inside his collar and straightened his tie. He wiped a bead of sweat from his brow. When he eventually climbed from his car, Janna smiled. He wore highly starched khaki pants and a new light blue short-sleeved shirt. He carried a handful of flowers.

Janna dropped the blind and shook her hands. She made a little spin and waited forever, for the doorbell to ring.

When it finally rang, she realized he had gone to the side door. Stepping out of the kitchen, she poked her head around the corner.

"Franky, over here," she said, waving.

A look of shock hit Franky's face. Janna was a beautiful woman. Her blonde hair, highlighted naturally from the sun, was luminescent in the evening light. Powder blue eyes were accentuated by a contagious smile. Her entire expression, like a choreographed dance involving several performers—nose, brows, lashes, and skin—converged in harmony to create the face of an angel.

Janna smiled and curtsied in her simple cotton sundress.

"Oh, hey," Franky said, extending the flowers. "These are for you."

"Wow! Thanks, Franky, that's really sweet," Janna said, taking the bouquet. "They're beautiful." She sniffed around them briefly. "How did you know I love lilies? Come on in."

Janna gave the total tour of her home with a simple wave of the hand. From the front door, the kitchen, dining room, and living room were visible.

"Back there are the bedrooms," Janna said, pointing down the hall. She went to the cupboard.

The floors were stripped to the original yellow pine; the refrigerator had a thousand pictures and finger paints. In the living room corner stood a play kitchen with a table, stuffed animals, and a little chalkboard. The furniture was smart and functional.

"I really like your place," Franky said.

"Thanks, me too," Janna said, putting the flowers in a vase.

• • •

Janna spotted Franky from the wings. The stage, also known as the altar on Sundays, had three microphones in stands at the front. Sunday's normal decorum of palms and candles had been changed out with a praise band set-up. After welcoming the audience, thanking everyone who helped set up, and praising the talented kids, Janna went into a five minute performance of her best material.

"Good evening, everyone," Janna said, standing at the mike. "Welcome to the God Squad's first-annual high school talent show fundraiser, or what I like to call the HSTSFR."

"Tonight, we are in for a real treat. We have singers, bands, dancers, and I think we even have someone who's throwing knives. The only problem is, he's throwing them at the audience. So no napping!"

"My name is Janna Sandler. I'll be your host tonight, and I must say what a thrill it is. I almost didn't make it. I was delayed unloading my car after a trip to the Costco this afternoon."

Janna pulled the mike from the stand.

"Can you believe the incredible savings at that store? I mean, I bought a case of whipped cream for only twenty-three dollars and a five-gallon jug of maraschino cherries for only twelve dollars. If I could purchase a truckload of bananas, I could make a banana split from here to Beach Boulevard."

"And don't get me started on the toilet paper; I bought a package so big I literally had to strap it to the roof of my car. My mattress is smaller than that thing."

Through the corner of her eye, Janna saw Franky smiling.

• • •

The restaurant engulfed Janna and Franky in the aroma of fresh bread and vanilla. The candlelit tables with linen tablecloths and cloth napkins were decorated for a romantic encounter. Franky held the chair for his beautiful date. Janna brushed her dress beneath her as she sat. An older couple who had run out of things to talk about, looked up from their coffee and smiled at the lovely couple. Janna and Franky were obviously on a first date.

"May I take your drink order?" the waitress asked.

Janna looked at Franky. She stayed fixed on his eyes; she wanted Franky to take the lead.

"I would like a cup of coffee and water."

"With lemon?"

"Yes, please."

"I'll just have water," Janna said.

"With lemon?"

"Yes, please."

"Thank you. I'll be right back with some bread while you look at the menu."

Franky opened his menu. His eyes caught Janna's.

"You know you could have gotten a drink," Franky said. "I'm trying to cut back, but if you…"

"No, I'm fine," Janna said. "Besides, the last time I went on a date and drank, I just lost all control and I…"

"Garcon!" Franky waved his hand in the air. "More wine, please!"

Janna smiled.

• • •

Throughout dinner, the conversation was casual. Janna kept things light by making a few interesting observations. Franky was cautious about sharing details of his life.

After dinner, the conversations turned a little more serious. Janna ordered a cup of coffee.

"So, Katie is at your folk's house?" Franky asked.

"Yes." Janna suddenly felt obliged to explain her first marriage.

"…and so I literally caught him red-handed. When I confronted him with the e-mails and text messages and all the stuff I had taken from the computer, he finally confessed, and I told him it was best if he moved out. It was two days later that I found out I was pregnant. Imagine that."

"That must have been tough."

"Well, it wasn't great. But, I had a lot of support. I can't say it was a mistake, with Katie and everything, but I knew the type of person he was, and…I guess I just was blinded by this urge to get married. I was thirty and well…"

"Yeah, I know what you mean," Franky said, nodding.

"So," Janna said, "what about you? What will I find when I google you later tonight?"

"Well, Janna, to be honest, there is no telling what you will find. I'm so afraid of what is out there; I've sworn to never even google myself."

"Really now? For example…"

"Well, you might find that I did indeed pass the bar."

"That's good."

"And you might find that I've never passed a bar…without stopping in."

"That's not so good."

"I've never been married."

"That's good."

"And, I've never had a really serious relationship."

"That's not so good."

"But," Franky said, raising his glass of water to make a toast. "I think that if Google were totally up-to-date, it would show that I spent today happier than I've been in a while because I scored a date with the prettiest girl in Mississippi."

"That's really good."

• • •

Driving back to Pascagoula, the conversation died out near the Mississippi-Alabama line. Janna looked over at Franky as he drove.

The lines in the median clipped along beside them at seventy miles per hour. The dashboard lights illuminated Franky's face and brought out grey flecks in his extremely dark eyes. Franky had become even more attractive with age. The air conditioner vent blew directly into his face giving his hair a slightly windblown look.

He looked over when he noticed her staring.

"What?" He smiled.

"I was just wondering. What do you remember about me from high school?"

Franky furrowed his brow in thought.

"I remember we had a few classes together."

"I'm not talking about that. Really, what do you remember, specifically?"

"I remember that I thought you were cute, and I had a crush on you…when we were juniors. And I remember you were on the bus when we went to see the Jackson Prep game."

"You were on that bus, the church bus?" Janna asked.

"Yeah, but you didn't notice because you were making out with a senior."

She slapped his arm.

"What do you remember about Wilson's party?" Janna asked.

He gave a blank look.

"Oh come on. Todd Wilson. His party on the river?"

Franky took a stern look.

"I remember you drove me home…and…that…I was rude." He turned to face her. "I'm sorry."

"You should be, you cad! You scarred me for life!" Janna said, in a Scarlet O'Hara imitation. She started laughing.

"Franky, you weren't that rude. I think I led you on a little bit."

Franky exited off of I-10 onto Hwy 90.

"The only thing I was really upset about, or maybe I should say, it was more like I was curious about, was why you didn't ask me out," Janna finally asked.

"I don't know. I guess I was scared that you would shoot me down," Franky said, looking over.

Janna moved over next to him and placed her head on his shoulder as she moved his arm around her neck.

"Silly boy."

● ● ●

The kiss at Janna's front door was long and passionate. No words were spoken beforehand. They walked holding hands from the car. At the porch, Janna stood on the first step so that they were eye-to-eye. Franky leaned forward, and taking her other hand, he closed his eyes, wanting to be respectful. However, temptation surged through his body with the first taste of her lips. He fought against moving his hands from her shoulders to her waist. He fought against opening his mouth.

Janna had tasted his lips long ago and did not fight this temptation. Slightly, softly, breathing in as she kissed, she slowly opened her mouth and allowed her tongue to gently caress the outside of Franky's bottom lip. Time slipped; they thought of nothing. All anxiety, all longing, all hope rested on a kiss that ended too quickly.

The kiss ended the date. With this knowledge, they held it for as long as possible. When it broke, when Janna saw Franky's still closed eyes in the light of a distant street lamp, she felt tingles run up the back of her neck. She was chilled.

The kiss, the embrace, and the glance she had stolen halfway through had great implications. Emotion and energy were infused in the firmness of his hands and in the way he held hers as long as possible before letting her enter her house. A silent goodbye gave her a new strength, a new hope, and an overwhelming desire to call him back.

CHAPTER 31

The ladies of the congregation wanted an early graveside service so that they could be home before the heat of the day. Ten ladies, varying in age from twenty-five to eighty, met at Christ Church early Saturday morning for a prayer breakfast and social. Wearing Sunday casual clothes, they carpooled to the grave site at Pine Crest Memorial on Ingalls Avenue.

Fred Norton took care of all the arrangements. Mrs. Brewer was delivered in a respectable casket to Pine Crest at nine thirty sharp. A little awning covered the grave. The morning dew glistened off the headstones and silk flowers scattered around. The smell of honeysuckle, mixing with the ten different perfumes of the ladies of Christ Church, was heavy in the air. Fred arranged for two dozen folding chairs to be set beside the grave. Dupree put twelve of them away before they started.

Those congregated by the grave sang a hymn. The pastor said a prayer.

"I know you don't know Mrs. Brewer. I never spoke to her. Our relationship started after she went into a coma," Dupree held an open Bible in his hands. "But rest assured, Jesus knew her."

Dupree's sermon spoke of Jesus and how he had gone ahead to prepare a place for her.

"…and came to take her there at the exact moment he planned. Not a minute too soon and not a minute too late. One may ask, why would Mrs. Brewer suffer in a coma for so long? What purpose would that serve?" Dupree proposed rhetorically. "We don't know God's purpose in many things, but I want to say that she ministered to me, in a special way, when I was in need of Jesus."

Dupree closed the Bible.

"It was a visit with Mrs. Brewer, when I…and I'm ashamed to admit this…when I was very selfish. I made a promise, and I treated it flippantly. I shrugged my responsibilities as a pastor. This visit served as a mirror; this visit showed me that this collar around my throat doesn't keep me from sinning."

Dupree pulled the clergy collar from around his neck and held it in front of the ladies from the church.

"So, the results of this particular visit with Mrs. Brewer, made me realize that this collar should humble me. It should direct me to my Lord and Savior Jesus Christ, every time I put the darn thing on."

Pastor Dupree kept his words short.

The ladies of Christ Church were appreciative.

Mrs. Brewer was finally home.

• • •

Dupree intentionally left his office dark when he prepared a sermon. He wished he could hang aluminum foil over the window to make it even darker. Still wet around the collar and abdomen from being outside at the gravesite service, he sat down to write the perfect sermon.

The sermon would be directed toward a special visitor to Christ Church, the one from last Sunday, Kenneth Schultz.

"Schultz is hurting, lost. He needs love, hope, purpose. Preach Jesus."

Dupree prayed that Schultz would visit one more time. He prayed that he would take communion this week.

"If we say we have no sin we deceive ourselves, and the truth is not in us."

Stick a communion wafer in his mouth and pull it out real quick.

The thought of getting a DNA sample kept running through Dupree's mind.

"But if we confess our sin…"

Dupree fell back into his chair, exhausted, and took a couple of painkillers.

Gregor's insane.

"He has to repent; he has to change. You've got to convince him to turn himself in."

Maybe a fingerprint from the communion chalice.

Dupree grabbed his Bible and turned to Revelation.

There's no way to get a mouth swab from someone against their will.

"You've got to explain the flaw in his motive."

• • •

Having been cleared to drive, Dupree parked in an empty spot in front of Kelly Mitchell's apartment.

The hot August evening made his hair damp with sweat, as he drove to pick up his date. The temperature in his car never dropped below 90 degrees during the ride.

Looking into the rearview mirror, with the air conditioning ducts still blowing on his face, he ran his fingers through his hair, fluffing it up a bit in front.

He grabbed the handful of flowers from the passenger seat. Exiting the car, he brushed the wrinkles out of his new pair of khaki shorts and gently shook his shoulders so that his Hawaiian shirt fell flat in front of him. He flip-flopped his way to the front door and knocked. He looked at his feet. A distinct tan line ran around his leg an inch above his ankle.

"Hey," Kelly said, opening the door. "Come on in. Oh, thank you, that's so sweet." She took the flowers. "How was it driving?"

"No problem," he said, rubbing his side. "Jeez, Kelly, your place is awesome."

"Thanks. I'm just about ready. Can I get you something to drink?"

Dupree sat on the sofa, below a ceiling fan, and sipped water.

Waiting for Kelly to finish, he racked his brain for ideas on getting DNA from Schultz.

"Dude, you're an ex-boxer. Just sneak attack him. He falls, you swab through his mouth with a Q-tip, done," Gregor suggested.

Dupree rubbed his knuckles. He had worked through the ranks of the golden gloves while attending seminary. However, his wins were from landing multiple blows and accumulating points. He logged only one TKO in his three-year career.

Standing and stretching, he stepped onto the back porch.

You could go through his garbage.

"And what exactly are you going to find? A toothbrush, a blood soaked rag from…"

"Who you talking to?" Kelly stepped onto the back porch.

Dupree smiled.

"You look terrific, wow." Dupree took in the scene. Kelly's auburn hair and light green eyes were complemented perfectly by a pastel green wraparound dress. The hospital scrubs had hidden her small waist and overall terrific figure. She wore white sandals on her newly pedicured feet.

She took his hand. "I looked up the restaurant and they have both inside and outside dining. I wanted to fix my hair, in case we want to sit outside. It's a little cooler with my hair up."

"Well, you look simply amazing." Dupree placed his hand on the small of her back and directed her back into the apartment.

"Thank you, Cooper."

• • •

The restaurant was casual. Located on the bay in Mobile, they were seated with a family of four at a picnic-style table. Dupree and Kelly were in the "romantic corner" overlooking the bay and the Fish River Bridge.

Conversation was void of awkward pauses on the forty-five-minute trip to the restaurant.

Drinking iced tea and eating crackers with butter, they waited for their entrées.

"…and the poor little guy. Of all the things I have to do, putting an IV in a small child is the worst." The conversation moved to the work Kelly did earlier that day. "Anyway, he was so sick, he didn't even flinch when I stuck him."

Dupree's mind wandered back to Schultz.

If only he were sick, I could just…

"…and then I had to go back up to the hospice wing."

If Schultz was in a coma, you could just go in and swab his mouth and…

"They really only needed me to start the IV."

Dupree studied the water behind her.

She turned to see what he was concentrating on so intensely. "And then do you know what happened?"

If only there were some way to induce unconsciousness, I could…

"What?" he said, out of reflex.

"Well, then they asked me to go topless into old man Weston's room to see if it would jumpstart his pacemaker," she said, smiling. "So I went in there…"

"What?" Dupree suddenly snapped back into reality. He returned a smile as he leaned across the table and took her hands. "I'm so sorry. I'm being such a jerk?"

"No. No. What's on your mind?"

"I've just been thinking about the shooting. I'm remembering some details."

"Really?"

"To be honest, I have a hunch about who it was."

"Oh my God!" Kelly said. "Who is it?"

"It's just a hunch. I'm not 100 percent sure. But, it's driving me crazy. Gregor says I need to get DNA and I've been obsessing on how I could get a mouth swab or a cigarette butt or something." Dupree paused, shaking his head slowly. "I don't think the guy even smokes and I don't feel like sneaking around his garbage cans." His face went flush verbalizing Gregor's idiotic plan.

"I just thought if I could get DNA from the guy secretly, then I could take it to the cops. I could ask them to analyze it, and if it turned out to be a match, then I would tell them who it is."

"The cops have the DNA of the guy that shot you."

"Yes," Dupree said. "It's the same person who committed the Hargood murder."

"You're kidding me."

"No. He confessed it, before he shot me."

"Then you've got to tell them," Kelly said, squeezing his hands. "This is a very dangerous man."

"I can't."

"Why not?"

Dupree frowned. "It's a long story."

Earlier when he discussed the case with Detective Campbell, Dupree refused to tell her that he suspected Kenneth Schultz. Dupree couldn't put anyone through the same torture that he endured after Sarah's disappearance.

Detective Campbell verified that the tracks behind Dupree's house did contain traces of blood, but the sample was too degraded to make a match with the sample in the Hargood house.

Dupree couldn't place Schultz in the canal. He refused to risk bearing a false witness.

"We've got time," Kelly said, releasing his hands and buttering another cracker.

"When Sarah, my wife, went missing. I was the prime suspect," Dupree said. "I was falsely accused and the detectives were relentless. I was sick with grief. I couldn't eat, I couldn't sleep. And all the while, they followed me, they hounded me, they interrogated me for hours. And, the press…the press nearly killed me."

"It must have been awful," Kelly said, reaching across the table to take back his hands.

"It was a long time ago." Dupree said, smiling softly. "But, even if he is the guy, if there's a chance that I'm wrong, I can't do it."

A long pause followed as Dupree studied Kelly's beautiful face.

"Is it too much to ask?" Dupree asked, smiling and making exaggerated hand gestures. "To get DNA from a complete stranger?"

Kelly laughed. It was a good sign that she didn't respond with a hand in the air and the words, "Check, please."

They dropped the subject during dinner.

Sharing a single piece of cake, they both sipped coffees.

"I know how you can do it," Kelly said, out of the blue. She flashed a beautiful, mischievous smile.

"Do what?"

"Get the DNA."

"Kelly, I should have never…"

"I can take it for you." She smiled. "Here's what you do. Call him at work and say that you're from HR or from a generic drug screen laboratory and that he's been selected for a random drug screen. You said he works at the refinery."

"Well, not at the refinery, but out by the refinery."

"Oh, where does he work?"

"I think he works at Biotech Labs." Dupree leaned close to Kelly, shifting their conversation to a whisper.

"Okay, same thing," Kelly said. "They all have a random drug screen policy. Call him up, or I can do it, and tell him to go for a drug screen within the hour. We give him a fake address. He shows up. I'll be wearing my 'Kelly the good nurse' uniform, and I'll get a sample."

"But I thought they just need a urine sample for a drug screen," Dupree said.

"Apparently, Biotech Labs' drug screening is a little more extensive."

CHAPTER 32

Franky Stevens reached into the base of the lady palm planted outside his front door and fished for his keys. His grey T-shirt was saturated at the neck and underarms. He lifted the front of the shirt to wipe his face and arms.

The run tonight was the highlight of his day. A Communy Street AA meeting at seven a.m. ushered him into a day of sobriety. Memories of his date last night, haunted him throughout the day. He really wanted to call Janna.

"But you've got to wait three days," he said, mimicking Dale.

Franky and Dale ate lunch at a new Mexican restaurant. Dale made sure Franky understood the rules.

"You don't want to seem needy," Dale said.

"But I am needy."

"That makes it even worse."

Franky unlocked the front door and tossed his keys on the counter. He spent most of the afternoon cleaning his apartment. The place smelled like Clorox and soap scum remover. He grabbed a Gatorade from the refrigerator.

"Three days."

Franky rested his elbows on the table, looking at the Ziploc bag containing a handful of barnacles that he had scraped from the pier.

Grabbing the phone, he dialed a number he knew well.

"Singing River Hospital, how may I direct your call?"

"Admissions."

"One moment, please."

"Admissions, this is Brenda. Can I help you?"

"Yes, ma'am, this is Franky Stevens. I was wondering if you could do me a favor. The other day I assisted a man who was injured on Beach Boulevard. He scraped his arm and chest and…uh…he was hurt pretty bad on the pier. I was wondering if you could give me his name? I have his watch. It's a very expensive Rolex and I'm sure he wants it back."

"Did he go to the emergency room?"

"Yes," Franky said, guessing. "Or no, I mean, I'm not sure because we wrapped the arm, and that's the last I've seen of him. He might not even have gone to the hospital."

"Did you say it was scraped on a piling?"

Franky heard frantic typing on a keyboard.

"Yes, ma'am, on the pier on Beach Boulevard."

"At the public pier?"

"Yes."

"I have a report of someone coming in yesterday and the incident happened at the public pier. But, I'm not allowed to give you his or her name or any information on whether or not he or she was even hurt or received treatment."

"I understand." Franky sat back in the chair and studied the baggie of barnacles. "Was it a he?"

"I can't tell you."

"Really? Because I really would like to return his watch. Like I said, it's very expensive," Franky said.

"Well," Brenda said. "I can't really…I tell you what. I can give you his…or her…phone number, and you can work it out from there."

"Thanks," Franky said, writing down the number.

• • •

By the time Franky showered and changed into fresh clothes, it was eight p.m. For the first Saturday night in a thousand, he was completely sober and sat down to watch TV and eat a bowl of cereal. Watching *COPS,* Franky grabbed the phone and dialed the number.

"Hello?"

"Hello, this is Willard Stevens. I hate to be a bother, but I'm a lawyer here in town, and I've been doing some studies on public safety and health risks, and I was wondering if this is the person who was seen injuring himself on Beach Boulevard the other day."

"Excuse me?" the voice was cold. "Who did you say this is?"

"This is Willard Stevens. I'm an attorney. Who am I having the pleasure of talking with?"

"What is it you want?"

Franky took a quick bite of cereal and swallowed without making a noise into the phone. On the television, a police officer was straddling a prostitute and cuffing her; the camera angle forced them to fuzz out her crotch.

"I'm looking into cases involving the city when people are injured on public property, and I was wondering if I could interest you in completing a survey form, perhaps, or maybe coming by my office for a visit."

"I don't think so," the voice said. "How did you get my name? How is it you…"

"No, sir, I don't know your name. You haven't given it to me. What is your name sir?"

"How did you get my number?"

"Like I said," Franky's brain fired on all cylinders. "A person I know, who, I could tell you his name, although the odds of you knowing him would be strange, saw you get injured…and wanting to help…followed you to make sure you were okay and…"

"This is ridiculous!!" the voice raged.

Uh oh!

"Who is this again? What is your name?"

Franky hung up the phone.

"Some other time," he said, getting up to pour another bowl of cereal.

• • •

Franky's room was not dark enough; his sheets were too heavy, his pillow too firm. When he rolled over, his eyes would open slightly, and light from the street lamps outside would shoot into his brain. Squeezing his eyelids tight, he rolled over and punched his pillow a few times. Kicking off his sheets, he cursed the little red light emitting from the clock. When he turned it over on its face, it read two fifteen a.m.

Franky twisted, pulled the pillow around his head, and sat bolt upright.

At the door, the kiss, the perfect kiss haunted him.

With his eyes closed tight, Franky saw Janna. His hand combed her hair back from her beautiful round face as he held her head and kissed her slightly parted lips. He felt her shoulders and the small of her back and…

"Good God!"

Turning to the side of the bed, he flipped on a lamp. He squinted at the blinding light.

He fumbled through the nightstand drawers looking for something to distract his mind. Grabbing a few pamphlets of AA propaganda, he restlessly flipped through the material. It left him little to contemplate.

Franky tossed the literature back in the drawer and headed for the kitchen.

Sitting at the kitchen table, head in his hands, palms covering his eyes, a dreadful thought struck Franky. Opening his eyes wide, he instantly wakened with intense anxiety. A sharp pain throbbed in his chest.

"The car," Franky said, into the empty room. "The night at the casino."

A distant memory flashed in Franky's mind. Reaching up to his chest with his right hand, he massaged his left pectoral muscle. His left hand tingled.

"Why didn't you just drive my car home? Why get your wife involved?" Franky said. He dropped his head to the table.

Because that's Dale. He would have never left me without a car. He knew when I woke up I wouldn't remember anything and if my car was missing I would have freaked out.

A lump developed in his throat as he tried to speak.

"He took me home. He called his wife to come get him. In the middle of the night, Rosie had to come all the way across town because of me."

Dale never mentioned the work that he and his wife did to get Franky home that night.

Pain ran through Franky's heart; he shook his left hand vigorously. He experienced the hurt that he inflicted on others for years.

Dale was a perfect friend, and Franky constantly dumped on him. Eddie, Sandra, Mom, and Dad had taken the brunt of Franky's selfish actions.

Janna Sandler would just be the next victim in a long line of people Franky mistreated.

"Dale's wife for Christ's sake had to…get…out of bed…to pick him up."

Franky's eyes started to water with pain and grief. He rubbed them violently with the back of his right hand. He squeezed his left hand.

Thoughts returned to the bridge and the intervention. He let out a loud painful moan.

He laid his head on the table.

It was then that the image of Janna, stepping from the men's restroom in Castaways, flashed into his mind.

Without the chance meeting, Franky would be dead. If the train would have caught her, if he left the AA meeting at Communy Street three minutes later, any ten-minute delay in Janna's Monday morning routine and Willard "Franky" Stevens III would have been a goner.

It was too much to take; Franky felt as if he would explode.

For the first time in his life, he let go and allowed himself to hurt. He pounded the table with his fist and then placed his hands on his ears. He pressed against his temples to simulate a vice.

He allowed himself to experience real shame.

In the kitchen of his Longfellow apartment, he finally understood the hand he was dealt. Every lousy decision, every alcohol-induced stupor, every lie was absolutely necessary to bring him to a table that faced the men's room at Castaways.

The relationship with Janna might not work. But Janna was in his life now; fate had rescued him, and he was not going to question it.

Franky's limbs were numb, and his face was swollen and red.

It took thirty minutes to compose himself. He made a pot of coffee.

Sitting at the kitchen table, he vowed in earnest to never drink again. He was a miserable drunk; that part would never change. However, he could take it to heart and deal with it.

With the coffee pot gurgling, Franky fell into a light, fitful sleep with his head resting on the kitchen table.

CHAPTER 33

"Miss Sandler, where are you?" Kenneth Schultz asked as he circled the block for a third time. "I don't like this."

Janna Sandler's work truck was in the driveway. She had even put her garbage can out the night before. But, there was no movement in the house.

"Where on...ah ha," Schultz said, looking into the rearview mirror. "There you are!"

At seven o'clock in the morning, Schultz wanted to check on Janna, before his shift at Biotech Labs. He would not be able to swing by at lunch. Also, Brad was expecting a report by the end of the day. Schultz planned on working late just to make his boss squirm.

Maybe she can stop by my office.

"No, I think they use Orkin," Schultz said, to no one.

Making the block, he took up his roost in front of the abandoned house. Soon, he would need to find a new place to stake out Janna's house. Some of the neighbors might think Schultz was actually interested in purchasing the dump.

Before leaving his house, Schultz destroyed the video of Janna. He hated himself for watching it so many times over the weekend. The first few viewings were entertaining. But soon he was disturbed by Janna's antics.

"Locking the door? Was that necessary?"

Schultz's whole body shook with shame.

"She didn't have to respond like that...she has nothing to fear."

The video showed that after Janna closed the door, she deliberately locked it. Spraying the room, a loud bump at the door made her spin around and point the spray nozzle like a weapon toward the door.

The camera didn't pick up Schultz listening from outside the room. It didn't pick up his injured knee giving out and him falling into the door.

With his car parked and idling, Schultz turned red just thinking about the video.

What a fool.

He wanted a fresh start; he wanted new memories of Janna Sandler.

He grabbed his phone and dialed Bay Pest.

"Good morning, Bay Pest. How may I help you?"

"Good morning, this is Kenneth Schultz. I live at 908 Eastwood Street. I need you to come out and spray. My wife saw some bugs this weekend, and I'm really upset because we bought the Gold Plan and…"

"Yes, Mr. Schultz, I remember. Let's see, Mark has an opening at one thirty, will you…"

"No, Janna Sandler sold me the policy. She said she would come back if I saw any…"

"I understand, Mr. Schultz, but that is Mark's territory and…"

"I don't care!" Schultz said. "Miss Sandler is a friend of my wife's, and she sold me the gold plan, and I don't want Mark. I want Janna."

"Yes, sir. Let me see here. She has an opening at two thirty. Will that be…oh wait, I'm sorry, my supervisor just told me that Janna has called in sick. She won't be in today. Can I send Mark out at…"

Schultz hung up the phone, watching Janna Sandler leave her house.

She loaded her daughter into the car seat. Wearing a freshly pressed Bay Pest uniform, with her pretty blonde ponytail hanging out of the back of her ball cap, she drove off in her work truck.

• • •

With a heavy hand, Schultz punched the send button. His report was on its way through cyberspace. At the speed of light, it landed in Brad's inbox, ready for him to pooh-pooh all over it. It was not his best effort. Seeds were stupid.

The office was bustling for a Monday. Two coworkers had even talked to him this morning. Schultz sloughed them off by pretending to be totally into writing his report.

His desk phone rang.

"Schultz."

"Mr. Schultz, this is Ginger Martinez with ABC Laboratories. You have been randomly selected for a drug screening. I'm recording the time as eight forty-seven a.m. We have verified with your supervisor, Mr. Bradley Philagen, that your calendar is free for the next two hours. Is there any reason why you cannot report to our office within the next two hours to complete this randomly selected drug screening?"

"I suppose not," Schultz said, looking at his calendar. He had a meeting with a process improvement team at ten, but apparently Brad didn't mind if he missed it.

"Okay. We will see you at our offices at 4380 Hospital Road, suite 31, on or before ten forty-seven a.m."

"That's suite 31?" Schultz asked.

"Yes, sir."

Schultz hung up.

The office was loud. A few of his coworkers were talking about their weekend. Schultz opened the yellow pages on his cell phone and thought about searching for ABC Laboratories.

"Attorneys." Schultz typed instead. He scanned through the fifty-plus entries.

"There you are," Schultz said. "Willard 'Franky' Stevens III." He grabbed a Post-it note and wrote down the address.

Schultz removed his lab coat and hung it on the back of his chair. He had only two hours before his drug screen, and he had several errands to run.

• • •

As Schultz navigated the streets of Pascagoula, heading for Down-town Plaza, he wanted to make sure he swung by Janna's house.

Maybe she really is sick.

"She may have gotten ready for work, felt sick, called in, and took the baby to the nursery so she could sleep and relax."

Schultz thought of stopping by Jerry Lee's and picking up some chicken soup and crackers.

That would be a nice gesture.

Calmness overtook Schultz when leaving Biotech Labs. A three-hour respite from work was just what the doctor ordered. His hands rested gently on the steering wheel; the BMW stayed under the posted speed limit. However, the instant Schultz saw that Janna's truck was not parked in front of her house, he pounded the steering wheel.

"That lying bitch!"

Schultz hit the accelerator, trying to squeal the tires right by her house. He wished she was in front of him.

"I can't believe the lies!"

• • •

It was just like Biotech Labs to send employees to the filthiest and most unorganized medical clinic in Mississippi. Brad would get an earful when Schultz made it back to the office.

When Schultz walked into the doctor's plaza, located across the street from the hospital, he had forgotten the suite number of ABC Labora-tories. The huge foyer with a giant spiral staircase that wrapped around the elevator shaft in the center of the building was decorated with palms and cheap paintings. Schultz sensed that the public toilets needed cleaning as he searched the index of practices posted near the water cooler.

"Oh good gravy," Schultz said. ABC Laboratories was easy to find. There was a Post-it note that said "Suite 31—under construction." All drug screening was being conducted at the rear parking area.

Schultz exited the building and walked toward the trailer in the northeast corner of the parking lot. A piece of plywood, with ABC Labs stenciled in spray paint, was propped up beside the door.

"You have got to be kidding me."

Traversing 100 yards of the parking lot, Schultz became enraged at the injustice. Besides, he wasn't a drug addict; the nerve of testing him was beyond forgiveness. Schultz would lodge a formal complaint to HR for hiring such a shoddy outfit.

Stepping into the trailer, he took a seat in the only folding chair in the room. A table with a sign-in sheet was the only other piece of furniture.

As soon as Schultz began reading his phone, a commotion, from the rear of the trailer, rattled the walls. Schultz stood quickly.

The door burst open to the waiting area.

"Like, dude, this is totally bogus." A sandy-haired man was arguing with the nurse.

"Mr. Gregor, please leave, or you will force me to call security."

"But I didn't do nothing. Like I told you, I'm anemic, and I'm like not supposed to get a cut because I could bleed to death, and if you stick me with a needle…"

"Sir that's not anemia, that is hemophilia." The nurse led him toward the door.

"That's what I meant," Mr. Gregor said, as the nurse pushed him out of the door and slammed it behind him. She locked it quickly.

"Are you here for a drug screening?"

"Yes," Schultz said.

"Sign the board and come with me."

"What was that all about?"

"Oh, he was just taking exception to getting blood drawn. He thought it was just a urine test. Follow me."

Schultz entered the back of the trailer.

"You're taking blood?"

"Of course. Have a seat. Let me get your blood pressure." The nurse grabbed a cuff.

"When did that start?"

The nurse held up her finger to quiet Schultz. She dialed her phone. "Yes. We were not able to get a sample from your employee Gregor Madison. That's correct. No. No. He showed up, but he refused the blood sample. Yes sir. Thank you. You too." She hung up the phone. "So what were you saying?" she asked, placing the blood pressure cuff on Schultz's arm. "What happened to your arm?"

"I scraped it." Schultz said, taking a seat. "I was asking when did they start taking blood."

"A while back. It's a lot tougher to tamper with, and it saves you the embarrassment of having me actually watch you urinate in a cup."

"I see," Schultz said, as he watched the nurse grab a rubber tourniquet and wrap it around his arm.

• • •

Schultz drove past Downtown Plaza at ten miles an hour over the posted speed limit. He wanted to stop by and pay a visit to the ambulance chaser, Willard "Franky" Stevens III, but his patience with the ineptness of so-called professionals had run completely out. The nurse could have more easily drawn blood out of his eye than out of his arm.

Her hand shook, her lip perspired, and she stabbed him three times to find his vein.

Ridiculous!

The light at Ingalls Avenue turned yellow; Schultz hit the accelerator and ran it just as it turned red.

If he were pulled over by the police, he would run. A car chase through the streets of Pascagoula might allow him an opportunity to run over a few of the residents.

Pain struck Schultz's temples again.

Driving down Beach Boulevard, he passed the Hargood house and spit into the floorboard of his car.

Hargood was a joke. Everything's a joke.

Pulling into his driveway, Schultz parked the car and saw his wife standing at the back door with her hands on her hips.

Close the door, you stupid bitch!

Schultz was fed up with her wasting electricity; he was tired of all her crap.

• • •

Kenneth Schultz's hands were sticky. Drenched moments ago, now the red, warm liquid no longer dripped from his fingertips.

He pressed his thumb against his middle finger, trying to see if blood worked like super glue. It was not very adhesive.

Picking up the phone, he watched his fingers press the buttons. Little red fingerprints were left everywhere he touched.

His hand was still, calm. They shook so violently when he was at Hargood's. Now, a wave of peace swept over his entire body—even while he was swinging the vase, his heart rate never elevated. His breathing was steady and relaxed throughout the whole ordeal, except when he had to exert so much energy hoisting her up onto the bed.

As Schultz listened to the ringing on the other end of the line, he massaged his lower back with his free hand. He identified the scent of the hand that held the phone…it was metal, or meat. The phone was uncomfortable in his grip.

"Hello?"

"Hello, Peg? This is Kenneth," he said to his mother-in-law.

"Hey, what's going on? Is everything okay?"

"Yes, fine. I was just calling to see if you could pick up the kids, I thought…"

"Where's Michelle?"

"She's at Jerry Lee's. I was just about to say, we were really wanting to get out of town for a night, and well, I was wondering if you could pick up the kids from school and watch them for the night. You'd have to take them to school tomorrow."

"I don't know. I mean, let me talk to Michelle."

"I told you she's not here. She'll be back soon."

"Well, have her call me," Schultz's mother-in-law said.

"Never mind."

"No, wait, I didn't say I wouldn't do it. I just wanted to talk to Michelle."

"We're leaving as soon as she gets back."

"On a Monday? Where are you going?"

"To the casino. We'll stay the night at the Beau Rivage. We should be back by noon tomorrow, but you would have to take the kids to school."

"Sure, I'll pick them up. You know I will. What time are you getting back tomorrow?"

"Noon."

"Won't they need fresh clothes?"

"You have some for the baby don't you?"

"Yeah."

"Wash Michael's uniform or he can wear it again tomorrow."

"Okay, what's the rush? When are you getting back?"

"Noon," Schultz said.

"You can't be late. I've got bunko tomorrow night, and Bernie won't watch them by himself."

"I said we'll be back by noon."

"What's the rush?"

"Never mind, Peg. I just thought it would be nice for Michelle and I to get away for an evening. But, I'll get…"

"No, I'll do it. Have Michelle call me as soon as she gets back."

"Fine."

Schultz hung up the phone. He waited for a few seconds and smiled when Michelle's cellphone started ringing.

Michelle Schultz was in no shape to talk on the phone. Schultz was sure that her lover would be upset. He had called her several times already.

• • •

The bedroom was a mess. The carpet was cluttered with broken pictures that had been knocked off the dressers. Near Schultz's closet the digital recorder was smashed on the floor. The wall was scarred where the equipment was thrown against it in a fit of rage. Michelle was on the bed. A large gash ran across her forehead. She was unconscious.

Schultz took a seat in a rocking chair beside the bed. He listened to her breathing, coming in gasps, each one becoming more spastic.

Kenneth Schultz had grown a lot in the past fortnight.

He rocked forward and touched the right forearm of Michelle. It was limp and nearly lifeless. He would have tried to feel for a pulse, but his position in the chair was cutting into his abdomen. Instead, he rocked back and propped his feet on the bed, being careful not to kick Michelle.

Two weeks ago, Schultz would not have been so spontaneous. He would have been frantically trying to cover his tracks by mopping up blood, wrapping her body in a sheet, and other such nonsense.

Now he was at peace.

It was a much different peace than he had anticipated. It was not the freeing peace of forgiveness. He had never done anything that warranted forgiving. It was a peace steeped in awareness, in self-knowledge. Now his conscience, his self-awareness, had grown to the deepest form possible—nothingness.

The sun was setting. Shadows formed in the bedroom. Michelle was starting to convulse. Before today, this would have irritated Schultz. All the gurgling and coughing would have sent him into a rage. Now he was in control of his anger, his hatred.

Michelle stopped breathing. Blood trickled from the corner of her mouth. He thought briefly of covering her with a blanket.

The police would appreciate it.

CHAPTER 34

Janna was loading the dishwasher when her phone rang. She moved quickly to answer.

"Hello," she said, cradling the phone between her shoulder and ear and sweeping a mass of blonde hair out of her eyes. Traces of soap bubbles dripped from her hands onto the linoleum floor.

"Hello, Janna; it's Franky."

Janna pumped her fist and grabbed a towel from the counter. She wiped her hands and forehead.

"Hey, Franky, so nice of you to call." Dropping the towel on the floor, she wiped up suds with her foot. She took a seat on the floor next to Katie, who was playing quietly with her kitchen set. When Janna loaded the dishwasher, the two-year-old felt the urge to finish her kitchen chores.

"Well, I really wanted to just call and tell you what a great time I had Friday night, I…uh…I mean it really was great watching you do stand-up and the dinner and everything."

"It was nice, thank you for dinner," Janna said, trying to disguise the fact that she had been angry at the "three-day rule" since Saturday. "I wanted to call you yesterday and invite you over," Janna said, suddenly verbalizing a thought that should have been left inside her head. "…but church ran a little long and I had a lot of…well I was exhausted and blah, blah, blah. So how was your day?" She cut her losses.

"Fine."

An awkward pause followed.

"Janna."

"Yes, Franky?"

"I really wanted to call you earlier, but my friend told me to wait so I wouldn't seem desperate. Well…now that I'm finally talking to you…I think the next time I see him, I'm going to punch him in the mouth."

"Oh that's sweet, Franky," Janna said, smiling. She motioned for Katie to come sit on her lap. "I mean the part about you wanting to call earlier…not the punching in the mouth part."

"I understand," Franky said. "Hey, I was wondering, if you're not busy, maybe I could take you and Katie to dinner."

"Tonight? Oh, I'm sorry; we just ate. Besides, she's about to zonk out any minute now—but we're free tomorrow night. Is that okay?"

"Sure, tomorrow's good."

"Franky," Janna patted her daughter's leg. Katie's head rested on her mommy's chest. She was slowly fading away. "Uh, would you like to come over tonight? Maybe for a cup of coffee, later, around, say, nine?"

"Nine o'clock? Sure, that would be perfect. I'll bring a pie."

Janna started laughing.

"You do that. Bring an apple pie; I've got vanilla ice cream that is just dying for a little company."

• • •

Janna smiled during the entire thirty minute phone conversation.

"Let's go, sweetie," she whispered as she gently lifted Katie. The child fell asleep as if she had no bones in her body and lay in a warm, twisted mass of limbs in Janna's lap. Both of Janna's legs had fallen asleep. Carefully standing, she held the child tight to her chest, shaking out one leg at a time as she walked to the bedroom.

She brushed the hair from Katie's face as she placed her in the crib. Leaning over to kiss her on the cheek, she held the rails of the crib for support.

She jumped when a popping sound came from the back of the house.

The sun was still throwing the last of its light into the room. Janna stood perfectly still listening for another sound. Katie's breathing was slow and methodical. A car drove down Polk Street; it needed a new muffler. Janna heard everything within a one-mile radius—cheers from the Twelfth Street softball fields, a wasp bumping along the window in the living room, the icemaker in the kitchen freezing another tray of water.

She waited forever for another pop.

Shifting her weight silently from one foot to the other, time slipped. The sun hoarded its scraps of light, saving them for another time, and Janna now stood in complete darkness. Sticking her head into the hall, she looked toward her bedroom—nothing. She stepped quickly into the den, grabbed her phone, and dialed.

"Hey, Janna. What's up?"

"Hey, Kelly, nothing. Where are you?"

"At home, just chilling. Why? What's wrong? Are you all right?"

"Yeah, I'm fine. I just put Katie to bed, and my imagination is running away with me. I thought I heard a sound in the back of the house but…"

"What kind of sound?"

"A popping sound…like maybe a window popping in or something."

"Grab Katie and get out. Walk over to Mr. Pat's."

"I don't know. It was like twenty minutes ago," Janna said, trying not to allow her paranoia to frighten Kelly. "It was really nothing. I guess I just wanted a reason to call you."

"Janna, get Katie and get out. I'll come by in a little while, and we'll go do something."

"That's not necessary. I've got to go," Janna hung up the phone.

Sitting forward on the chair, she placed her hands on her head.

The phone rang. It was Kelly calling back. Janna pushed the 'answer' button.

"Don't answer that."

Janna shrieked. Jumping from her seat, she spun, frantically waving her arms. She threw her phone at the face of the masked man, striking him in the eye.

"Ahhh!" she screamed. Lunging forward, driving with her legs, she lowered her shoulder.

The intruder was between her and her child. She landed her shoulder in his abdomen and grabbed around his waist. Pushing, pushing, the wall stopped her momentum. Lifting her chin, she smashed the crown of her head into his face, twisting her head, pressing it deeper into his mouth and nose.

Screaming her lungs out, she kicked her knee into the thigh of the attacker, trying to drag him to the floor. She didn't see the gun.

Using her weight, she fell toward the floor, pulling the man toward the hall. He landed with his full weight on top of her. She swung madly with both fists, landing them on the side of his head.

"Janna! Janna!" A voice from the phone was yelling.

One more blow to the face, and then, darkness.

Janna managed to knock the breath from the intruder and land a few blows, but it took only one strike of the butt of the pistol on the back of Janna's head to knock her out cold.

CHAPTER 35

Pastor Dupree fell into his couch, holding his side and clutching a little vial of blood—Schultz's blood. The highs and lows of the day rattled around in his head as he allowed the painkillers to work their magic.

Pulling a blanket over his torso, the room began to buzz with cool light coming in from the setting sun. He pushed the recovery of his abdomen too hard with the walk through the bayou behind his house. The packet of bloodstained dirt was the last in a series of evidence he collected throughout the day.

Schultz was guilty. It was Schultz who murdered Hargood. It was Schultz with his thin hands and his icy blue eyes that shot Dupree.

"And I've got all the pieces."

The pain in his side was subsiding. The room thumped to the beat of his heart. His teeth began to tickle a little bit as he ran his tongue across the front of his smile.

Dupree rolled the vial of Schultz's blood through his fingertips.

Earlier in the day, Dupree wrote a detailed description of his own attacker—voice, mannerisms, eyes, fingernails, etc. He outlined Schultz's motive in the murder of Hargood. He also explained the serendipitous visit of Schultz at Christ Church when Dupree preached on Revelation, giving Schultz a motive to shoot Dupree.

Only one question in Dupree's mind remained unanswered: Why did Schultz position the body with the hands directly above his head rather than spread out like a real cross?

Dupree fell back into the couch, his head spinning. A euphoric feeling buzzed around his temples. His side no longer hurt.

"Theory one," he said aloud. He held one finger toward the ceiling. "He only had two spikes," he said, adding a finger to his count.

Maybe he just ran out of time.

"But why go to so much trouble and not do it correctly?"

One last visit to the Hargood's house could provide the answer.

Breathing heavily, he rolled to his side and grabbed the cellphone sitting on the edge of his ottoman. He dialed Detective Campbell.

"Hello, pastor."

"Hey, detective."

"I'm glad you called," Detective Campbell said. "How are you feeling?"

"Good. I'm really good. Hey, I was wondering, could we swing by the crime scene?" Dupree asked, sitting up. He blinked wildly trying to get his eyes to stop thumping.

"Wow. News travels fast."

"I guess."

"I was just about to call you, to see if you could come up with anything."

"Well, I'll do what I can." Dupree opened one eye at a time in an attempt to focus.

"That's all I can ask. I can be there in about fifteen minutes." Detective Campbell hung up.

Dupree stood and caught his balance.

"Detective, can you make it thirty? I need to get a shower."

He walked to the kitchen, placing his phone on the counter.

He grabbed the bottle of pain-killers. "Just one more Coop," he said, shaking another pill into his hand.

• • •

Dupree walked out to the police cruiser carrying a computer case filled with evidence that would put Kenneth Schultz in prison for the rest of his life. The pastor/detective shaved and put on fresh clothes. He had all intentions of turning in Schultz on his way to the Hargood house. He wasn't sure if they would allow him in the police interrogation room. But if they did, he wanted to look his best on the film.

"Hey, detective," he said, sitting beside Detective Campbell. "Long day, huh?"

"It's been awful. Waiting on you isn't making it any better."

Dupree put on his seat belt and placed the bag on the floor between his feet.

"Were you waiting long?"

"Never mind. What's the computer for?" Detective Campbell asked.

"It's not a computer. I'm just using the case to carry some things."

He paused. Detective Campbell pulled away from the curb.

"I think I know who killed Jerry Hargood and who shot me."

"Really?" Detective Campbell looked at Dupree. "We do too."

"Seriously? Is it who I think it is?"

Detective Campbell turned right onto Washington Avenue. "Probably. Kenneth Schultz?"

"Jeez," Dupree said, astounded. "That's it! That's incredible. Have you picked him up?"

"We don't know where he is."

They turned left onto Eastwood Street.

"Are you staking out his house?"

"No," Detective Campbell gave Dupree an inquisitive look.

"Then why are you going this way? He lives right up there."

"I thought you knew," Detective Campbell said.

"Knew what?"

"Didn't you say you wanted to go by the crime scene?"

"Sure," Dupree said. "But we don't really have to now. Why are…"

They started slowing down as they approached Schultz's house.

"What crime scene are you talking about?" Detective Campbell glanced over.

"The Hargood house."

"Then you haven't heard?"

"Heard what? What?"

"There's a new crime scene."

Dupree's heart sank when she stopped in front of the Schultz's house. Crime scene tape crisscrossed the front door.

"No."

"I'm sorry," Detective Campbell said.

Dupree had been to a few gruesome crime scenes, but never one with small children. A picture of Schultz holding his two-year-old daughter in one arm and patting his son on the head on the steps to Christ Church flashed in his mind. He wasn't sure he could handle it.

"Did you know Michelle Schultz?"

"No, I never met her. I just met him and the two babies, Michael and…" Dupree paused, trying to remember. "Ashley, Allison…"

"Amber."

"Yes, I met them at church a couple Sundays ago."

"Well, the children are fine; they're with the grandparents."

"Oh thank God!" Dupree interrupted.

"But Michelle…it's not good. You'll see." They pulled up into the driveway. The same yellow crime scene tape was wrapped around the entire back of the house.

"It's that bad?"

"Yes."

Detective Campbell and Dupree entered the side door and were hit with a noxious odor. The body had not yet been removed.

"It only gets worse as you go that way," Detective Campbell said, trying to speak and breathe through her mouth.

Every light in the house was on as crime scene investigators milled about looking for evidence. The décor of the living room included portraits of the children, functional kid-proof furniture, an archaic television, and accessories from Pottery Barn.

"The crime scene is actually in the bedroom." Detective Campbell said.

"Just a moment." Dupree dropped to one knee and said a silent prayer for the victims of the crime, the family, the children, and Michelle. A few minutes elapsed until, by the Spirit, he was moved to say "amen" and open his eyes.

He was staring directly at a stuffed fish. Tucked away in the corner of the room, nestled beside a dominating bookcase, a little bass hung mounted on a plaque.

"I will make you fishers of men."

"Jesus's calling of Peter," Dupree said.

"Excuse me?" Detective Campbell asked.

"Nothing, I was thinking of something Schultz said to me, right before he shot me."

"You're sure Kenneth Schultz is the one that shot you?"

"That's what I was calling you about," Dupree said, standing slowly. He held his side with both hands. "I suspected it a few days ago. I was able to verify it this morning. Anyway, looking at that stuffed fish I remembered he quoted Jesus saying 'I will make you fishers of men'. He's a fisherman. Schultz is a fisherman, that's all."

• • •

Spending only a few minutes in the Schultz's house, Dupree realized that Kenneth Schultz, in a fit of jealous rage, cracked his wife's head open with a vase. Dupree spent as little time as possible inside. The case was closed, and as soon as they found Schultz, Dupree could go back to pastoring Christ Church without all the distractions that come from investigating crimes and being shot.

Stepping outside, Dupree was met with a welcome blast of warm, August air. The police had intentionally turned the air conditioning in the house to sub-arctic levels to preserve evidence and reduce the smell.

"Hey! Detective Campbell!" he yelled back into the house. "I'm going to walk home."

"Okay. I'll call you tomorrow to go over the case."

"Sounds good. I'm leaving the bag in your car. Is that all right?"

"Sure. Good night."

Dupree left the Schultz house on foot and headed toward the seawall. Pascagoula was dark, quiet. At the seawall he turned right, away from his house; the water was calm and reflective. A sense of separation washed over him. He had missed his dance lesson last Friday; Mrs. Frisk never even called. The image of Michelle Schultz lying dead, cold, covered in blood, flashed in his mind; Dupree's side started hurting again. He walked with determined steps toward the shipyard. The moon was just above the horizon and reflecting off the surface of the Mississippi Sound. Dupree's eyes picked up the light, invoking an uneasy feeling. An enormous gantry crane hoisted metal onto the deck of a navy cruiser sitting in dry dock. Dupree studied the silhouette of the ship as he picked up the pace of his walk.

"How do they start building something like that?" he asked himself.

They built a great ship by placing two pieces of sheet metal together and striking an arc. A craftsman, in a shop nowhere near the water, took two pieces of metal (that on their own would sink like a stone) and connected them with material that would also sink. Then another piece would be attached. Eventually, a giant rust-covered hull emerged, matching to scale the model outlined on the blueprint that was unrolled in the dock foreman's office.

Dupree stopped and turned back east. It was time to build his own great ship.

Sarah was gone, forever.

Tomorrow, from his office at Christ Church, Dupree would call Kelly Mitchell and see if she was free for a second date.

• • •

Dupree was only a few strides from his house when his cellphone rang. It was Kelly Mitchell. He took a seat on the front porch.

"Hello."

"Cooper, oh my God, Coop you've got to get here quickly. Janna's gone. She's missing and the police are here, and Cooper, I need someone to…"

"Kelly, Kelly, slow down," Dupree said, jumping to his feet. He started fumbling for his car keys. "Where are you? Are you all right?"

"Yes, I'm at Janna's house, my best friend, Janna Sandler. She's gone, and I need you to come help me. I think it was Schultz. The guy we got the blood from, I think it was him. Oh my God, I never realized…"

"Schultz! Is he there? Where are you, Kelly?"

"I'm at Janna Sandler's house, and the police are here, and can you get here as soon as possible? Please."

"Of course. Where is it?"

"It's on the corner of Tenth Street and Polk about two blocks north of Jerry Lee's. Do you know where that is?"

Dupree was running toward his car. He was only a mile from Jerry Lee's. "I'm getting in my car now. I can be there in a minute. What's going on?"

Kelly was speaking as if she were in tears. "Janna called me and she was scared, and when she hung up I called back and I heard a struggle. Oh my God, I got here as soon as I could, and the front door was wide open and the baby was asleep in bed. She was here all by herself, and there's blood in the dining room. Oh, Cooper, there's blood in the dining room. Please get here quick."

"Kelly, I'm on Belair now. I'm almost there. Who is Janna?"

"Janna's my best friend. She's my very best friend, and, Cooper, she's gone."

"Stay on the line, Kelly. I'm turning onto Ingalls Avenue now."

• • •

The little house on the corner of Tenth Street and Polk was surrounded by police cars. Dupree parked as close as possible. Kelly bolted from the front door, when she saw his car.

"Oh my God, Cooper. She's gone. He's taken her."

"Easy, Kelly, easy. It's going to be all right," he said, holding her tightly and scanning the scene behind her. The police officers in the house were walking around quietly, talking in whispers.

"I'm so glad you're here. Katie was all alone and I just died when I thought she was hurt, but she's fine and I…"

"Katie is the baby?"

"Yes, she's still asleep inside."

Dupree pulled himself away from the embrace. Kelly's eyes were puffy and red; mascara ran down the side of her face. He brushed her hair behind her ears and used his thumb to wipe off some of the makeup.

"We'll find Janna," Dupree said. "Believe me, if it's Schultz, we'll find her." He took her hands and gave them a gentle squeeze. "What makes you think it was Schultz?"

"I finally put it all together," Kelly said, pulling him back into an embrace. "Janna had to go to the Schultz house to spray, and he's been stalking her or something and then this morning…"

Kelly started crying.

"It was him all right—Schultz. I just never realized the guy we got the blood from was the same one that had been giving Janna such a hard time."

"It's okay, Kelly. We'll find her."

"I don't know, Cooper," Kelly said, pulling him tighter. A long pause followed. "I called you because I need your help."

"What is it?"

"I need you to call the guy she's been seeing and give him the news. I can't do it," she said. "If the police contact him, they'll treat him like he did it or something. Can you call him?"

"Sure. What's his name?"

"Franky Stevens."

CHAPTER 36

Franky Stevens walked past the beer cooler at Jerry Lee's for the first time in his life without looking like a kid in a candy store. Although sometimes he would just walk at full speed and grab a twelve-pack without breaking stride, nights like tonight, when he had extra time to kill, he would study and smack his lips and agonize over picking the perfect beer. But those days were long gone; the beer cooler was no longer a comfort.

The only solace that it would provide tonight was to cool him off as he walked toward the bakery.

He promised Janna an apple pie, and that's exactly what he would deliver.

The bakery, located on the back wall of the store, smelled like barbecued chicken, having been located next to the deli. The pies, baked earlier in the day, were assorted and stacked on a table in the middle of the aisle. With the same persistence he took with choosing between lager and pilsner, he studied crumb topping versus lattice.

Carrying the pie back to the registers, he checked his look in the mirrors behind the meat counters. His face was getting tan, and his eyes were much clearer, reflecting the deep blue off his shirt. His stride was confident; Franky was no longer ashamed of his purchases. He smiled at the cashier as she rang up the pie and the pack of breath mints he grabbed at the last second.

"Hot date tonight?" the cashier asked. "That'll be six dollars and forty-two cents." She was in her mid-thirties, not very attractive, but she had a mischievous smile. She bagged the pie.

"Uh...well," Franky said, caught off guard. "Yes."

"I thought so. You smell really good, and you're buying mints."

"That's observant."

"Actually, not really," she said, handing Franky his change. "I pretty much guess the same thing with everyone who buys Certs. Have a great evening."

Franky smiled as he grabbed the bag and headed for the door. His cellphone started vibrating in his pocket. The number was not familiar.

"Hello?" Franky said, stepping into the heat of the parking lot.

"Uh. Is this Franky Stevens?"

"Yeah. Who's speaking?"

"This is Cooper Dupree. I've got some bad news I need to give you concerning Janna Sandler."

"Janna?' Franky said. He stopped in the middle of the parking lot. "What about Janna?"

"She's missing."

"Missing? What do you mean—missing? I just talked to her an hour ago. I'm on my way to her house right now," Franky said. He took off in a sprint to his car. "I'm two blocks away."

"We're at the house now. Come meet us."

Franky jumped into his car, throwing the pie into the passenger seat.

"What about Katie?"

"Katie is here. We don't..."

"Without Janna? She would never..."

"Franky! We're outside of her house by the street. It's me and her friend Kelly."

"What are all the cops doing there?" Franky said, in reaction to turning onto Tenth Street.

"The police are here. They're investigating."

"Investigating what?"

"Franky, Janna's been kidnapped. She's been taken," Dupree said.

"Oh my God, no," Franky said, screeching to a stop a few hundred feet from Janna's house. He jumped from the car and took off in a sprint toward the police barricade. A redhead was moving toward him, holding her hands up. Behind her was a clergyman on a cellphone. Breathless, panicked, Franky ran past them, blocking the redhead with a sweep of his arm. Two strides later, he was tackled onto the front lawn from behind.

"Franky!" the preacher yelled, pinning him to the ground. Franky's face was pushed into the grass. He struggled under the man's weight.

"Enough, you two!" A police officer pulled the preacher off Franky as another pulled Franky to his feet.

"It's okay. He's a friend of Janna," the preacher said, to the cops. "I'm Cooper Dupree," he said, turning his attention to Franky. "This is Kelly, Janna's best friend. Katie's inside sleeping. The police are looking for a man named Schultz."

Franky breathed heavily, trying to catch his breath. He bent over, wanting to vomit.

"Schultz?" Franky said, heaving. "Schultz is the…he's the guy that's been calling her…always wanting her to spray his house. Oh God, that's the creep that…"

"You're the boyfriend?" A lady asked, walking up to the group. She wore a PPD polo shirt and a holstered gun.

"Detective Campbell," Dupree said. "This is Franky Stevens."

The lights of the squad cars continued to light the scene.

"Mr. Stevens, I'm going to need to ask you a few questions."

CHAPTER 37

Kenneth Schultz's desk at Biotech Labs was clean and orderly. Although it was customary to give a two-week notice, Brad would understand that circumstances didn't allow for a proper turnover. Schultz needed to leave town now. The unread memos and documents were stacked neatly in piles. Pencils and pens were aligned next to the phone. He grabbed the box he had been packing and headed toward the exit.

"Where you off to?"

Schultz jumped, caught off guard by an unfamiliar voice. A janitor was walking toward him carrying an industrial-size garbage bag. He bent over to grab Schultz's wastepaper basket filled to the brim with discarded documents.

"Home," Schultz said, frowning at the man for frightening him.

"You quitting or something?" The man emptied the contents into the large green garbage bag.

"No," Schultz started toward the exit again.

"Looks to me like you're quitting."

"Well, I'm not. Goodnight."

"Goodnight, Mr. Schultz."

Schultz tucked the box under one arm. Grabbing his badge from his lab coat pocket, he swiped it across the scanner and heard the familiar *beep*. He hurried through the parking lot, trying to dodge the circles of light thrown from lamps thirty feet above his head.

"Okay, all that's left is to…crap! The recording!"

Schultz dropped the box next to his car and headed back toward his desk. He had forgotten to download a copy of the recording.

• • •

Although the lighting was poor quality, the camera angle had been perfect.

If there were another opportunity to shoot the scene, Schultz would have installed additional lighting and turned off the audio—the incessant moaning and gasping on the tape was a distraction. The images of his wife flopping around on the bed and doing unmentionables with another man were actually entertaining. But the constant "that's it baby, oh yeah, that's it," made Schultz want to smash his head into the television screen.

It was the sound that drew Michelle into the bedroom to see what Schultz was watching. He could have been more discreet. But he wanted Michelle to see his new motion picture.

"What on earth are you watching?" Michelle asked, walking into the bedroom. "I told you I won't allow pornography in this house. It's disgusting."

About that time she recognized the voices.

"Michelle, how could you?" Schultz wanted to ask with big crocodile tears falling from his face. "I am so…so…please, what's my line?"

"Jealous and hurt," the director would have said.

Instead, the scene played out much differently. Michelle went into shock at seeing the images on the screen. Schultz was silent. Enraged, Michelle found the video equipment, ripped it out of the wall, and threw it at Schultz. He blocked it with his good arm. When she turned her back to jerk more equipment from the closet, Schultz smashed her head with the base of a crystal vase. When she spun to face her husband, he hit her once more across the forehead, shattering the vase.

"Cut!" the director would have shouted. "We must do the scene all over again!"

But Schultz had only one wife.

The footage would have to suffice.

• • •

Schultz finished transferring the file and shoved the jump drive deep into his pocket. If he were to make any headway with Janna Sandler, she would want to know why Schultz and his wife were separated. The recording was proof that Michelle was unfaithful and that Janna could trust him.

"Back so soon?"

Schultz jumped. The janitor had snuck up on him again.

"Why do you keep doing that?" Schultz said, raising his voice. "I forgot something. Now go scrub a toilet or something before I report you to your…what is your name?"

"Grady. What's yours?"

"Schultz," Schultz said, flying into a rage. "You know that! Now scram, before I call security."

"Call 'em. See if I care. They're the ones that just called and asked me if you were still up here. I told 'em you left. But now…"

"What?" Blood rushed from Schultz's face.

"They're looking for you. Security is. They told me that they need to get your badge."

"You're insane. Now get out of my way." Schultz pushed Grady aside. "I'm calling your supervisor first thing in the morning."

Schultz ran toward the exit, pulling his badge from his pocket. He swiped it across the card reader and pushed on the door.

Locked.

He swiped it again and a third time.

"Come on! Come on you…"

The reader never beeped.

Grabbing a fire extinguisher, he rammed the glass door, shattering an enormous hole through the center. Alarms sounded. Schultz used the extinguisher to clear glass away and climbed through. He sprinted toward his car.

"Schultz! Stop!"

Grady the janitor was in pursuit.

"Schultz!"

Thirty seconds later, out of breath and sweating profusely, he jumped into his car and locked the doors. He fumbled with his keys.

"Come on, come on, Schultz!"

The box of personal items was by the trunk.

"Forget it."

He didn't risk getting out of the car to grab it.

"Schultz!" Grady was banging on the driver's door; he was trying to smash in the window with his fists.

Schultz cranked the car and jammed it into drive.

"Security Five, this is Williams. He's in the east parking area, near Biotech Labs Post Three! Biotech Labs Post Three!"

Punching the accelerator, the tires skidded as the silver BMW started hopping toward the exit.

"Let's go. Let's go," Schultz said, over and over again to his car.

Schultz briefly entertained the idea of turning back around and slamming Grady into another car, but there was little doubt that the police were on the way. Besides, he didn't have time for that. There was no telling how long Janna Sandler would remain unconscious.

CHAPTER 38

Janna Sandler opened her eyes very slowly; she was blind. Pain shot from the base of her skull into her jaws. Blinking wildly brought more darkness. She screamed. Unable to open her mouth, the sound remained captured in her throat. Breathing frantically through her nose, her nostrils flared.

Memories returned at the speed of light. She was attacked.

Katie!

She screamed again, stretching her lips to free them from the tape that bound them. Her head was exploding with pressure. A tiny dot of light appeared. Her eyes focused on the dot, a star perhaps, a million miles away.

Her eyes watered. Her nostrils spewed snot as she breathed frantically.

Entombed in darkness, with only a tiny beacon of light guiding her, she wiggled her hips. Her hands were bound in front of her.

You've got to get Katie.

She was attacked. He wore a mask. She fought.

If he's got Katie. Then he's got both of you. Be calm. Be calm.

Her breathing slowed. Keeping her eyes on the tiny dot of light.

Be calm.

Images of Katie, her parents, Kelly, and…Franky…flashed through the darkness. The back of her head throbbed and the images bounced with every beat of her heart, slowing, slowing.

She was lying on her side, with her legs curled behind her and bound at the ankles. She reached her hands up to her face and wiped her nose. Using a thumb nail, she gently, removed tape from her bottom lip. Moving her hands in all directions, she recognized that she was hemmed in. Rolling was impossible. She was entrapped.

Another dot of light appeared near her feet. She blinked wildly. She was not blind; she was in the base of a closet. However, the smell of gasoline and rubber, or asphalt, was strong. The heat made her think that she was in a shed.

Out of the complete silence, footsteps slapping the ground, faint at first, grew louder and louder.

She started to scream. She bit her lip instead. Her breath stayed calm, steady.

Keys jangled and then were pushed into a lock. A car door slammed and shook her entire body.

She was in the trunk of a car.

"Schultz!"

"Come on, come on."

It was Kenneth Schultz's voice. She was in the trunk of his car.

"Biotech Labs Post Three."

Someone named Williams was trying to get Schultz. They were in the parking lot at Biotech Labs.

The car skidded off. The trunk filled with noise and smoke. Janna was thrown forward onto her hands; her knees jammed into something hard.

She muffled a scream.

He worked at Biotech Labs. His wife said in agriculture at Biotech Labs.

Janna leveled her weight. She assumed that she was facing the rear of the car when the door was slammed behind her.

Biotech Labs is on Hwy 611.

She was thrown toward her head as the car practically went up on two wheels to make a turn.

Calm, Janna, calm, calm, he's turned right. He's going north on 611.

Janna closed her eyes tight. The roads in Bayou Cassotte flashed in the darkness. She knew every street in every town south of Interstate 10. She began counting.

"One Mississippi, two Mississippi..."

Her head was slammed into the rear-quarter panel again. Schultz slammed on the brakes, then threw the car into a hard right.

At forty-five seconds. Old Creosote Road.

She was thrown forward, toward the rear of the car, as Schultz smashed the accelerator. After 75 seconds, Schultz broke hard, made another hard right. Janna was illuminated in bright red.

60 seconds is a mile. We're on Parker Road South. One Mississippi, two Mississippi...

Janna braced for acceleration. Schultz shut off all the lights. Janna was once again engulfed in darkness. The car continued to move. From the level of the road noise, she guessed he was going about thirty miles per hour.

Five minutes later, at 300 counts, Janna felt the car take another right.

Roy's Fishing Camp.

They made several turns within seconds of one another. At one point Janna was sure Schultz had made a complete circle. The car finally stopped after traveling forty-five seconds on a gravel road.

Schultz cursed as he got out of the car. He popped the trunk.

"Okay, Miss Sandler, time to wake up," Schultz said. He began shaking Janna. She didn't respond. He felt her neck for a pulse. Janna held back wincing from the pain.

"Let's get you inside where it's a little cooler," he said, bending over. He tugged on her arms; Janna assisted slightly without being detected. From her calculations, she was fifteen minutes from the Biotech Labs parking lot.

"Upsy, daisy," Schultz said, with a final lift. Janna flopped over his shoulder. Her legs were numb and began tingling as blood regained a flow back to her feet.

She took a quick peek - a single room camp with a window unit air conditioner, two kayaks chained to the back awning post, a red Weber kettle grill.

Somewhere at Roy's.

Schultz kicked open the door and dropped Janna onto the bed. She laid quiet, eyes gently closed, pulse calm.

"Good night, Elizabeth," Schultz said. He gently brushed the hair out of Janna's eyes. "I'm sorry for the last time. It won't happen again. I promise."

Janna remained perfectly still as Schultz began gently kissing her mouth. Motionless, calm, she said a prayer of thanks for not ripping off the tape.

"I love you, Lizzy," he said. He rolled off the bed. He unbuttoned his shirt. "And I know you love me. Things will be different this time."

• • •

Schultz stripped to his underwear. He checked the tie wraps around Janna's hands and ankles. Covering her with a blanket, he fell asleep facing her on top of the covers.

Janna kept watch with her eyes open in slits. Thirty minutes passed, when, with a grunt, he rolled over. With his back to her, Janna slowly raised her hands above his head. With one quick, smooth movement, she could slide her hands down the sides of his head and strangle him to death with the tie wraps.

A lump rose in her throat. She wanted to scream. Her hands shook violently. She slowly lowered her hands and placed them under her chin.

Using her thumb, she slowly removed the tape from her mouth.

"Kenneth." She gently nudged Schultz. "Kenneth, you need to wake up. We need to talk."

"We'll talk in the morning."

She nudged him more aggressively.

"Kenneth."

He jerked from sleep. Jumping out of bed, addled, he looked down at Janna.

"Kenneth," Janna said, firmly. She rolled up to a seated position, holding her knees with her hands. "I'm not Elizabeth. I'm not Lizzy! Look at me. Kenneth, please just look at me."

Schultz turned toward the window, confused, perhaps still asleep.

"Kenneth, I'm not Elizabeth."

He turned toward Janna. His eyes were darker; his lips were pursed and quivering.

Janna kept a stern expression. She brushed a mass of blonde hair from her eyes with her hands. Schultz's right eye twitched. His loss was evident. He was reliving a traumatic experience.

"Kenneth, Elizabeth is dead," she said, gambling with every word. "She's been dead for some time now. Come here. Please. I want you to hold my hand for a second." Janna lifted her hands toward him, palms down in a sign of submission. Schultz was an animal and could turn at any moment.

Schultz dropped his eyes to the floor and stood motionless for a very long time. Janna's arms began to burn; she refused to drop them and ruin the invitation. Schultz shook his head a few times. He wiped his eyes with the back of his hand. Walking toward Janna, he reached out and touched her fingers.

"You see, Kenneth, I'm not Elizabeth. My hands are warm," she said in a soft but firm voice. She read Schultz's face. She could sense the guilt and pain. "Elizabeth is dead. I know you had something to do with that, but that was a long time ago."

She curled her fingers in, giving Schultz a slight squeeze with her middle finger. She waited a long time before speaking.

"This won't end the same way, Kenneth."

Looking up with his dark, lifeless eyes, he saw Janna smiling. Her expression displayed compassion, her eyes soft and sisterly. "It can't end the same way."

"How do you know, Janna?" Schultz said, dropping his hands to his side and walking back toward the window.

"Because Elizabeth loved you," she said, allowing her words to trail off. "…and I don't."

"You might…with time."

"No, Kenneth, I won't. I love someone else."

"Who?"

"That doesn't matter. The fact is Elizabeth and I are much different," Janna said. "You can't redo the past…but you can change the future. You can do the right thing."

Schultz turned his stare back toward Janna. "And what is the right thing, Miss Sandler?" An evil smile flashed across his face.

Fear struck Janna's heart; she wanted to blurt out, "Let me go! Let me go home to my daughter! Free me!" But something deep inside told her this was not the moment to be selfish. Her response, her advice to Schultz had to be what was right for him. A prayer circled back through her mind. Her heart warmed, and her smile grew even larger.

"In a word Kenneth…repent."

"Ah, Miss Sandler." Schultz turned back toward the window. "Repent."

He stared out the window for an eternity. Janna remained perfectly still.

"I'm afraid it's too late for that."

Schultz reached into his pocket and pulled out a cellular phone. He grabbed a knife from the table.

Janna's heart sank. A lump formed in her throat, preparing to scream. She kept her eyes on Schultz as he walked slowly toward her.

"Give me your hands."

Janna raised her hands toward him and in a quick move he cut the tie wrap that bound them together. He handed her the phone.

"Would you like to make a call?" He took a seat beside her on the bed.

Janna's mind raced for the correct answer.

Call the police! Call Mom and Dad! Call 911!

She stared at the phone for a moment.

"So, would you?"

"No, thank you," Janna said, attempting to hand the phone back.

"Go ahead, make a call," he said, standing quickly. "Just one and make it quick." Walking a few steps, he removed a small handgun from his front pocket and took a seat on a little stool by the door. Crossing one leg over the other, he rested the gun on his knee. "By the way, are you going to call the one you love?"

"I don't know his number."

"Why not?"

"It's in my phone. I never memorized it."

"Doesn't sound much like love. What's his name?"

Janna remained silent.

"Never mind. Just make it brief. You've got two minutes," Schultz said, waving the gun slightly with his wrist.

CHAPTER 39

Pastor Dupree let out an audible grunt and awoke quickly, grabbing his stomach in pain. His hands were soaked in blood. In a nightmare, Schultz had walked in on him and Kelly and ran a knife right through his abdomen.

He let out a sigh of relief, rubbing his hands together. He would not bleed to death in his own bed.

Morning was breaking in Pascagoula.

Three hours earlier, Dupree's head hit the pillow like a rock. Exhausted, delirious, fighting abdominal pain, that returned while searching for Janna Sandler, he fell asleep without taking any pain medication.

With the light streaming into his bedroom, he fought getting up.

Groaning, he rolled his feet off the side of the bed and doubled over. Falling to the floor, he pulled his knees in tight to his chest. He scooted a couple of feet to the bedside table. Reaching into the drawer, he fished out a bottle of pills. He swallowed two, without water.

Watching the shadows of the blinds move across the ceiling, his abdomen slowly became more flexible.

Rolling onto his knees, he slowly stood. Walking to the kitchen, hunched over at the waist, he poured a large glass of tap water.

His Bible rested on the kitchen counter. He grabbed it and took a seat on the floor.

"Lord, I need help." He prayed. His prayers focused on Janna and her family. He implored God to protect her, keep her safe, and bring her home to her child.

"Guide me Lord to find her."

The painkiller was taking effect; the pastor's teeth began to feel numb, his abdomen more elastic. He rolled over onto his knees and grabbed the counter.

"Direct me, Lord. Just like in the past. Help me to find Janna Sandler."

He groaned as he stood. He walked to the bathroom to shower.

He needed the sanctuary; he needed to shave.

• • •

The sanctuary at Christ Church was exceptionally warm. Dupree's face was flush and smooth. He took a seat in the first pew and meditated on the altar. Jesus was surrounded by angels, who were worshipping him or tending to him. Dupree wasn't exactly sure what the angels were doing. But it was apparent that Christ was in His glory, in heaven, watching over His flock.

Dupree picked up his Bible and opened it to Psalms.

"Guide me, Jesus."

He skim read several psalms but then fixed upon Psalm 23…"He leads me beside the still waters."

"Jesus is the good shepherd." He repeated the term over and over in his mind.

He flipped quickly to Matthew Chapter 7 and read the account of the good shepherd.

"The good shepherd knows his sheep, and they know his voice," he said. "Help me, Jesus, I'm listening. What am I missing? I'm listening to only you."

Dupree fell into a deep meditative prayer, allowing all his thoughts to focus on the term *"I'm listening"*.

"Lord, to whom shall we go? Yours are the words of eternal life."

As his body began to slip deeper into prayer, he opened his eyes and fixated on the angels.

"They're listening," he said. "I'm listening."

And then, a pain hit his groin. Moved by the Holy Spirit, he flipped the pages to the words of Peter the Apostle.

"Lord, to whom shall we go?"

It was Peter, the fisherman. Schultz was a fisherman.

"Schultz is a fisherman," Dupree said, almost in a trance.

A long pause followed. Falling deeper into a meditative state, focusing on the angels in the painting, Dupree mumbled, "Schultz is at a fish camp."

He slowly closed his eyes. Prayers of thanks rolled through his heart. Dupree was so thankful to be alive, so thankful for Kelly, for Sarah. He was thankful for their certain reunion. He loved his church and Gregor and Jesus and Mrs. Fritz. Falling into the pew, he curled into a ball and hugged himself.

"Schultz is at a fishing camp," he said, smiling.

CHAPTER 40

The elevated landing of Castaways Bar rose high above the long morning shadows. Franky Stevens was blinded as he stood nervous and sweating, engulfed in a whirlwind of light and humidity. The oyster shell parking lot surrounding the dive sat far below Franky's feet. He took one last look around.

It was as if he were floating above all his troubles. Franky had not slept all night. It didn't matter to him if he ever slept again. The last time Franky had a drink, however, was eight days and twelve hours ago, exactly eight days too long.

Stepping through the front door, he allowed it to close behind him. It took only a moment for his eyes to adjust to the darkness.

"Hey, Franky," his friend Matt said. He was sitting on the beer cooler, watching the *Today* show on a television above the bar. "What'll it be?"

"Let me think," Franky said, studying the wall of bottles behind the bar.

Driving through the streets of Pascagoula, searching motel parking lots, and canvassing trailer parks proved totally worthless. If he were going to continue his efforts to find Janna, he needed help from an old friend.

He leaned heavily on the bar.

"Let me have a double Jamison and a glass of ice water."

"You got it."

Franky pulled his cellphone from his pocket and placed it on the bar.

Janna was being held captive; Franky was useless.

"What good is a lawyer or a boyfriend?"

"Excuse me?"

"Nothing, I was talking to myself."

All the petitioning and briefs and lawyer crap were not going to find her or keep her safe. If he professed his undying love for her, she would still be held captive.

"Words, words, and more words," he said, as Matt placed the water in front of him.

Janna was gone. Franky could do nothing. And he couldn't bear to think about it.

"Here you go, buddy."

"Hold up."

Franky took the ice water and drank it down.

"I'm dehydrated," Franky said, handing the glass back to Matt.

"No problem, water's cheap," Matt said, filling the glass again.

"Thanks."

Franky pushed the cellphone on the bar next to the shot of booze and waited. The neon bar signs and soft lighting gave Franky a sickly, tired look. He picked up the clear glass; the caramel liquid caught the light. Swirling it carefully, a beautiful, intoxicating fragrance of vanilla was released. He felt a bite in his jaws, a warming sensation ran up the back of his spine as he brought the glass to his lips. A brush across the rim and Franky immediately felt the tingling on his upper lip. As a sip of the liquid poured into his mouth, all Franky's senses were peaked—sight, smell, taste, touch, all working together to create a euphoric experience.

The liquid warmed his throat. Franky smiled up at the television. And, then, he doubled over in pain, spilling the drink onto the bar.

The instant the booze hit his stomach, he glimpsed the men's room in the mirror behind the bar. Janna was not going to walk out and save him.

Janna was gone.

Franky placed the shot glass back on the bar. He bit through his upper lip and held back a tear.

Matt wiped the bar with a rag. He talked, questioned. He poured Franky another shot. His words fell silent.

Janna was gone.

Franky dropped his head into his folded arms.

"Whatever it is, it'll be all right."

Franky jumped when his phone started vibrating madly, crawling slowly across the bar. He answered it without looking at the number.

"Hello?"

"Franky Stevens?"

"Yes."

"Franky, this is Earl Sandler, Janna's father. She asked me to call you."

"Janna? Oh my god! Is she there? Is she okay?"

"Franky, listen to me. She called a few minutes ago and said that she's fine. She's safe and well taken care of. But Franky…she was obviously calling, with the guy who took her, telling her what to say."

"Schultz?"

"She didn't say. She basically asked about Katie. Her mother and I told her she was fine. She asked to speak to Katie but then suddenly said no. Before the phone was grabbed from her, she asked me to call you. She said you were coming over last night and she didn't want you to worry. The entire conversation took less than a minute."

Franky couldn't speak. He held back a lump in his throat.

"Franky?"

"I…"

"Franky, I'm worried sick," Earl Sandler said, after a long pause. "Janna's mom and I are going on Channel 13 news in a few minutes. They tell us to say her name as many times as we can. 'Janna, we love you. Janna, please come home.' Stuff like that. But…I… Franky, they say he's killed two others. I'm so…"

"Mr. Sandler," Franky said, standing suddenly. He wiped his eyes with the back of his hand and then pushed the rest of his drink down the bar. "We're going to find her. I've been out all…"

Franky's phone rang with another call. He looked at the display. "Mr. Sandler, we're going to find her. I've got to go. I'll call you back."

Franky hung up suddenly and took the incoming call.

"Pastor Dupree?"

"Franky. I wanted to let you know the latest. We're currently looking for any connections that Schultz might have with a fishing camp."

"Okay," Franky said, throwing a few dollars on the bar to cover his tab. "I just talked to Earl Sandler. He's gotten a call from Janna and…"

"Yeah, Detective Campbell talked to him," Dupree said. "Can you come get me? I'm at Christ Church on the corner of Pascagoula and Convent. If you can come get me, I think we might be able to find her."

"Really?" Franky said, heading toward the door. "I'm on my way."

• • •

When Franky pulled into the parking lot of Christ Church, Pastor Dupree was seated on the steps to the sanctuary with his laptop. Wearing a T-shirt and shorts, he was hunched over the keyboard, with a baseball cap pulled down tight over his head. The preacher looked like he should be seated in a coffee shop rather than in the shade of a steeple. Franky parked and walked up quickly.

"Hey," Franky said, from the base of the steps. "What'd you find out?"

"Good morning," Dupree said, looking up briefly. "Schultz has a fishing camp or has access to one. I'm sure of it." He began typing frantically on the laptop. "Now I've searched property records and there's no Schultz at any of the bigger camps around Pascagoula. I'm looking in Gautier now. I was going to search under his wife's maiden name next to see…"

Franky's phone rang. "Hold on," he said, answering on the second ring. "Hello?"

"Hello, Mr. Stevens, the lawyer?"

"Yes."

"Uh…this is Detective Owens with the Pascagoula Police Department. I was wondering if you have a moment to speak." The voice was authoritative. Franky mouthed the words "it's the police" to Dupree, who went back to searching his computer.

"Yes, of course. Any news on Janna?"

"Uh…"

"Janna Sandler? My girlfriend, any news?"

"Uh…did you say…did you say your 'girlfriend'?"

"Anyway. Yes. I would say my 'girlfriend'."

"No one cares that she's your girlfriend."

"What the hell?" Franky shook his head and pointed at the phone. Dupree looked up briefly, then returned to his computer.

"Mr. Stevens. Are you the lawyer that works for the Fineburg's?"

"Yes."

"Did you recently call the hospital and request information on a patient?"

"Excuse me?"

"Did you know it is illegal to obtain medical records without the expressed written consent of the patient?

It's HIPAA rules. There are felony offenses that…"

"Excuse me, Owens did you say?"

"Yes."

"I thought you were calling about Janna Sandler. Are you working with Detective Campbell?"

"Uh…yes, we are working together. But…you must understand… for us to work with you, we need to make sure that you are reputable. I mean, it wouldn't look good on the police department if we worked with someone who habitually played fast and loose with felony laws."

"Detective Owens, I answered enough questions like that last night," Franky said, raising his voice. Dupree looked up from his laptop. "We're working on a real lead. Pastor Dupree and I are tracking down fish campsites as we speak, and wasting my time with more…"

"Fish campsites?"

"Yes, Schultz is likely holed-up in a fishing camp he owns. You did say you were working with Detective Campbell?"

"Uh…he's actually the one who told me to call you."

A chill ran up Franky's spine. Suddenly, the voice on the line sounded familiar. "Excuse me," he said, in a weak voice.

"Yes, yes. I'm working with Detective Campbell."

Franky's abdomen suddenly contracted. His knees went weak. He recognized the voice; it was the man he called about the barnacle injury. With wide eyes, he pointed frantically at the phone, getting Dupree to come listen. He punched the speaker on his phone.

"Well, you see, uh…Detective Campbell and I have been searching fish camps all morning," Detective Owens said. "And we're really thinking this is a…it feels like it's a…we think it's a dead end. Are you by yourself?"

"I am," Franky said, holding a finger to his mouth to keep Dupree silent.

"Where are you?"

"I'm at my office."

"Really? Because I just called there to get your cellphone number."

"You must have just missed me."

"Are you going to be there all morning?"

"Yes."

"Okay, I may call you back later. But as far as that fish camp thing goes. We're going to move in a different direction."

"And Detective Campbell agrees?" Franky asked. "I mean, he was pretty sure we were on to something last night."

"No, no, uh…he agrees. I need to go. Bye."

"Wait, wait," Franky said, trying to keep the line open. Dupree had mouthed the words that he was calling Detective Campbell.

"I said I have to go!"

The phone hung up.

"That was him!" Franky yelled. "That was Schultz."

Dupree was on the line with Detective Campbell. "Roy's Fishing Camp," Dupree said, pushing the speaker button.

"Did you say Roy's?" she asked.

"Yes, Roy's Fishing Camp in Bayou Cassotte. We're headed that way," Dupree said, as he moved quickly toward Franky's car. He waved Franky along.

"You need to wait for me!" Detective Campbell was saying as Dupree hung up his phone.

"What is it?" Franky said, running toward his car.

"Schultz's brother-in-law, his wife's brother, owns a fishing camp in Bayou Cassotte," Dupree said, handing his phone to Franky. "This is his Facebook page. Check out who's standing behind him at the end of the pier. That's Kenneth Schultz!"

Ten minutes later, Franky was driving on Highway 90, at seventy miles per hour, into a blinding sunrise. The brackish marsh of the Pascagoula River delta reflected the orange and blues of the sky that was peaking in color above the pine trees bordering the eastern shore. The massive grasslands looked inviting with cool bayous meandering through eight-foot high grass patches. At this speed they would get to Roy's Fishing Camp in five minutes.

"Look up the number for the Bayou Cassotte volunteer fire department," Franky said, to Dupree. "If anyone knows that area, it'll be them."

"We should probably wait for Detective Campbell."

Franky applied the brakes and made a hard right turn onto the main road running south into Bayou Cassotte. Dupree, letting out a little groan, held onto the dash with one hand and his side with the other.

"Never mind," Franky said, handing Dupree his phone. "I've got it plugged in. Just let me know when the turns are coming up."

"Franky, we should wait for the cops."

CHAPTER 41

Kenneth Schultz stormed out to the pier to eat his sandwich.

When he jerked the phone from Janna's hand, she was sobbing uncontrollably, blowing her nose all over her lips and mouth. It was very unattractive. That's why he had to smack her across the face with the back of his hand, twice.

"Blathering on about that idiot!" he said, kicking off his flip flops at the entrance to the little pier. "I'm the one that's been violated. Willard "Franky" Stevens? That god-damned ambulance-chaser! That's her boyfriend? This is the one she's screwing?"

He plopped down on the pier. Ripping into a tuna sandwich, he tossed the plastic wrap into the water at his feet. The taste of tuna and the smell of the river filled his senses. Barely chewing, he swallowed the sandwich in wads.

The marsh rolled out for miles; Schultz's legs dangled over the pier. His toes barely reached the surface. Kicking violently at the water, he flicked droplets out for about twenty feet. Shoving the last of his sandwich in his mouth, Schultz finalized his plans. They would escape to Costa Rica.

In the most beautiful of countries, the scene unfolding before him would change drastically in his tropic paradise. Instead of a flat, putrid swamp, there would be lush mountains that stretched to the sky. Rather than pine trees and possums, there would be palms and monkeys. The dead and dying swamp would be transformed into a scene of fishing boats moored to their anchoring, afloat on clear, blue-green water.

Yes, a thick, lovely Tico would tempt him to leave Janna. They were incredibly warm and brown and accommodating.

"Janna probably tans easily," Schultz said, watching a chunk of bread escape his mouth and land on the surface of the water.

"But with the security. It's impossible, especially if she's going to fight you all the way."

Think, Schultz, think.

They needed fake identities. He could become Mr. Kenneth Sandler, husband and colleague of the esteemed Miss Janna Sandler—exterminator extraordinaire.

Ridiculous.

Then there was the kid problem and the shyster lover problem and the border crossing problem and the…

One at a time, Schultz.

Schultz looked at his cellphone. He had four bars and a fully charged battery. Using only his right thumb, he used his phone to place a very important call. He dialed Willard "Franky" Stevens III, Esq.

"Fineburg, Fineburg, and Fineburg."

"Hello, this is Dustin Massey. I'm a new client of Mr. Stevens."

A few seconds later, he had Franky Stevens' cellphone number. He dialed it immediately.

"Hello."

"Hello, Mr. Stevens, the lawyer?"

"Yes."

"Uh…this is Detective Owens with the Pascagoula Police Department."

CHAPTER 42

Through a lush, green live oak Janna Sandler watched a thunderhead stretch toward the sky. Her heart was beating uncontrollably, causing the side of her face to throb with pain. Silently, she worked her hands, gently making a fist and then relaxing as her arms lay beside her. She drew in a deep breath and released it slowly; her hiding place smelled like tar. Stealth was the key to safety.

A cumulous cloud, the giant mountain of water vapor, climbed to new heights. Janna focused on the tip of a peak, closing one eye, then the other, working to calm her heartbeat, breathing in one lungful, then another and exhaling quietly, slowly, not disturbing even the mosquito that had landed on her cheek.

She didn't dare swat it; absolute stillness was essential.

"I said I have to go!"

Schultz ran down the pier, his feet striking the boards with loud spats. They suddenly silenced, when he reached the grass. He landed heavily on the front porch. "Janna, we've got to go!"

A squirrel barked at her from a limb twenty feet closer to the clouds than where she lay. Sweat formed on her lip; her bed was excruciatingly hot. Janna remained still, flat, hot, like the shingles she was imitating.

Schultz trusted her for one minute too long.

"Janna!"

The front door slammed, shaking the entire one-room building.

"Janna Sandler!"

Schultz was destroying the shack, cursing, screaming, throwing furniture around.

"Janna!" Schultz shouted into the wilderness that surrounded the camp. It echoed for a second. Schultz was suddenly still.

The fishing camp returned to the sounds of birds chirping and bugs buzzing, of water lapping against the pilings of a lost pier. The mosquito had filled its belly and was now on its way.

When Schultz had stepped out onto the front porch to make his phone call, Janna got up quietly and hopped out the back door. She couldn't run; Schultz had never unbound her ankles. No worries. Her hiding place was not far.

When Schultz carried her into the camp, when she was riding on his shoulder, the quick glance she took of her surroundings revealed the destination of her escape.

Janna smiled. Her pulse was slow, calm. Fear, adrenaline, and hoisting herself onto the flat roof, using only her upper body strength, had spiked her heart rate. Now, watching her cloud and hidden by a six-inch precipice, she listened to Schultz curse.

"Janna Sandler, get back here this instant!"

Schultz's voice was farther away; he was walking back toward the pier.

Stealth was the key. Janna smiled.

Thank you, Lord. Thank You.

• • •

Squealing tires, kicking up dirt and gravel, was the final indicator that Janna would soon be released from her hiding place. For twenty minutes, the squirrel jumped from limb to limb. She marveled at the magnificence of nature—oak trees, Spanish moss, black ants, all working in harmony to the tune of locusts and bumblebees. Janna prayed and meditated on the beauty while lying perfectly still, breathing in petroleum-based roofing materials and frying atop a fishing camp.

Kenneth Schultz made a valiant effort to find her. He cursed the bayou and the woods. She followed his voice, staring up at the clouds, as he circled the camp. Finally, he walked the floor below her, collecting his things. He made several trips to the car, before screeching off in his silver BMW, the same car Janna had seen several times at the abandoned house a hundred yards from her home.

Waiting until she could no longer hear the car, she peeled herself off the roof and stood. The warm breeze blowing from the bayou sent a chill up her spine.

Dusting her clothes off, she stood at the edge of the roof. She circled the perimeter to find a soft place to land.

She heard a car coming back up the road toward the camp.

Janna dropped to her knees and crawled back to the same location. Rolling over, she fell silent once again and listened. The car stopped farther away than before. Janna took a deep breath.

"Janna!" A voice yelled. "Janna, Janna!" Another voice yelled. She recognized the first one instantly. It was Franky!

Sitting up, she spotted Franky and another man, both yelling at the top of their lungs.

"Up here! I'm up here! Oh, God, Franky!"

Franky turned and bolted toward Janna.

"Up here!" Janna couldn't stop screaming. Tears filled her eyes; her voice cracked.

"Janna, where's Schultz?" the other man asked.

"He's gone. I don't know." Franky was holding out his arms to catch her.

"Katie? Where's Katie? Is she—"

"Katie's fine. She's fine. She's at your mother's. Come down."

Sobs of joy, relief, suddenly incapacitated Janna. Her knees buckled. She couldn't get down.

"Here, take my hand." Franky climbed onto the window unit. "Throw your legs over." He removed a pocket knife and cut the tie-wrap that was around her ankles. "We'll call Katie right now."

Falling over the edge of the roof, Janna fell into Franky's arms. He carried her toward the car.

"It's the second entrance past the giant Roy's Fishing Camp sign," the other man said. He handed Janna a bottle of water and smiled at her. "The second left. Yes, left. I can hear the siren. When you turn, go all the way to the end."

Franky set Janna down and handed her his phone. She dialed her parents.

"Hello, Franky?" Her mother answered.

"Mom, it's me," she could hardly speak. Her voice cracked on every syllable.

"Oh God, Janna! You're with Franky!" Her mom started crying on the other end of the line.

"Mom, where's Katie?"

"She's here. She's right here. Katie, do you want to talk to mommy?"

"Mommy?" A tiny voice spoke through the phone.

Janna put her hand up to her mouth and shook uncontrollably, trying to hold back her sobs. "I'm right here, honey. Mommy will see you soon. Okay? Okay? Bye-bye."

"Bye-bye."

Janna fell into Franky's arms. A squad car pulled into the camp with lights flashing.

"Yes, yes, she's fine. Okay, we'll see you soon," the other man said.

The police were getting out of the squad car, guns drawn.

"He's gone," Franky said. He held Janna tight. It would be another half hour before they were released to go get her daughter.

• • •

Franky held Janna in the back seat as Dupree drove.

"Your face?" Franky asked. "He did this to you?"

"He hit me a couple times, after I called my mom and dad this morning," Janna said, patting Franky's knee. "But I'm fine. I really am. The back of my head hurts." She dropped her chin to show him.

"Yeah, you've got a pretty bad bruise." He kissed her forehead. "I'm so glad you're okay."

"Me too." Janna looked out the window. "I can't believe you found me."

"It was Pastor Dupree. The guy's a genius."

"Did you hear anything that might lead to where he was planning to go, anything at all?" Dupree asked.

"No, not really," she said. "He left the cabin and I escaped to the roof. I didn't hear anything."

"I'm sure he's past Mobile by now," Dupree said, obviously thinking out loud.

"How long was Katie by herself?" Janna asked Franky.

"Maybe twenty minutes. Kelly heard the struggle when you were on the phone. She went straight there."

"Poor Kelly…went to check…" The tears came back to Janna. "And you," she said, looking toward the front seat. "You're the one she's been talking about. You're the Pastor…Cooper…"

"Janna," Franky said, pulling her closer. "It's over; everything is fine."

"Thanks, Pastor," she said, toward the front seat. "Thanks for everything."

CHAPTER 43

Kelly Mitchell's apartment was alive with the joy of reunion. When Janna stepped in the front door, Earl Sandler grabbed his daughter like she was a two-year-old. Trying to cradle her in his arms, he failed to get her a little more than a foot off the ground. His wife interrupted his attempt by hugging them both and squeezing the life out of her daughter.

When Katie ran into the room, Janna was breathless. She hoisted the child up and embraced her, kissing her smiling face all over.

The air buzzed with euphoria as Dupree took a seat on the couch.

He made eye contact with Kelly and smiled. She moved across the den and sat next to him.

"Nice job, Cooper," she said, taking his hand. She rested her head on his shoulder and listened as Janna explained how she woke up in the trunk of a car, and befriended Schultz, and then eventually made her escape.

"She looks great, doesn't she?" Kelly said.

"Yeah," Dupree said, as he patted Kelly's knee. "She sure does."

"Look at the way she looks at Franky. She was telling me the other day that she and Franky actually went to high school together and that…"

Dupree's cellphone rang. It was Detective Campbell. "Hold that thought," he said to Kelly.

"Hey Detective."

"Pastor Dupree, I just wanted to call and let you know that we've got a hit on the BMW in Gulf Shores. It's in a motel parking lot off Highway 59, and we're heading that way."

"That's terrific," he said. He placed his hand over the phone. "They've found Schultz," he said to Kelly.

"Yes!" She said, clapping quietly.

"How's Janna doing?" Detective Campbell asked.

"She's good. I think she and the baby are going to stay at her friend's house tonight, just to play it safe."

Kelly was nodding as she listened.

"Sounds good," Detective Campbell said. "I'll let you know when we get him in custody."

"Okay. Thanks, detective."

"Hey everyone," Kelly said, standing. "They've got Schultz." She looked at Dupree.

"They've located his car at a motel in Gulf Shores, so keep your fingers crossed," he said, standing to make the announcement. Everyone in the room nodded and smiled with satisfaction.

Franky was working his way across the room toward the pastor.

"Hey, pastor, I just wanted to thank you one more time," Franky said, extending his hand.

"My pleasure."

"Kelly," Franky said, "I was wondering if maybe I could stay here tonight, on the couch of course, just to make sure everything's all right. I won't be any trouble."

"I don't mind if it's alright with Janna."

"It was actually her idea."

"Sounds good to me."

"Can you do me a favor first?" Dupree asked Franky.

"Name it."

"If it's not too much trouble, can you run me over to the church to get my car?"

"Sure," Franky said, holding out his hand to help the pastor get up from the couch. "Let's go so we can get back."

"Great," Dupree said. He leaned over and gave Kelly a kiss on the forehead. "We'll hurry back; we've got some celebrating to do."

• • •

"I'm just going to run by my office to check on a few things," Franky said, as he pulled out of the church parking lot. "See you in twenty."

Dupree climbed into his car and dropped it into gear. He headed toward Kelly's apartment. Sitting on Pascagoula Street, waiting on the light at Downtown Plaza, a wave of dread suddenly hit Dupree. Something had been dropped; someone in his direct care was in danger. His fingers tingled as he steered the car through the intersection. Completing a mental inventory, he couldn't pinpoint who it was that troubled him.

Well, Schultz, of course.

But Kenneth Schultz didn't trouble him in that way.

Kelly and Janna.

Janna and her parents, the baby, Kelly all of them were safe. It wasn't anyone at the apartment.

Stevens?

It couldn't be Stevens.

Stevens!

Dupree made a sudden right and looped into the back parking lot of the Downtown Plaza, unsure of what he was really doing.

Dupree possessed a debilitating gift of being overly concerned to the point of neuroses. Since his youth, if his heart was troubled by someone, he acted. A call or text usually did the trick. When a sick child grabbed his attention, he would write a short note on a postcard and send it through the mail. Or, he would simply grab Red, jump in the car, and make a surprise visit. The older members in his congregation loved Red.

The only time it failed was when Sarah went missing.

As he drove through the parking lot, one model of car came to the forefront of his mind, a BMW. Driving behind a series of law offices provided him plenty to look at. There was a red one and a blue one. The sun was setting and shining brightly in his face. There was a silver one.

Dupree parked the car and walked quickly toward Stevens' office.

There's a white one and another...

Dupree's heart froze. It was Schultz's car.

Scanning the parking lot for the madman, he grabbed his cellphone and dialed Stevens.

No answer.

He immediately dialed Detective Campbell's cellphone.

"Yes, pastor?" she answered.

"Detective, I'm at the Downtown Plaza. I'm standing here looking at Kenneth Schultz's car."

"Are you sure?"

"Positive. I'm not sure where he is, but I just dropped off Franky Stevens. I'm going to check on him."

"No! Pastor, find a safe place! Go back to your car. I'm sending help over right now."

"Fine, but I'm still checking on him," Dupree said, hanging up.

"Pastor, don't..."

Running and keeping low, Dupree ran through the parking lot. He hugged the wall of the breezeway and peered around the corner toward Franky's office. He took off in a dead sprint down the plaza. Holding his left side, he arrived at the offices of Fineburg, Fineburg, and Fineburg in about fifteen seconds.

Opening the door, he stepped inside and froze. The receptionist was hiding under her desk, watching the front door from a crack that ran along the floor.

Dupree quietly closed the door behind him and made an okay sign. She returned the gesture. Rotating his fingers in an old rotary phone style, he mouthed 911.

Voices came from behind Franky Stevens' office door. Schultz was talking. Dupree gently placed his hands on the door.

"Lord Jesus, bring a peaceful end to this situation," he whispered. He continued to pray, having no real power of his own over the situation.

CHAPTER 44

Moments after entering his office, Franky Stevens found himself staring at the end of a gun. He focused so intensely on that one point that all things in his peripheral vision started to fade into black. His insides knotted. He was close to wetting himself.

And yet, the man behind the gun kept talking.

Franky's ears pulsed so loudly he could make out only every other word. The gun didn't waver, bob, or shake. It was so steady and calm that soon Franky would lose his sight all together. Until one word broke him from his trance: *Janna.*

"Is that true?" the man asked.

"What?"

"Didn't you hear me?"

"No."

"Are you in love with Janna?"

Background scenery started coming back. Franky was in his office. He was seated at his desk. A slender, dark-haired, greasy man was standing just inside his door, pointing a gun at him. To his right stood his bookshelf and the bat that he was going to give to his brother.

"I don't know, maybe. Who are you?" Franky asked.

"I'm her boyfriend."

"Oh," Franky said, nodding slowly. It was Schultz, no doubt. "She didn't tell me she had a boyfriend."

"Are you saying she's a slut?"

"No, no, nothing like that," Franky said. He sat back in his chair and started massaging his hands. "Janna and I are old friends. We went to high school together."

"How sweet," Schultz said. He started waving the gun, directing Franky to stand and move around the desk. "I want to sit there."

"Sure."

Franky stood. For an instant he thought about grabbing the bat.

"She says she loves you," Schultz said, moving around the opposite side of the desk to keep his distance. "Do you want to know where she is? Hands up!"

Franky raised his hands up quickly and positioned himself in front of his office door. The light from the window behind Schultz made him look dark and sinister. His silhouette was outlined by the public works department entrance across the street.

"We found her."

Schultz took a seat and placed his elbows on the desk, keeping both hands on the gun that was directed at Franky's chest.

"Did she tell you she gave herself to me?"

"No," Franky said. His arms started to drop a little. "She was mostly concerned about her daughter. We didn't talk much except about that."

"I see."

Schultz remained silent for a long time. He licked his lips and studied the gun. He examined Franky's expression.

Franky maintained eye contact the entire time. In the background, the front window in the public works department opened slightly, the mini-blinds raised a half-inch, and a long, black barrel of a rifle, with a sight, stuck out from inside.

Franky never broke his stare. There was so much activity going on in the mall. One side-glance would ruin it all.

"Why do you think she loves you?" Schultz asked.

"I don't know," Franky said. He had actually thought a lot about that very question. And since this could be the last conversation he had on earth, he might as well be honest. "Maybe, she's a crusader."

"What do you mean?"

"Listen, Schultz, that's your name right?" A pause followed. "Anyway, I'm a basket case. I've always been one. There is absolutely nothing in me that anyone could love. I drink. I womanize. I'm negative. Basically, I'm the most self-centered person on the planet.

There is not one socially redeeming feature about me." Franky's hands grew heavy; he lifted them again. He paused for a moment.

"But apparently, she sees something in me that I don't. She's just wired that way."

Schultz nodded slowly.

"I know she's a Christian and everything, but hell, I'm a Christian. I think maybe she just gets it more or something." Franky looked at the floor.

"You know," he said, "all that Jesus loves me and doesn't judge me…he knows we're all flawed, but loves us anyway. All that stuff. Well, I think she takes it to heart and…that frees her to love and be loved. It's just not that difficult for her. Maybe that's how she can love me."

Franky looked up and smiled. "I guess, Mr. Schultz, I don't know why she loves me, but I guess I can see now how she *can* love me."

Kenneth Schultz looked at his hands; the gun began to vibrate slightly.

"So," he said, "do you think she could love me?"

Franky's shoulders burned with pain; he could no longer hold his hands up. Dropping them slowly, he said, "If anyone could love you, if not Janna, then it would be someone much like her."

Schultz nodded slowly at Stevens and smiled. His shoulders and elbows looked like they too began to hurt, as he lowered the gun. He folded his arms in front of him, pointing the gun away from Franky.

"Maybe one day I'll…" Schultz said, as the window pane behind him shattered. He was catapulted forward, his forehead bounced off the desk.

"Holy!" Franky yelled.

The door behind him burst open. Franky was knocked to the floor. In an instant, he was covered by Dupree. An army of cops entered yelling, guns drawn. Franky remained perfectly still under the weight of the pastor and watched as a little stream of blood ran from his desk to the carpeting below.

The End

CRAIG S. MORGAN is a second career writer and tree farmer. Having spent 35 years working in oil refineries, he is now dedicated to improving his carbon foot print by growing hardwood trees and writing organic novels. He lives in Pike County Mississippi with his wife, Kathryn.

For more information on Craig S. Morgan, visit his website or follow him on social media:
www.CraigSMorgan.com
Craig S Morgan Author on Facebook
CSMorganAuthor on Instagram

Other Books By Craig S. Morgan Include:

Thou Shalt Not Mysteries:
Thou Shalt Not Desire
Thou Shalt Not Escape

Satirical Fiction
Robot Tom

Historical Fiction
Three Headstones

www.ingramcontent.com/pod-product-compliance
Lightning Source LLC
Chambersburg PA
CBHW070454300726

48975CB00007B/2165